CAPTIVES

and

latest

Booker

winners

NEW RUSSIAN WRITING 11

glas

Editors:
NATASHA PEROVA
ARCH TAIT

Cover design: Emma Ippolitova
Camera-ready copy:
Tatiana Shaposhnikova
Copyeditor: Joanne Turnbull

FRONT cover: Sergei Potapov,
"Wanderers," oil on oilcloth
BACK cover: Sergei Potapov,
"Virgo," oil on oilcloth

GLAS Publishers (Russia)
Moscow 119517, P.O.Box 47, Russia
Tel./Fax: (095) 441 9157
Email: perova@glas.msk.su

GLAS Publishers (UK)
Dept. of Russian Literature,
University of Birmingham,
Birmingham, B15 2TT, UK
Tel/Fax: 121-414 6047
Email: a.l.tait@bham.ac.uk

North American
Sales and Editorial office,
Zephyr Press, 13 Robinson St,
Somerville MA 02145, USA
Tel: (617) 628-9726
Fax: (617) 776-8246
Email: edhogan@world.std.com

ISBN 5-7172-0027-7

Back issues of Glas
are available:

1. HISTORY IN REVERSE
2. SOVIET GROTESQUE
3. WOMEN'S VIEW
4. LOVE & FEAR
5. BULGAKOV & MANDELSTAM
6. JEWS & STRANGERS
7. BOOKER WINNERS & OTHERS
8. LOVE RUSSIAN STYLE
9. THE SCARED GENERATION
10. BOOKER WINNERS & OTHERS

© Glas: New Russian Writing 1996
Copyright reverts to authors and
translators upon publication

CONTENTS

Vladimir Makanin
The Captive of the Caucasus 5

Victor Pelevin
The Tambourine for
the Upper World 39

Vassily Aksyonov
Palmer's First Flight 57
Palmer's Second Flight 73

Zinovy Zinik
The Moth 87

Alexander Terekhov
The Rat-killer 125
Happiness 139

Mark Shatunovsky
The Discrete Continuity
of Love 152

1995 BOOKER WINNERS:

Georgy Vladimov
A General and His Army 169

Oleg Pavlov
An Official Tale 183

Evgeny Fyodorov
The Odyssey 193

Stanislav Rassadin
A Subjective Substantiation
of a Subjective Choice 207

Sergei Potapov 207
A Painter with a Cosmic
Consciousness 217

Gummerus Printing,
Jyväskylä, Finland, 1996

Vladimir Makanin's "The Captive of the Caucasus", which gives this collection its name, is one vivid example of the illusory nature of man's freedom. We are all in some sense captives: captives of a political system, of circumstances, of our obligations or our illusions, to say nothing of those who are captives in a literal sense. The world seems to be full of misplaced people trapped in captivity of one kind or another, sometimes self-imposed, but feeling nonetheless alienated from a hostile world around them.

In Makanin's novella the invaders find that they are the captives of the country they have conquered. In Victor Pelevin's "Tambourine for the Upper World" enterprising girls resuscitate foreign corpses from the battlefields of World War II so as to marry them and get themselves out of Russia. Emigres too are eternal captives of their former homeland and their Soviet past, their loyalties torn between a Russia they are losing touch with and the land that gave them asylum but where they are unable to strike roots (Zinovy Zinik's "The Moth", Vassily Aksyonov's "Palmer's First Flight").

Georgy Vladimov, winner of the 1995 Booker Russian Novel Prize, features a decent Second World War army commander caught in a web of intrigue, with all his subordinates spying on him for the army's secret police ("A General and His Army"). Oleg Pavlov, recently released from the army, depicts a platoon guarding a present-day prison camp where the convicts and the guards are both equally prisoners of the huge, merciless state machinery ("An Official Tale"). Yevgeny Fyodorov, who spent many years in Stalinist gulags, describes his personal experiences in surviving and preserving his sanity in "Odyssey".

Alexander Terekhov sets his novel "The Rat-killer" in post-perestroika provincial Russia where not much has changed for the little man and totalitarian rule effortlessly prevailes.

Mark Shatunovsky depicts a man and a woman locked into their private lives and not venturing out into a warring world they are little interested in.

Despite the unifying theme the aim of this, as of the other issues of Glas, is to present contemporary Russian literature as it happens. Traditionally we have offered excerpts from the novels short-listed for the Booker Russian Novel Prize to give publishers abroad an opportunity of acquainting themselves with what Russian critics have considered the best novels of the previous year. In his notes Stanislav Rassadin, Chairman of the jury of last year's Booker Russian Novel Prize, shares his thoughts on the current state of Russian writing. **The Editors**

Vladimir
MAKANIN
The Captive of the Caucasus
Translated by Arch Tait

It was Dostoevsky who said, "Beauty will save the world". Most likely the soldiers had not heard that, but what beauty was they both had a fair idea. Among the mountains they were only too aware of it, and found it daunting. A stream leaping without warning out of a crevice. Right now an open clearing, dazzlingly yellow in the sun, testing their nerves. Rubakhin, more experienced, led the way.

The mountains were suddenly gone. The sun-drenched expanse ahead spoke to Rubakhin of a happy childhood he had never had. Proud southern trees whose names he did not know rose up in isolation above the grass, but what most stirred his plainsman's soul was the tall grass, rustling, breathing in the slight breeze.

"Hold back, Vovka. No hurry," he warned softly.

Cross an open place you're unfamiliar with and you can bet you're in someone's sights. Before emerging from the dense scrub Hot Shot Vovka raised his rifle and made a leisurely sweep with it from left to right using the telescopic sight as binoculars. He held his breath, surveying this expanse so generously flooded with sunlight. He noticed a small transistor radio by a hillock.

"Aha!" Hot Shot Vovka exclaimed in a whisper. (The glass on the little radio had glinted in the sun.)

In short bursts the two soldiers raced in their camouflage tunics to the half dug (and long abandoned) trench of a gas pipeline and the gingery hillock with its autumn colouring. They turned the radio over in their hands, already recognizing it. When Corporal Boiarkov was drunk he liked to go off and lie down somewhere on his own, cradling this antiquated transistor radio in his arms. Parting the tall grass they looked for the body and found it nearby. Boiarkov's corpse was weighed down by two rocks. Death had found him. He had been shot at point blank range, most likely before he even had time to rub his drunken eyes. His cheeks were sunken. It had been decided in the unit that he must have done a runner. His documents were missing. That would have to be reported. But why hadn't the fighters taken the radio? Because it could incriminate them? More likely it was too old and tinny for them. Not worth taking. The irrevocability of what had happened (death is one thing that is plainly irrevocable) made them move, made them want to get it over with. Dredging with flat stones, they hastily dug a grave for the murdered man, equally hastily shaped the mound of earth above him into a conspicuous man-made hill, and continued on their way.

Again they are coming out of a defile, again there is tall grass which hasn't shrivelled at all. It sways gently and birds call joyously to each other in the sky above the trees and above the two soldiers. Perhaps beauty is already saving the world, a reminder from another place which keeps a man on the right path (walking not far away, admonishing him). Keeping him on his toes, beauty also keeps him mindful.

This time, however, the sunny open space is familiar and not dangerous. The mountains recede and ahead the path is level. Slightly further on is a dusty fork in a road much driven over by military vehicles where their unit is stationed. The soldiers unwittingly march faster.

Lieutenant-Colonel Gurov is not in the unit but at home. They will need to see him there. Without pausing to recover their breath the soldiers get themselves over to where Gurov lives, the undisputed ruler of these parts, and of all the beautiful sun-soaked adjacent parts of this earth. He lives with his wife in a fine wooden house with a vine-draped veranda on which to relax. A smallholding adjoins the house. It is noon, the hottest time of the day. Lieutenant-Colonel Gurov and a local man, Alibek, are sitting out on the open veranda. Somnolent after lunch, they are dozing in light cane chairs and waiting for tea to be brought. Rubakhin, faltering and nervous, makes his report. Gurov looks dozily at these two dust-covered privates who have landed in on him and whose faces, another minus, are unfamiliar to him. For a moment he is young again. Suddenly raising his voice he shouts at them that nobody will be receiving reinforcements, for Christ's sake what do they take him for! He will be sending none of his soldiers out to rescue trucks up shit creek as a result of their own stupidity!

Worse, he is not going to let them off that easily. Angry now, he orders the two soldiers to get to work shifting sand. They can do some honest hard work on his smallholding. About turn! Quick march! Spread that pile of sand by the gate on all the paths leading to the house and the vegetable garden. There is so much frigging mud everywhere, you can't walk down them... The lieutenant-colonel's wife is pleased, as any smallholder would be, to have unpaid soldierly labour. Anna Fedorovna promptly appears with cries of joy in the vegetable garden with her sleeves rolled up, wearing muddy, broken men's boots, and urges that they should also help her on the vegetable beds.

The soldiers wheel the sand out by the barrow load and shovel it over the paths. It is hot, and the sand is damp, evidently brought from down by the river.

Vovka perches the radio of the murdered corporal on a pile of sand and finds music with a good beat to lighten the work, but not too loud. He does not want to upset Gurov and Alibek who are talking away on the veranda. Judging by what reaches them of Alibek's drawl, he is negotiating for guns, a serious matter.

The radio on its sandy eminence reminds Rubakhin of what a beautiful spot Boiarkov chose to get killed in. The witless drunk had been scared to sleep in the wood, so instead he had gone out into the clearing, and even on to a hillock. When the fighters came for him he pushed the little radio (his one true friend) aside so that it should slide downhill into the grass. He didn't want to lose it. He himself could take his chances. No. It was hardly likely. He had simply been drunk, fallen asleep, and the radio had fallen from his hands and rolled away down the slope.

They had shot him point blank. Youngsters, no doubt, who wanted to get their first kill in as soon as possible, to get the taste for it, even if the guy was asleep. Now here was his radio perched on this pile of sand, and Rubakhin saw again the reddish, sun-drenched mound with two bushes growing tenaciously on its northern slope. The beauty of the place had been breath-taking, and Rubakhin would not let it go from his memory. He drank it in more and more, the slope Boiarkov fell asleep on, the hillock, the grass, the golden leaves on the bushes, and all of it one more invaluable lesson in survival. Beauty strives constantly to save us, calling to a man through memory, reminding him.

At first they tried to force the wheelbarrows through the muddy soil, then had the sense to put boards down on the paths. Vovka came first, chirpily pushing his barrow along, and behind him Rubakhin shoving an enormous barrow with a mountain of sand in it. He had stripped to the waist. Wet with sweat, his muscular body gleamed in the sun.

2

"I'll let you have ten Kalashnikovs. I can give you five crates of ammunition. Hear that, Alibek? Not three, five crates."

"I hear."

"But I must have those provisions by the first of the month..."

"My dear Colonel, I like to have a little nap after lunch. You too, as I know. I do hope Anna Fedorovna has not forgotten our tea."

"No need to worry about that."

"What do you mean, no need to worry?" his guest laughed. "Tea is not the same as war. Tea gets cold."

Gurov and Alibek return gradually to their conversation, which shows no sign of concluding, but the sluggishness with which they talk and a certain laziness in their arguing are deceptive. Alibek has come to get weapons, and Gurov, his officers and men, are in desperate need of provisions. What they have to barter is, of course, arms, sometimes petrol.

"I want the food by the first. And cut out those idiotic ambushes in the mountains. I'm not bothered about wine, but we must have at least some vodka."

"There is no vodka."

"Find some, Alibek, find some. I'm finding ammunition for you."

The lieutenant-colonel calls his wife. "How's the tea coming along?" "Ah, I'll just be getting you some good strong tea this very moment." "Anna, what are you saying? I thought you called to us from the garden that you had made it already!"

While they wait for the tea the two of them unhurriedly light up, basking in postprandial torpor. The smoke trails indolently over the cool veranda to the vine, wafting thence towards the vegetable garden.

Vovka signals to Rubakhin that he is going to try to get them a bottle of something (to make the best of a bad job), and edges towards the wattle fence. He has an infinite repertoire of ingenious signals and gestures. On the other side of the fence is a young woman with her child. Vovka gives her a wink. He jumps over the fence and gets talking. Well, good luck to him! Rubakhin gets on with pushing his barrow full of sand. Each to his own. Vovka is one of those impetuous soldiers who cannot stand slogging away at a dull job (or any other job, come to that).

Already they are on the best of terms. Amazing, the way she came round, as if all she was waiting for was a soldier to come along and say a kind word to her. Of course, Vovka is a likeable guy who smiles a lot and puts down roots in an instant.

Vovka puts his arms round her. She smacks his hands. The usual stuff. They can be seen, and Vovka understands he needs to get her into the darkness of the hut. He tries sweet talking her, tries dragging her in. The young woman resists. "Not so fast, you!" she laughs, but step by step they are both moving towards the hut with its door half-open because of the heat. Now they are there, and not far from the door her toddler goes on playing with the cat.

Rubakhin meanwhile is labouring away with his barrow. Where the path is too muddy he moves boards from where they were before and lays them end-to-end in the new position. He wheels the barrow over them carefully, balancing the heavy sand.

Lieutenant-Colonel Gurov continues his unhurried dealing with Alibek. His wife (after washing her hands and putting on a red blouse) has served each of them tea in a separate elegant little oriental teapot.

"Anna Fedorovna brews a fine cup of tea," Alibek compliments her.

Gurov says, "Why are you being so pig-headed, Alibek! To an outsider you could seem to be our captive. You need to remember where you are: right in the middle of my territory."

"What do you mean, your territory!"

"I mean just that: the lowlands here are in our hands."

"The lowlands are yours, but the mountains are ours." Alibek laughs. "What sort of a captive am I? It is you who are the captive here." He points laughingly at Rubakhin, busily wheeling his barrow. "He is the captive. You are the captive. Every last one of your soldiers is the captive." He laughs once more. "But I, I am not a captive."

He starts right in again.

"Twelve Kalashnikovs, and seven crates of ammunition."

Now it is Gurov's turn to laugh.

"Twelve, ha-ha! What sort of a number do you call that? Twelve! Where do you get a number like that from? Ten I can understand. Ten is a proper number, one you can remember. Right then, ten rifles."

"Twelve!"
"Ten...!"
Alibek sighs with delight.
"What an evening it is going to be. My goodness!"
"It's a long time yet till evening."
They slowly sip their tea, two people talking unhurriedly who have known and respected each other for a very long time. (Rubakhin is wheeling another barrow load of sand. He tips it out, spreads it level with the soil.)
"You know, Colonel, what our old men are saying? We have some wise old men in our villages."
"Well, what are they saying?"
"They are saying it is time for another campaign against Europe. It is time to fight there again."
"You certainly think big, Alibek. Europe, eh?!"
"Why not? Europe is only Europe. The old men say it is not so far away. They are not happy. The old men say, where the Russians go we should go too, and how is it we are shooting at each other?"
"You'd better ask your own people that!" Gurov exclaims, irritated.
"Oh, oh you are offended. Let us drink tea and our hearts grow kinder..."
They are silent for a time. Alibek returns to his theme, unhurriedly topping up his cup from the little teapot.
"It's not so far away. Every now and again you need to invade Europe. The old men say it will immediately bring peace to us and life will get back to normal."
"Some chance, Alibek. Don't hold your breath!"
"The tea is truly excellent. Oh, Anna Fedorovna, please make us some more. I beg you."
Gurov sighs.
"It really is going to be a lovely evening. You're right, there."
"I am always right, dear Colonel. Okay, ten Kalashnikovs. I agree. But seven crates of ammunition."
"You're at it again. Where do you pluck these numbers from? There is no such number as seven!"
The mistress of the house brings out the left-overs from lunch (in two white saucepans) to feed to her fortuitous soldiers. Rubakhin is keenly appreciative. "Oh yes, thank you very much!" When did a

soldier ever refuse food? "But where is your mate?" The inarticulate Rubakhin lies cloddishly that he thinks his mate has an upset stomach. As an afterthought he adds, only marginally more convincingly, "Really going through it he is, poor guy." "Perhaps he ate too much greens or fruit?" the lieutenant-colonel's wife asks solicitously.

The cold okroshka soup is really good, with egg and pieces of sausage. Rubakhin gets stuck in to the first saucepan, rattling out a signal with his spoon.

It is a signal which Vovka hears and, of course, correctly interprets, but eating is not the biological function presently uppermost in his mind. The young woman in turn hears (and also correctly interprets) the hysterical miaowing which comes from the yard, to be followed by the wail of her toddler ("Mu-um!"), evidently scratched in return for pulling the cat's tail. She is in thrall to her senses. She has languished for want of love and now clings ecstatically to Vovka, not wishing to miss this chance of happiness. As for Hot Shot Vovka, he is in his element, every inch a soldier. The child's petulant shriek is heard again, "Mu-u-um..."

The woman tears herself from the bed, sticks her head out the door, shushes the little pest, and shuts the door again more firmly. Padding across the floor in her bare feet she returns to her soldier and bursts into flames all over again. "Wow, you're hot! You really put out," Vovka tells her in delight, but she closes his mouth: "Shhh..."

Vovka explains his simple errand to her in a whisper, asking the young woman to pop down to the shop and buy him some of their terrible fortified wine. They won't sell it to a soldier in uniform, but it's no problem for her.

He shares his main worry with her too: right now they could do with not just a bottle but a whole crate of wine.

"What for?"

"To buy ourselves out of trouble. We're stuck at a roadblock."

"Well, if you need to buy wine what did you come to the colonel for?"

"Because we're idiots."

The young woman is suddenly crying. She tells Vovka she lost her way recently and got gang raped. Vovka gives a whistle of amazement. Having expressed proper sympathy, he asks (with considerable curiosity) how many of them there were. "Four," she sobs, wiping her eyes with a corner of the sheet. He is eager for more detail but she doesn't want to talk about it. She nuzzles her head in his chest, kissing it, hungry for words of comfort. A simple wish.

They talk some more. Yes, of course she will buy him the bottle of wine, but only if he comes to the shop with her so she can hand it straight over to him. She can't be seen coming home with a bottle after what happened to her. People know all about it. They will get ideas.

There is a lot of food in the second saucepan too, boiled barley and tinned beef. Rubakhin polishes off the lot, but without indecent haste. He washes it down with two mugs of cold water. This leaves him feeling slightly chilled, and he puts his shirt back on.

"Time for a little nap," he says to himself and retires to the fence.

He lies down and soon drifts off. Through the nearby open window of the house Vovka disappeared into a murmured conversation carries to him.

Vovka: "I'll give you a present, a nice headscarf, or I'll get you a shawl somewhere."

She: "But you're just now leaving." Weeping.

Vovka: "Well I'll send you it, then. 'Course I will!"

For a long time Vovka tries to get her to bend over. He is a bit stocky and has never made any secret of the fact that he likes to screw large women doggy fashion. He has readily described it to the other soldiers. Can she really not see what he's on about? It's such fun with a big woman. She fends him off coyly. To the sound of their incessant torrid whispering (he can no longer make out the words), Rubakhin falls asleep.

Outside the shop, the moment his girl handed over the bottle of wine, Hot Shot Vovka shoved it deep into a good strong pocket in his soldier's trousers and ran for all he was worth back to the deserted Rubakhin. The young woman had done him more than one favour and now shouted reproachfully after him, apprehensive about raising her voice in the street, but Vovka just waved. 'Bye. See you around. Now he had other fish to fry. He ran off down the narrow street, taking a short cut between the wicket fences, back to Lieutenant-Colonel Gurov's house. He had news for Rubakhin (and what news!). While he was hanging around minding his own business outside their dismal little shop (and also waiting for his bottle of wine) he had overheard some soldiers walking past.

Jumping over the fence, he found Rubakhin asleep and gave him a shake.

"Rubakhin, listen. This is straight. Savkin is taking a posse into the woods to disarm the competition."

"Eh?" Rubakhin looked at him blearily.

Trying to wake him up, Vovka blustered,

"They're going disarming. Let's get in on it. Nab a cloth-head and we've got it made. You said yourself..."

Rubakhin was now wide awake. Yes, he got the point. Yes, it was just what they needed. Ye-es, they would more than likely strike it lucky. They should move. The soldiers quietly absented themselves from the lieutenant-colonel's estate, carefully collecting their knapsacks and the guns they had left by the well. They climbed over the fence and left by someone else's gate so as not to be seen and called back.

The two men on the veranda did not see them, and did not call them back. They carried on sitting where they were.

It was hot, it was still, and Alibek was quietly singing "Midnights in Moscow" to himself. He had a clear voice.

It was still.

"People do not change, Alibek."

"You believe this?"

"They just grow older."

"Hah! Like you and me." Alibek refilled his cup with a thin stream of tea from his teapot. He no longer felt like haggling. He felt sad. He had in any case already said all he had to say, and now his words would (with their own unhurried logic) find their way to the heart of his old friend Gurov. There was no need to say them aloud.

"Good tea has completely disappeared. You can't get it any more."

"Too bad."

"Tea is getting more expensive, food is getting more expensive, but the times are not a-changing," Alibek drawled.

Gurov's wife was just at this moment bringing another two pots of tea. It was true. Tea was getting more expensive. "But whether the times are changing or not, you will bring us those provisions, my

The Captive of the Caucasus

friend," Gurov thought and also, for the moment, did not bother to say the words out loud.

Gurov knew that Alibek was brighter and craftier than he was. Against that his own thoughts, if not numerous, were solid and had been thought through over a period of many years to such a degree of clarity that they were no longer mere thoughts, but as much a part of his body as his hands and feet.

In the good old days (of the Soviet Union) if there was any disruption of the army supplies, or even if the soldiers' rations were merely delayed, Gurov would promptly don his dress uniform. He would pin on his medals. In the Gaz army jeep (the dust! the draught!) he would hurtle along the twisting mountain roads to the regional administrative centre, finally drawing up at a colonnaded building, sweeping in at full speed, looking neither at the visitors nor the petitioners worn down by long waiting, straight in to see the man at the top. If it wasn't the regional Party committee, it was the local Soviet. Gurov knew how to get what he needed. When necessary he would drive over to the warehouse himself, grease a few palms, and even sometimes persuade someone in power to see things his way by presenting them with a distinctive pistol. "Could come in handy: this is the Orient, you know!" he would say, little dreaming that one day his joke would become deadly earnest. Except that nowadays one pistol counted for nothing. Nowadays ten rifles got you nowhere, they wanted twelve. Gurov had soldiers to feed. As a man grows older he grows more resistant to change but, in compensation, more tolerant of human weakness. It keeps him on an even keel. He had himself to feed, come to that. Life was moving on, and Lieutenant-Colonel Gurov was giving it a helping hand, no more than that. Bartering weapons with the local fighters, he gave no thought to the use they would make of them. What was that to do with him? Life had moved on into a world of dealing (trade anything you like for anything you like) and Gurov was dealing. Life had moved on into a world where wars were fought (ghastly wars, neither one thing nor the other!), and Gurov, naturally, was there to fight in those wars. He was there to fight, but there was no shooting. Only from time to time he would disarm the competition when ordered to do so. Or shoot if the order came from the top. He could handle even this period. He was up to his job but... of course he missed the old times. He missed the old times when you knew where you stood, when you jumped into your jeep, swept into that office, could turn the air blue with oaths and then, condescending to make peace, flop down in a leather armchair and smoke with the regional official as if he were an old friend. While the petitioners waited their turn outside the door. One time he didn't find the Party boss in his office or at home. He was away on a business trip, but his wife wasn't. She was sitting there at home when Gurov arrived, and he got all he needed from her. She gave dashing young Major Gurov, whose hair at that time was just beginning to be streaked with grey, what only a bored wife left alone for a whole week in summer can give. All that and more, he thought, remembering the keys to the cavernous No. 2 cold store at the regional meat processing plant where they kept the freshly cured meat.

"Alibek! I've just remembered. Get us some smoked meat as well, would you?"

3

Since Tsarist times disarming expeditions in the Caucasus had been known as "horse-shoeing". Russian troops would surround the fighters but not fully close the encirclement. Just one way out would be left. Bolting down this path the fighters would become extended into a straggling single file. Mounting an ambush to the right or left it was then possible, if not exactly straightforward, to pick them off one at a time, dragging them into the bushes (or leaping out and knocking one off the path into the ditch and disarming him there). The operation was, of course, carried out to the accompaniment of much firing in the air to encourage them to leave the encirclement.

They both managed to infiltrate the disarming squad, but Vovka was spotted and chucked out: Lieutenant Savkin only trusted men he knew. His eyes flickered over the solid physique of Rubakhin without snagging, and no rasping order to take "Two paces forward!" ensued, most likely because Savkin simply hadn't noticed he was an outsider. Rubakhin was standing among a group of the most powerfully built soldiers. He fitted in well.

The minute they started shooting Rubakhin moved fast into position in an ambush. He had a quick smoke in the bushes with a

The Captive of the Caucasus

corporal called Gesha. They were both old timers and reminisced about others who had already been demobbed. They didn't envy them. Why the fuck should they? Who was to say who was better off anyway?

"Nifty movers, this lot," Gesha said, not bothering to raise his eyes to the shadows flitting past in the bushes.

At first the fighters ran by in twos and threes, crashing noisily through scrub that had sprouted up on the little used path, but now one or two stragglers were being caught. A shriek, a scuffle... and silence. ("They took him?" Gesha's look asked, and Rubakhin answered with a nod, "Yup".) The sound of someone again crashing towards them through the scrub was growing louder. The fighters could still just about shoot (and, of course, kill), but charging through scrub clutching a rifle and with an ammunition belt round your neck while under fire is not good for morale. Scared shitless and running into sporadic fire from the ambushes, the fighters needed no urging to keep to a path which seemed to be getting narrower, leading to the mountains and out of trouble.

"This one'll be mine then, okay?" Rubakhin said, half rising and moving fast towards the light.

"Go get him!" said Gesha, hastily finishing his cigarette.

"This one" turned out to be two running together, but having leaped out of the bushes Rubakhin could not change his mind. "Halt! Halt!" he yelled terrifyingly as he ran after them. He had not got off to much of a start. He was a muscleman not a sprinter, but once he built up speed neither the trampled bushes nor the loose scree underfoot could slow him. He flew like a bird.

He was pounding along six yards or so behind the second fighter. The first one was nippier than Rubakhin and pulling away. The second he was not too worried about (he was very close to him now). He could see the tommy gun round his neck, but either he was out of ammunition, or perhaps he just didn't know how to fire it on the run. The first was more dangerous. He did not have a gun, so he must have a pistol.

Rubakhin turned on the heat. He could hear running feet behind him. Gesha. Great! Two against two...

Catching up, he made no attempt to grab or tackle the fighter. By the time you had wrestled him to the ground, the other would be miles away. With a murderous left hook he sent him spinning off the path into the brittle bushes, shouting to Gesha, "One in the ditch! Get him!..." and raced after the first one with the long hair.

Rubakhin was running flat out, but his opponent was a good runner too. Whenever Rubakhin started gaining on him he speeded up, keeping a steady eight to ten yards between them. Half turning, Rubakhin's quarry raised his pistol and shot at him. Rubakhin saw he was very young. He took another shot at him (and lost ground. If he had not tried shooting he would have got away).

He was shooting over his left shoulder and the bullets were going very wide. Rubakhin did not even bother crouching when he saw him raising his hand. The fighter had enough sense, however, not to use up all his cartridges. He started pulling away again. Rubakhin saw his chance and without more ado flung his tommy gun at the fighter's legs.

The fugitive cried out in pain, jerked and started to fall. With a single leap Rubakhin was on top of him, immobilizing the hand that held the pistol with his own right hand, except that the pistol had vanished. He must have flung it aside as he fell, a fighter to the last! Rubakhin twisted his arms behind his back, wrenching his shoulder painfully, of course. "Ouch!" his prisoner cried, and stopped resisting. Rubakhin, still on a high, pulled a thong out of his pocket, tied the prisoner's hands, and sat him down by a tree, pushing his slight body against the trunk to tell him to sit still. Only then did he straighten up and walk back along the path, recovering his breath and scanning the grass, his attention already refocussed on the search for his own rifle and the discarded pistol.

Rubakhin again heard the approach of pounding feet. He leapt from the path back to the gnarled and stunted oak where his captive was sitting. "Not a squeak!" he commanded. The next instant several luckier fleet-footed fighters ran past, followed shortly afterwards by grunting and cursing Russian soldiers. Rubakhin left them to it. He had done what he came for.

He glanced at his captive's face, and was surprised. Firstly by how young he was, although it was not uncommon to find youngsters of sixteen or seventeen among the fighters. He had regular features and his skin was soft, but there was something else about the Caucasian's face. What? He had no time to think about it.

"Let's move," Rubakhin said, helping him to his feet (since his arms were tied behind his back).

As they marched back he warned him:

"Don't try to escape. Don't even think about it. I won't shoot you, but I'll hit you. Hard. Understand?"

His young prisoner was limping, his leg injured when Rubakhin threw the rifle at him. Or was he putting it on? Prisoners when caught often attempt to enlist their captor's sympathy by limping. Or heavy coughing.

4

A lot of fighters had been disarmed, twenty-two in all, which may have been why Rubakhin had little difficulty holding on to his prisoner. "This one is mine!" he repeated, resting his arm on the boy's shoulder among the general commotion and that final hubbub when attempts are being made to get the prisoners lined up to take them back to base. There was no falling off in the tension. The prisoners crowded together fearing that they were about to be split up. They held on to each other, shouting among themselves in their own language. Some did not even have their hands tied. "What do you mean, he's yours? Look how many we've caught. They belong to all of us!" Rubakhin shook his head, making it clear that while those might belong to all of us, this one belonged to him. Hot Shot Vovka appeared, as always, at just the right moment. He was miles better than Rubakhin at pulling the wool over someone's eyes while more or less telling the truth. "We've got to have him. Leave him be. We've got a note from Gurov... exchanging prisoners," he lied with his customary panache. "Well, you'll have to see the lieutenant about that." "We already have. He says that's okay!" Vovka effused, adding that the lieutenant colonel was presently at home drinking tea (which was true), and that the two of them had just come from there (also true), and that Gurov had signed this note for them personally and it was at the command post...

Vovka looked all in. Rubakhin glanced at him in puzzlement. He, Rubakhin, had just chased this long-haired lad through the scrub. He was the one who had caught and bound him. He had sweated blood, and here was Vovka looking knackered.

Having finally managed to line the prisoners up, the soldiers led them to the trucks. The weapons were carried well away from them, and somebody was counting: seventeen Kalashnikov rifles, seven pistols, a dozen grenades. Two of theirs had been killed during the hunt and two wounded. One of ours had been wounded, and Korotkov killed. The covered trucks were drawn up and, with an escorting armoured personnel carrier fore and aft, the column headed off, picking up speed, back to the unit. The soldiers in the trucks talked excitedly about the day's events and yelled at each other, and they were all ravenous.

The minute they arrived and climbed down from the trucks, Rubakhin and Hot Shot Vovka got themselves and their prisoner over to one side. Nobody argued. The prisoners were no great prize in themselves. The youngsters would be set free. More seasoned fighters would be imprisoned for two or three months in the guardhouse. If any of them attempted to escape they would be shot, not without some satisfaction. There was a war on. It could quite well have been these fighters who shot Boiarkov in his sleep (or just as he was opening his eyes). There wasn't a scratch on his face, just ants crawling over it. That first moment, Rubakhin and Vovka had started brushing them off. When they turned him over there was a gaping hole in his back. Boiarkov had been shot at point blank range, not sprayed with bullets. They had been pumped into his chest, shattering his ribs and blasting out his innards. On (and in) the ground was a mish-mash of ribs with his liver, kidneys, and loops of his guts on top of them, all in a great pool of coagulated blood. Several bullets had been stopped by his still steaming intestines. Boiarkov lay where they had turned him over with an enormous hole in his back, his guts and the bullets impacted in the ground.

Vovka turned to head for the canteen.

"He's a hostage. Lieutenant-Colonel Gurov has approved an exchange of prisoners," Vovka rattled out, pre-empting questions from the soldiers they met from Orlikov's squad.

The soldiers, full from their meal, shouted, "Say hello to the guys." They wanted to know who had been captured. Who was he being exchanged for?

"Exchange of prisoners," Hot Shot Vovka repeated uninformatively.

Vania Bravchenko laughed:

"Exchange of hard currency, you mean!"

Hook-nosed Sergeant Khodzhaev shouted,

"Well done, guys, he's quite a catch. They like ones like that. Their commander," he nodded in the direction of the hills, "likes ones like that very much." To make himself quite clear Khodzhaev laughed, showing his strong white soldier's teeth, and added: "You can get back two, three, five men for one like that. They love them like girls." Coming alongside Rubakhin, he winked suggestively.

Rubakhin grunted. He suddenly realized what it was that had been nagging him about the boy he had captured. He was very beautiful.

The prisoner did not speak Russian too well, but of course he understood everything. With squawking, guttural sounds, he shouted something back at Khodzhaev. His face and his cheekbones flushed, which only made it even more obvious how beautiful he was, with his dark, shoulder-length hair an oval frame for his face, with the set of his lips, and his straight, slender nose. Rubakhin's gaze was arrested by his large hazel eyes, wide set and with a slight oriental slant.

Vovka quickly talked the cook round. They needed a good meal to set them up for the return journey. Their fellow diners at the long plank table were a noisy, sweaty bunch, and it was very hot. They sat down at one end and Vovka immediately slipped the half-full bottle of wine out of his knapsack and furtively passed it under the table to Rubakhin who wedged it between his knees and finished it off unobserved by the others. "I left you exactly half, Rubakha. I trust you appreciate my bigheartedness."

He put a plate of food in front of the prisoner too.

"Not want," he responded curtly and turned away with a toss of his head.

Vovka pushed it nearer to him. "At least get stuck into the meat. It's a long march."

The prisoner said nothing. Vovka was afraid he was going to shoulder the plate away and the extra ration of stew and barley which he had coaxed from the cook with such skill would end up on the floor.

He quickly scraped the third portion on to his own and Rubakhin's plates. They finished it up, and it was time to go.

5

They drank at a stream, taking turns with a plastic cup. The prisoner must have been very thirsty. Advancing purposefully he fell to his knees, the pebbles grinding under him. He did not wait for them to untie his hands or give him a drink from their cup. Kneeling and bowing his face to the fast-flowing water, he drank at length. His hands tied behind his back were raised high in the air and were turning blue. He seemed to be praying in some bizarre manner.

Then he sat on the sand wet faced and pressed his cheek against his shoulder, trying his best to rid himself of the remaining drops of water on his face without the use of his hands. Rubakhin came over.

"We would've let you drink all you wanted, and untied your hands. What's the hurry?"

No reply. Rubakhin looked at him and wiped the water from his chin with his hand. His skin was so soft that the soldier's hand jerked back. He had not been expecting that. It was true. Just like a girl's, he thought.

Their eyes met, and Rubakhin immediately looked away, caught out by a sudden and none too moral impulse.

A sudden breeze blowing through the undergrowth put Rubakhin on the alert. Was someone there? His irresolution subsided (but it had only gone to ground: it was still there). Rubakhin was a simple soldier. He had no defence mechanisms to protect him against sheer human beauty, and now the same new and unfamiliar feeling seemed again to be coming over him. He remembered very well what Sergeant Khodhzaev had shouted, and the way he had winked. He really was going to have no option but come face to face with his captive in a moment. His prisoner could not cross the stream on his own. There were loose stones on the riverbed, the current was fierce, and he was bare-foot. His ankle had swollen so much that he had had to take off his excellent trainers just as they were setting out. (They were in Rubakhin's knapsack for the time being.) If he fell once or twice in crossing the stream he might be lamed completely. The current might drag him downstream. There was obviously no choice, and of course it would be for Rubakhin to carry him over. It was, after all, Rubakhin who had hurt his foot in the first place when he threw his gun at it in taking him prisoner.

A feeling of compassion came to Rubakhin's aid at just the right moment from somewhere up above, possibly heaven (although from the same quarter there again flooded over him the sense of irresolution, together with a renewed awareness of the boy's subversive beauty). Rubakhin was lost for only a moment. He caught the youth up in his arms and carried him over the stream. He resisted, but Rubakhin's muscular arms were strong.

"Now, now, stop kicking," he said, in much the same rough way as he would have spoken to a woman in a similar situation.

As he carried him he could feel the boy breathing. His prisoner had pointedly turned his face away, but his arms (untied while they crossed the stream) held on to Rubakhin tightly. He did not, after all, want to fall into the water or on to the rocks. Like anybody carrying someone in their arms, Rubakhin could not see where he was going and trod warily. Squinting sideways he could see only the water of the stream flowing in the distance, and against that background of leaping water, the profile of the boy, soft, pure, with his unexpectedly full lower lip pouting sulkily as if he were a girl.

They made their first halt on the other side. For safety they moved downstream from the path and sat in the undergrowth, Rubakhin's gun on his knees with the safety catch off. They were not hungry for the moment, but drank water several times. Vovka lay on his side fiddling with the dial on the little radio. It chattered barely audibly, gurgled and miaowed and exploded into alien speech. Vovka relied implicitly on Rubakhin's experience. He could hear a stone crunch under a stranger's foot a mile away.

"I'm going to have a kip, Rubakha. All right?" he warned straightforwardly, and instantly fell into a soldier's light sleep.

When the eagle-eyed Lieutenant Savkin winnowed him out of the disarmament squad, Vovka, having nothing better to do, went back to the young woman's shack (next to the lieutenant-colonel's house but Vovka was suitably discreet). Not surprisingly she berated the lover who had so unceremoniously abandoned her at the shop, but a minute later they were again looking into each other's eyes, and a minute after that they were back in bed. Vovka was consequently now pleasantly fatigued. He was all right for marching, but whenever they halted he immediately fell asleep.

Rubakhin found it easier to talk when they were on the march.

"... when you think about it, how can we be enemies? We are all one family. For heaven's sake, we were friends only recently, weren't we?" he asked agitatedly, even insistently, hiding the feeling which was so unsettling him behind hackneyed (Soviet) utterance. They were marching at a cracking pace.

Hot Shot Vovka snorted,

"Long live the indestructible friendship of the peoples of the Soviet Union..."

Rubakhin registered the sarcasm, but just said tersely,

"I wasn't talking to you."

Vovka dried up, but the boy too said nothing.

"I am just the same kind of human being as you, and you are the same as me. So why should we fight each other?" he persisted, but to no avail. He might as well have been mouthing his platitudes to the scrub and the path which, since the stream, was heading straight up into the mountains. Rubakhin wished the boy would at least disagree with him. He wanted to hear his voice, he wanted him to say something. (Rubakhin was feeling more and more disquieted.)

Hot Shot Vovka (without pausing) moved a finger and the radio in his knapsack twittered back to life. He tuned it some more and found a marching song, but Rubakhin went on talking. Eventually he tired and gave up.

Marching up a mountainside with a sore ankle and your hands tied behind your back is not easy. The captive was stumbling and finding it hard going. In one place where the ascent was steep he suddenly fell. He got himself up somehow and didn't complain, but Rubakhin saw his tears. He suddenly blurted out, "If you won't try to escape, I'll untie your hands. Promise me."

Hot Shot Vovka heard (through the music on the radio) and exclaimed,

"Rubakha, have you gone nuts?"

Vovka was marching ahead of them. He swore, registering his opinion of Rubakhin's soft-headedness. The radio was playing loudly.

"Vov. Turn it off. I need to be able to hear."

"Right."

The Captive of the Caucasus

The music was turned off.

Rubakhin untied the prisoner's hands. He wasn't going to get far from him, Rubakhin, with an ankle like that.

They were moving along at a fair pace, the prisoner in front, the semi-somnolent Vovka next to him and, slightly behind them, Rubakhin, wordless, his instincts ablaze.

You get a good feeling from freeing somebody, even if it is only their hands, and only for the duration of a march. There was a sweet taste in Rubakhin's mouth as he swallowed his saliva. It was a moment to remember. For all that his eye was as sharp as ever. The path became steeper. They skirted the mound where they had buried that piss-head Boiarkov. It was a lovely spot, bathed in the evening sunlight.

When they halted for the night Rubakhin gave the boy his woollen stockings to wear. He would wear his boots on bare feet. Everyone needed to get a night's sleep (they kept the campfire very small). Rubakhin confiscated Vovka's radio (not a sound at night). As always he kept the gun on his knees. He sat shoulder to shoulder with the captive and with his back to a tree in a huntsman's posture he had long favoured which allowed you to be ready for anything, but also to fall into a light slumber. It was night. He seemed to be asleep, but in parallel to sleep he was aware of the boy sitting by his side. He was so alert to him that he would have reacted instantly had his charge thought of making even the slightest unusual movement. But the captive was not thinking of escape. He was very downhearted. (Rubakhin could sense what was going on in his heart.) Now the two of them fell into drowsiness (trusting each other), and Rubakhin could again feel the boy being overwhelmed by sadness. During the day he had tried to appear disdainful, but now he was plainly sick at heart. Why should he be so sad? Rubakhin had earlier hinted unambiguously that they were not taking him off to a military prison or for some other dark purpose, but purely in order to hand him back to his own people in return for safe passage for themselves. No more to it than that. They would hand him back to his own side. Sitting here next to Rubakhin he had nothing to fear. Even if he had not actually been told about the trucks and the blocked road, he must surely know, he must be able to feel, that he was in no danger. More than that, he must know that he, Rubakhin, liked him. Rubakhin was suddenly again overcome with confusion. He squinted sideways. The boy was looking miserable. Darkness had fallen now and in the firelight the captive's face was just as beautiful, but very sad. "There, there," Rubakhin said kindly, wanting to raise his spirits.

He slowly reached out. Afraid of disturbing that face half-turned towards him and the breath-taking beauty of that motionless gaze, Rubakhin barely touched the fine cheekbone with his fingers, as if brushing back a long braid of hair flowing over his cheek. The boy did not pull away. He said nothing. It even seemed, but perhaps it only seemed so, as if his cheek responded, oh, barely perceptibly, to Rubakhin's touch.

Hot Shot Vovka had only to close his eyes to relive those sweet elusive minutes which had flown so swiftly in that village hut, moment by moment, the throbbing, too fleeting joy of intimacy with a woman. He could sleep sitting up, on his feet, even on the march. It was no wonder that he fell soundly asleep at night (even though it was his turn to keep watch), and failed to register an animal charging past them, quite possibly a wild boar. That made them all sit up. The sound of it crashing off through the undergrowth died away very, very slowly. "Do you want all of us to get shot in our sleep too?" Rubakhin gently tweaked the soldier's ear. He stood up listening intently. All quiet.

Adding more wood to the fire, Rubakhin walked round in circles, stood for a time looking up the defile, and came back. He sat down next to the prisoner again. After their fright he was sitting there looking tense and hunched. His handsome face had been swallowed up by the night.

"Well now, how do you feel," Rubakhin asked almost too straightforwardly. Under such circumstances a question as to his welfare is asked primarily as a means of keeping the prisoner under surveillance. Was his drowsiness perhaps feigned? Had he found himself a knife? Was he contemplating escape under cover of darkness while his captors were asleep? (Only if he was mad. Rubakhin would have caught up with him in an instant.)

"Fine," he answered laconically.

Neither of them spoke for a while.

Having asked the question, Rubakhin stayed there sitting next to him. He couldn't be forever changing his position by the fire.

Rubakhin patted his shoulder.

"Don't let it get to you. I told you, when we get you back we'll hand you over to your lot straight away. All right?"

He nodded. Yes, all right. Rubakhin gave an awkward chuckle, "You really are good-looking, though."

They sat in silence some more.

"How's your foot?"

"Fine."

"Right. Get some sleep. We're short of time. Let's get a bit more kip before it's morning."

And then, as if agreeing they needed to get a bit more kip, the young captive slowly inclined his head to the right and lowered it on to Rubakhin's shoulder. It didn't mean anything. It was just the way soldiers always make the best of their short sleep, huddled against each other. But now the warmth of his body, and with it a current of sensuality, in separate waves, began to reach Rubakhin, flowing through, wave after wave, from the boy's shoulder into his own. No, of course that wasn't it. The lad was asleep. He was simply sleeping, Rubakhin told himself, wrestling with temptation. He suddenly tensed as a great charge of warmth and unexpected tenderness passed through his shoulder and into his tremulous heart. Rubakhin froze, and the boy, feeling or guessing his alarm, also delicately froze. Another minute and the sensuality had gone from their contact. They were simply sitting side by side.

"Yes. Time to sleep," Rubakhin said to no one in particular, his eyes firmly fixed on the little red flames licking up from the fire.

The captive changed position, settling his head a little more comfortably on Rubakhin's shoulder, and almost immediately the flow of warmth, yielding and inviting, was there again. Rubakhin detected that the boy was trembling slightly. What could that mean, he wondered in turmoil, and again ran for cover, holding himself back, fearful of being given away by his own answering trembling. But that was not his real fear. He could cope with that. What terrified him was the thought that at any moment the boy would quietly turn his head. (All his movements were quiet and insidious, while at the same time seemingly without significance. Someone shifts while half asleep, what of it?) He would turn his face to him, almost touching him, and Rubakhin would inescapably feel his young life breathing in him and the closeness of his lips. That moment was very near. Rubakhin experienced a moment of weakness. His stomach was the first of his organs to protest at such an unwonted overloading of his senses and spasmed. Immediately the feel of the battle-scarred soldier's shoulder became as unyielding as a washboard. He was next convulsed by a fit of coughing, and the boy, as if taking fright, lifted his head from Rubakhin's shoulder.

Hot Shot Vovka woke up.

"You're booming like a cannon, you maniac. You can be heard half a mile away."

The carefree Vovka promptly fell asleep again and, as if in response, himself began snoring and wheezing sonorously.

Rubakhin laughed, as if to say, that's my fighting partner for you. Sleeps all day, sleeps all night.

The captive said slowly and with a smile,

"I think he had woman, yesterday."

Rubakhin feigned amazement: you reckon? Then, thinking back, he promptly conceded,

"You just might be right."

"I think yesterday in afternoon."

"You're right. Spot on!"

They laughed together, man to man.

But immediately afterwards, and very cautiously, Rubakhin's captive asked him,

"And you, you have woman long ago?"

Rubakhin shrugged.

"Long ago. A year ago, near enough."

"Not good-looking? A stupid cow? I think she was not good-looking. Soldiers have no good-looking women."

The pause that followed was long and awkward, and Rubakhin felt as if a great rock were pressing down, down on the back of his head...

Early in the morning the fire was completely out and Vovka, freezing cold, moved over to join them, pressing his face and shoulder against Rubakhin's back. The captive was snug by Rubakhin's side, and his sweet, warm body had beckoned him through all the hours of darkness. Thus the three of them, giving each other warmth, saw out the night.

They put a billycan full of water on the fire to boil.

"Tea-time everybody," Rubakhin said, a little guiltily after the unusual experiences of the night.

This guiltiness had come alive in him at first light, unsure of itself but now out in the open. Rubakhin had suddenly started courting the boy. (He was perplexed. This was the last thing he had expected of himself.) There was a restlessness in his hands, like a sickness. He twice made him tea in the plastic cup, dropping in pieces of sugar, stirring them noisily with a teaspoon, and serving it to him. He let him keep the stockings, evidently for good. "Wear them. You needn't take them off. You can walk on in them today." That was how considerate he had suddenly become.

He had started fussing, and kept stoking up the campfire to keep the boy warm.

The captive drank the tea, sitting on his heels, his eyes following Rubakhin's hands.

"These warm socks. Fine," he praised them, shifting his gaze to his feet.

"My mother knitted them."

"Oh..."

"Don't take them off. I told you, they'll help you walk. I'll find something to wind on my own feet."

The boy took a comb out of his pocket and busied himself with his hair, combing it at great length, proudly shaking his head from time to time, and then again with a practised hand smoothing it down to his shoulders. Taking pleasure in his beauty was as natural for him as breathing the air.

In the strong, warm woollen stockings the boy walked noticeably more confidently. In fact all in all he had perked up considerably. The sadness had gone from his eyes. He undoubtedly knew that Rubakhin had been thrown into confusion by the way their relationship was taking shape. He might even have been pleased a little. He would glance sideways at Rubakhin, at his arms, and his gun, and smiled a fleeting smile to himself, as if having gained a playful victory over the huge, powerful yet hopelessly bashful soldier.

When they again came to a stream he did not take the stockings off, but stood waiting for Rubakhin to come and catch him up. The boy no longer only clung to Rubakhin's collar. His gentle arm unashamedly circled the soldier's neck as he forded the stream and sometimes, as they lurched forward, he slipped his hand under his shirt to be more comfortable.

Rubakhin again took the radio off Hot Shot Vovka, and signalled them to silence. He was in charge. Here where the much trodden path widened out he would trust nobody until they made it to the white cliff already in sight. This was a dangerous spot, redeemed precisely by the fact that two narrow paths went their separate ways there (or, depending on how you looked at it, came together).

The cliff was known to the soldiers simply as the Nose. A large white triangular promontory of stone, it now bore down, looming towards them like the prow of a ship.

They had already begun climbing up through the tangle of scrub at the very foot of the cliff. This mustn't be happening, flashed through the soldier's mind when he heard danger bearing down on them from up there (from the right and the left simultaneously). People were coming down both sides of the cliff at once. Their steps were sure-footed, rapid and irregular. The enemy. Shit! For two hostile detachments to coincide minute for minute, blocking both paths at once, just mustn't be happening! The cliff's one saving grace was that you could hear someone coming and pass them unseen up the other track.

Now, of course, they had no time to get through either way, or even to dart back from the cliff across the open ground and into the woods. There were three of them, one a prisoner. They would be spotted straightaway and all instantly shot down, or simply chased into a thicket and surrounded. This mustn't be happening, his reason cheeped piteously for a third and final time before deserting him. Now everything was down to instinct. He felt a prickling in his nostrils. He was aware not only of their steps but, in the almost total absence of a breeze, he could even sense the slow straightening up of the grass they had trodden.

"Shhh."

He pressed a finger to his lips. Vovka understood, and nodded in the direction of the prisoner. What about him?

Rubakhin glanced at the boy's face. He too had instantly taken in the situation (his side were coming). His cheeks and forehead slowly flushed (an indicator of unpredictable behaviour).

"Oh, to hell with it!" Rubakhin murmured to himself, quickly readying his gun for action. He felt his cartridge belt, but the idea of taking them on (like any other idea in a moment of danger) also moved aside (deserted him), shying away from responsibility. Instinct told him to listen, and wait. The prickling in his nostrils, the quiet, meaningful straightening of the grass, the steps coming nearer. No. There were a lot of them. Too many... Rubakhin glanced once more at his prisoner's face, trying to read from it how he would react, what he would do. Would he keep down and stay silent (which would be fine) for fear of being killed or would he rush out towards them with mindless joy in huge half-crazy eyes and (the killer!) with a yell?

Without taking his eyes off those coming down the left path (this detachment was already close and would be the first to pass them), Rubakhin moved his hand back and cautiously touched his captive's body. The boy trembled slightly, like a woman anticipating love. Rubakhin touched his neck and felt upwards to his face. Gently touching the beautiful lips, he put his hand over the mouth which must stay silent. The boy's lips were trembling.

Rubakhin slowly drew the boy closer to himself (never taking his eyes off the approaching rank of men on the left path). Vovka was following the progress of the right-hand detachment whose steps could already be heard. Pebbles were cascading down. One of the fighters had slung his gun over his shoulder and it kept rasping against the gun of the man behind.

The boy did not resist. Putting his arm round his shoulder, Rubakhin drew him round to face him. The boy (less tall) moved closer, pressing towards him, his lips crushed against the spot under Rubakhin's unshaven chin where an artery was throbbing. He was trembling, not understanding. "N-n," he breathed, like a woman whose "No" did not mean no, but only testified to her modesty, while Rubakhin watched him and waited for any sign of a shout. How his eyes widened in fear, trying to avoid Rubakhin's look and see, through the expanse of air and sky, his own people. He opened his mouth, but did not shout. Perhaps he only wanted to breathe deeply, but Rubakhin had lowered his gun to the ground, and with his other hand smothered the half-opened mouth and the beautiful lips and the quivering nose. "N-neh", the captured boy wanted to tell him something, but was given no chance. His body stiffened, his legs straining, but there was no longer anything for them to strain against. Rubakhin had lifted him clear of the ground. He held him tightly in his arms, not letting him kick against the telltale bushes or the stones which would have gone clattering down. Rubakhin hooked the arm with which he held him round the boy's neck and crushed him. His beauty could not save him. A few convulsions and it was over. Had Rubakhin been in too much of a hurry? Or not? Accursed hands. Rubakhin's mind, which had deserted him in his moment of peril, now came stumbling back with a phrase half-remembered from his schooldays.

Beneath the cliff where the paths joined up guttural cries of amity were soon to be heard as the enemy detachments discovered each other. The two Russian soldiers could hear salutations and questions. How come you are here?! Which way are you going? The fighters slapped each other's backs. They laughed. One of them, taking advantage of the halt, decided to relieve himself and ran over to the cliff where it was less public, not suspecting that he was in a Russian gunsight. He was standing only a few yards from a clump of bushes behind which two live men and one dead boy lay stretched out. He urinated, hiccupped, did his trousers up, and hurried back.

When the detachments had passed and the sound of their voices and their feet marching down to the open ground had died away completely, two soldiers with tommy guns carried a dead body out of the bushes. They brought it to a sparse nearby wood along a path to the left where Rubakhin remembered a clearing, a dry patch of bare, soft, sandy earth. They dug a hole, dredging the sand out with flat stones. Hot Shot Vovka asked Rubakhin if he wanted to take his stockings back. Rubakhin shook his head. They said not a word about a human being to whose presence, in all truth, both of them had become accustomed. They sat half a minute in silence by his grave. What more could they do? There was a war on.

6

No change. As they approached Rubakhin could see the two trucks still stuck where they had been.

The road narrowed down to a tight corridor between two rock-faces, but the strait was guarded by hillmen. The trucks had been shot at in a desultory sort of way (but if they attempted to come any nearer they would be riddled with bullets). The trucks had been stranded here for three days already, waiting.

The fighters want weapons before they will let them through.

"We are not transporting guns! We haven't got any weapons," they shout from behind the trucks. A shot from the cliffs is their reply. Or a hail of bullets, a long burst of machine gun fire, capped with laughter, gusts of joyful, jubilant, childish laughter echoing from the heights.

The escorting soldiers and the drivers (six men in all) have settled in by the roadside bushes, shielded by the bodies of the trucks. They are leading a simple nomadic life, cooking their food on a campfire and sleeping.

When Rubakhin and Hot Shot Vovka get nearer, Rubakhin notices a pale, day-time campfire, up on the cliff where the fighters lie in ambush. They are cooking their lunch too. It is a low-key war. Why not eat properly if you can, and enjoy a mug of hot tea?

Of course, those up on the cliff have also observed the approach of Rubakhin and Vovka. The fighters are keen-eyed. Even though they can see that the same two who left have returned (without visibly bringing anything back with them), they loose off a couple of rounds from the cliff just to be on the safe side.

Rubakhin and Hot Shot Vovka make it back nevertheless.

The sergeant-major sticks his belly out and asks Rubakhin,

"Reinforcements on their way, then?"

"Like fuck."

Rubakhin does not elaborate.

"You didn't manage to get a prisoner?"

"Nah."

Rubakhin asked for water and drank long from the bucket, splashing it on to his tunic and his chest before blundering off and collapsing among the bushes to sleep. The grass was still flattened there. It was the same place where he had been lying two days before when someone prodded him in the side and he was sent for reinforcements (with Vovka as back-up). He sank face down with the crushed grass tickling his ears and deaf to the sergeant-major's grumbling. He was pissed off. He was tired.

Vovka sat down in the shade of a tree, stretched his legs in front of him and tilted a panama hat over his eyes. He started winding the drivers up: what had they managed to do while he was away? Hadn't they found an alternative route yet? Seriously? There was no alternative route, he was told earnestly. The slow-thinking drivers were lying in tall grass. One deftly rolled himself a cigarette from a piece of newspaper.

Sergeant-Major Beregovoi, bugged by the unsuccessful outcome of the foray, attempted to re-open negotiations.

"Hey, listen, guys. Hey," he shouted in a voice calculated to instil immediate trust. "I swear, we haven't got anything in these trucks. No weapons, no food. We are empty. You can send someone down to check it out. We shall show him everything, and we won't shoot him. Hey, are you listening?"

His reply was a burst of shooting, and merry laughter.

"Fuck your mother's soul," he swore.

There was sporadic fire from the cliff which went on for so long and so pointlessly that the sergeant-major swore once more and called, "Vovka. Come over here a minute."

The two drivers lying in the grass came to life. "Vovka, Go on. Show those cloth-heads how to shoot."

Hot Shot Vovka yawned, lazily detaching his back from the tree. (He had found a really comfortable position.)

As soon as he took up his rifle, however, every trace of lethargy vanished. He settled himself comfortably in the grass and, raising his rifle, centred in the telescopic sight now one, now another of the figures prancing about on the cliff towering over the road from the left. They were all in full view. He could have picked them off even without the telescopic sight.

At just that moment one of the hillmen standing on the cliff edge started ulullating mockingly.

"Vov, do you feel like giving it 'im?" a driver asked.

"I don't give a fuck about him," Vovka snorted.

After a moment's silence he added, "I like aiming at them and squeezing the trigger. I don't need a bullet to know when I've scored."

The impossibility of it all didn't need putting into words. If he did kill a fighter the trucks would have no chance at all of getting through.

"That one who's kicking up all that din, consider him rubbed out." Vovka pressed the trigger of the unloaded rifle. He was enjoying himself. He aimed again, and again recklessly pulled the trigger. "That's another off the list. And this one, I could rip half his arse off. Not waste him, no, he's got cover from that tree, but half his arse, all yours on a platter!"

Sometimes, if his eye was caught by some possession of the hillmen glinting in the sun, a bottle of vodka, say, or (since it was morning) a prized Chinese thermos flask, Vovka would meticulously take aim and shoot the conspicuous item into tiny pieces. Just at the moment there was nothing tempting.

Rubakhin meanwhile was sleeping fitfully. The same guilty, disconcerting vision kept coming back to him (or was Rubakhin, burrowing there in the grass, conjuring it himself): the handsome face of the captive.

"Vovka. Let's have a

moke." (What sort of fun was just aiming at them anyway?)

"Hang on a second." Vovka was well away by now, aiming at one after another, sweeping his cross-hair along the skyline of the cliff, down the edge of the rock, over the mountain scrub, along the trunk of a tree. Aha! His eye lighted on a scrawny fighter standing by the tree and snipping away at his greasy locks with a pair of scissors. Cutting your hair is a deeply personal matter. The mirror flashed, signalling to him, and Vovka instantly loaded the rifle and took aim. He pressed the trigger, and the silvery puddle fixed to the trunk of the elm tree shattered into a thousand pieces. The response was a volley of curses and the invariable random gunfire (as if a flock of cranes were calling beyond the cliff overhanging the road, giyaow, kiyaow, liyaow, kiyaow...). The tiny figures up on the cliff started running about, yelling, ulullating, but suddenly (evidently on a command) quietened down. For a time they did not show themselves so brazenly (and were generally better behaved). And, of course, they deluded themselves that they had taken cover, although Hot Shot Vovka could see not only their supposedly hidden heads, but the Adam's apples on their throats, their stomachs, even the buttons on their shirts, and he playfully moved his cross-hair from one button down to the next.

"Vovka. Pack it in," the sergeant-major restrained him.

"Sure," Vovka responded, lowering his rifle and heading back to the tall grass (with the soldier's eternal simple intention of having a sleep).

But Rubakhin was losing something: he could no longer hold the boy's features in his mind's eye for long, the face broke up almost as soon as it appeared. It lost definition and left behind only a general sense of prettiness, blurred and uninteresting, just somebody's forgotten face. His presence was melting away. But then, as if in farewell (perhaps, too, in forgiveness) the boy's features again became more or less clear. How his face now blazed, but not only his face, the boy himself stood there physically present before Rubakhin as if he were about to say something. He stepped even closer and suddenly threw his arms round Rubakhin's neck (as Rubakhin had done to him at the cliff), only his slight arms were as soft as a young woman's, impulsive but tender and Rubakhin (alert to the danger) had just time to register that man's weakness was about to come over him now in his sleep. He ground his teeth, forcibly driving the vision away, and immediately woke up, aware of an aching fullness in his groin.

"I need a smoke," he said hoarsely as he woke, and suddenly heard the shooting.

Perhaps it was the shooting that woke him. Tuk-tuk-tuk-tuk-tuk, a thin stream of rifle fire sent the stones flying and raised fountains of dust from the road beside the forlorn trucks. The trucks were going nowhere. (Rubakhin was not too bothered. At some point they would have to let them through.)

Hot Shot Vovka was asleep in the grass not far away, his rifle cradled in his arms. He had strong cigarettes for once (bought in the village shop at the same time as the wine), and they were conveniently sticking out of his breast pocket. Rubakhin selected one as Vovka snored quietly.

Rubakhin inhaled slowly. He lay on his back looking up at the sky, while to left and right (crowding in on his peripheral vision) the mountains of the Caucasus had him surrounded and would not set him free. Rubakhin had served out his time in the army, but whenever he decided to send it all to the devil and go back home for good (to the steppes beyond the Don), he would pack his belongings into his battered suitcase, and then stay. "What is it about this place anyway? The mountains?" he said out loud, with a vindictiveness directed solely at himself. What was so great about the monotony of life in the barracks, or the mountains themselves, for that matter, he wondered rattily. He was going to add, after all these years, but thought instead, after all these centuries... A slip of the tongue. The words had come up out of the darkness, and the startled soldier now mulled over this quiet thought which had been lying there somewhere in the depths of his mind. Grey, moss-covered gorges, the poor, grubby little huts of these mountain people, moulded like birds' nests. Was it the mountains? Their summits yellowed by the sun, crowded randomly together. The mountains. The mountains. The mountains. For how many years their majesty, their mute grandeur had given him no peace. What was it their beauty was trying to tell him. Why had it called to him?

June-September 1994

Published in Russian in *Novy Mir*, No 4, 1995

Vladimir Makanin is among the best known Russian writers of the last 20 years. Born in 1937 in the Urals, he was trained as a mathematician and later as film-maker. His first passion was chess and then the cinema, but he made his name with his highly individual stories which won him instant fame among the Russian intelligentsia during the years of the Thaw. Makanin became widely known with the publication in 1982 of his **Forebears**, a novel about a faith healer. Many of his novels have been outstandingly successful in translation in Germany, France, Spain, Eastern Europe and elsewhere. His better known works are available in English: **Voices** (in **Dissonant Voices**, Harvill, 1991), **Antileader** (Abbeville, USA), **Blue and Red, The Laggard, Two Solitudes.**

His novel **Manhole** was shortlisted for the Booker Russian Novel Prize in 1992 and published by Ardis (US), his **Baize-covered Table with Decanter** won the Prize. in 1993 and was published in English by Readers International in 1995.

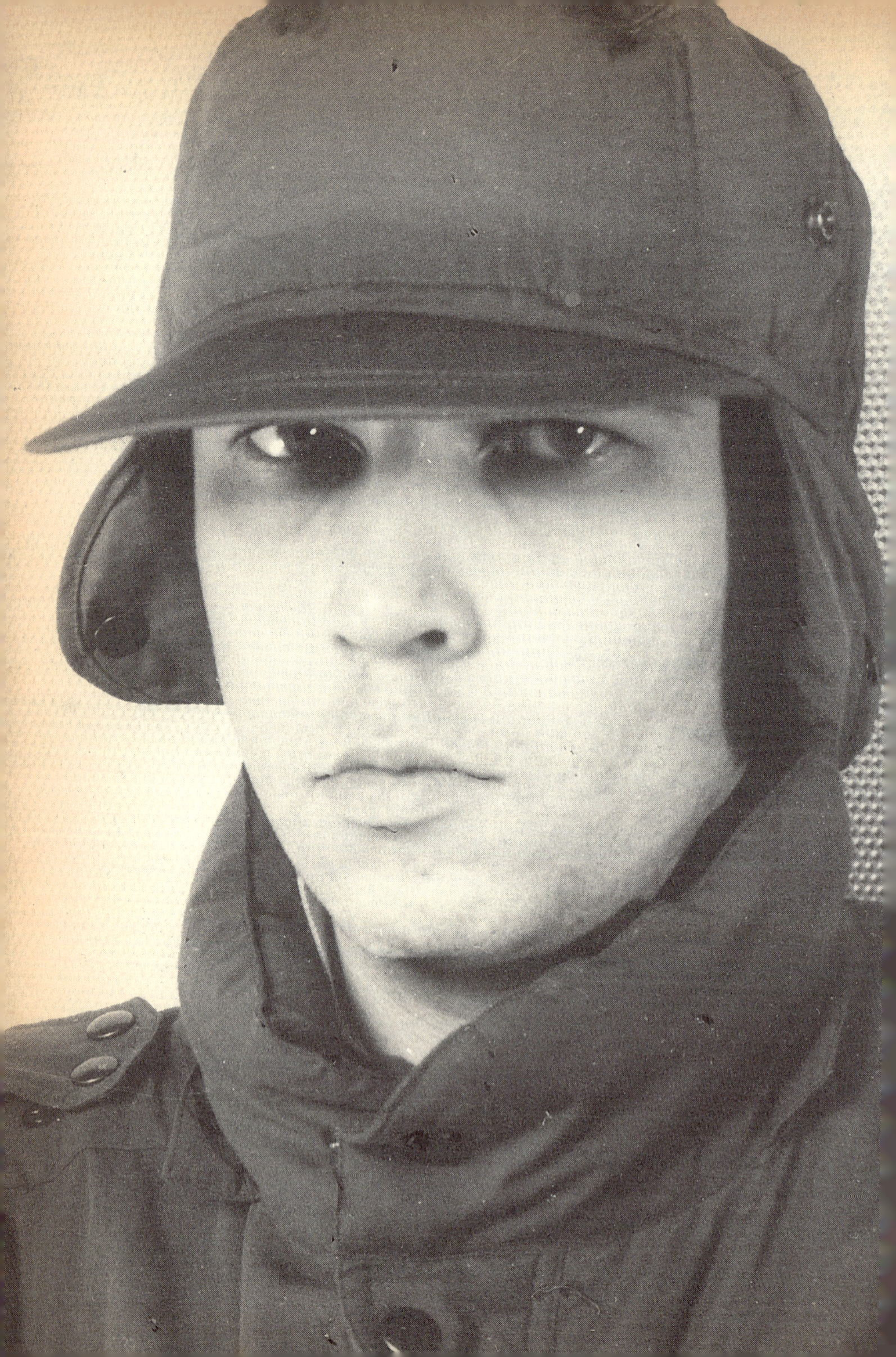

Victor PELEVIN

The Tambourine for the Upper World

Translated by James Escombe

Entering the railway carriage, the policeman cast a cursory glance at Tanya and Masha, looked over into the corner, and stared dumbfounded at the woman sitting there.

She did look pretty wild.

It was impossible to tell her age from her Mongol face, which resembled a stale pancake turned up at the edges. The more so, since her eyes were hidden behind dangling leather thongs and threads of beads. In spite of the warm weather, she was wearing a fur hat with three broad strips of hide attached to it. The first went round her forehead, and from it hung ribbons with small copper figurines on them, little bells and brasses. The other two strips of hide were joined across the crown of her head, and at the join was fastened a crudely fashioned metal bird with its twisted neck stretched upwards.

The woman was dressed in a hand-woven shift, adorned with strips of reindeer fur, embroidered with rawhide laces, and hung with shiny discs and any number of little bells, which made a pleasant tinkling sound with every lurch of the carriage. Apart from this, all sorts of small objects of no discernible purpose were fastened to her shift — serrated metal arrows, two Orders of Labour, bits of tinplate with mouthless faces beaten into them, while from her right shoulder, on a crepe ribbon, hung two long rusty nails. In her hand she held an oval tambourine, also made out of hide and embellished with many little bells, while the edge of another tambourine protruded from the capacious tennis-bag on which she was sitting.

"Your papers, please," the policeman finally said.

The woman produced absolutely no reaction to his words.

"She's with me," interjected Tanya. "She doesn't have any papers. And she speaks no Russian."

Tanya spoke wearily, like someone who has to repeat the same thing several times a day.

"What do you mean, she hasn't any papers?"

"Why should an elderly woman carry her papers with her? All her papers are in Moscow, at the Ministry of Culture. She's here with a folklore group."

"Why does she look like that?" asked the policeman.

"It's her national costume," answered Tanya. "Her culture."

"Ah," said the policeman, "national culture, I see. We had a

Chechen down at the station the other day, explaining why he had a sawn-off shotgun on him. He said it was part of his national costume: battle-green trousers, you know, leather jacket and an automatic rifle!"

"That was a bandit," Tanya said. "This is an honoured artist. She even has a medal, look, there, to the right of the bell. She's an Honoured Reindeer Breeder."

"So what? This is not the tundra. Here we'd call this a breach of the peace," said the policeman.

"What peace?" Tanya's voice rose. "The puddles of piss here on the platform? Or those thugs over there?"

She nodded in the direction of the connecting doors, from behind which drunken cries were clearly audible.

"Just sitting in the compartment is terrifying, but rather than keeping some sort of order, you go about checking old ladies' papers."

The policeman looked doubtfully at the person Tanya referred to as an "old lady". She sat there silently in the corner of the carriage, rocking in time with the train's movement, and taking no notice whatsoever of the scene she was creating. Despite her bizarre appearance, her small figure radiated such peace and contentment that, after looking at her for a minute, the policeman softened, smiled to himself at some distant memory, and relaxed his clutch on the truncheon hanging from his belt.

"What's her name?" he asked.

"Tuimi," answered Tanya.

"OK," said the policeman, pushing open the heavy door to the next carriage. "Only, just watch it..."

The door closed behind him, and the shouts from the next carriage grew a little fainter. The train braked, the doors opened, and for a few damp seconds the girls glimpsed an uneven asphalt platform. Behind it stood some low buildings with numerous chimneys of different shapes and sizes; smoke curled weakly from a few of them.

"Crematovo Station," announced an impassive female voice over the loudspeaker, when the doors were already closed. "Next station, 'Nameless Heights'."

"Is that ours?" asked Tanya.

Masha nodded and looked at Tuimi, who continued to sit in the corner, taking no part in the proceedings.

"Has she been with you long?" she asked.

"Three years," answered Tanya.

"Is she difficult?"

"No," said Tanya, "she's quiet enough. She sits all day long like that, in the kitchen watching television."

"Does she ever go out?"

"No," said Tanya. "She just sleeps on the balcony sometimes."

"But doesn't she find it hard? I mean, to live in a town?"

"Yes, she did at first," said Tanya, "but then she got used to it. She used to beat her tambourine all night, fighting with invisible ghosts. Now they seem to obey her. See those two nails hanging from her shoulder? She's defeated everybody. Now she only hides when there are fireworks, in the bathroom."

The station platform at "Nameless Heights" fully lived up to its name. Usually there are at least a few signs of human habitation alongside a railway station, but here there was nothing, except for the brick ticket office. Immediately beyond the fence enclosing the platform the forest began, and it stretched as far as the eye could see. God knows from whence the few shabby passengers on the platform could have come.

Masha, staggering under the weight of the tennis-bag, led the way. Tanya followed, with just such another bag on her shoulder, and Tuimi brought up the rear, her bells tinkling, and lifting the hem of her shift as she stepped over the puddles. On her feet she wore blue Chinese sneakers, and her legs were clad to the knee in thick leather leggings, stitched with beads. Turning round to look, Masha saw the round face of an alarm clock on the left legging, and on the right, hanging from a length of toilet chain, was a hoof, reaching almost to the ground.

"Listen, Tanya," she asked quietly, "what's that hoof for?"

"It's for the underworld," said Tanya. "She says everything's covered in mud down there. The hoof's so she won't sink in."

Masha wanted to ask about the clock-dial, but thought better of it. Somehow, its purpose was clear enough.

A good paved road led into the forest, lined with two rows of old birch trees. But after three or four hundred yards any order in the way the trees had been planted was lost. The asphalt petered out, and wet mud squelched beneath their feet.

Masha thought that, sometime, some local party functionary must have given the order to pave a road through the forest, but then it had become obvious that the road led nowhere, and so they had forgotten about it. The sight of it depressed Masha. Her own life, begun twenty-five years before by whose will she knew not, seemed to her like this road – first straight and even, lined with rows of simple truths, then forgotten by some unknown authority, before turning into a winding path that led she knew not whither.

"Must get away from here," she murmured, "must get away from here, never mind who with..."

"What's that?" asked Tanya.

"Nothing," answered Masha, "I'm just mumbling."

A length of white tape gleamed in front of them, tacked to a birch branch.

"Here we turn right into the forest," said Masha. "Another five hundred yards or so."

"It's so close," said Tanya doubtfully. "I can't understand how it's still there."

"Nobody comes this way," said Masha. "There's nothing here, and half the wood's surrounded by sagging barbed wire."

Indeed, there soon appeared before them a low concrete post, from which barbed wire stretched in both directions. Several more posts then became visible. – They were old, and all around them the undergrowth grew thickly, so that the barbed wire could only be seen when you got right up to it. The girls walked wordlessly along the wire fence, until Masha stopped beside yet another piece of white tape hanging from a bush.

"Here," she announced.

Several strands of the wire had been pulled together and twisted. Masha and Tanya climbed underneath without difficulty, but Tuimi crawled through backwards, getting her shift caught on the barbed wire, and her bells tinkled as she slowly negotiated her way through the narrow aperture.

On the other side of the wire the forest was just the same, without any sign of human activity. Masha walked confidently ahead, and

43

after a few minutes stopped at the edge of a gully with a small stream gurgling at the bottom of it.

"We're here," she said. "Over there, in the bushes."

Tanya looked downwards.

"I can't see anything," she said.

"There's the tail sticking out," said Masha, "and there's the wing. Come on, there's a way down here."

Tuimi did not go down. She sat on Tanya's bag, leaned her back against a tree and froze into stillness. Masha and Tanya, hanging on to the branches and slipping on the wet soil, went down into the gully.

"Listen, Tanya," said Masha in a low voice. "What's up with her? Doesn't she need to look? How's she going to do it?"

"Don't you worry," said Tanya, looking into the bushes. "She knows better than we do... Yes, there it is, it's still there."

Behind the bushes lay something a dirty dark brown in colour, and very old. At first sight it suggested the humped grave of some minor tribal chieftain who at the last moment had been hurried into conversion to some rare form of Christianity. From this long narrow hump there emerged askew a broad, cross-shaped construction of twisted metal, in which it was possible to discern the half-destroyed tail of an aeroplane, which had become detached from the fuselage at the time of the crash.

The fuselage was almost buried in the ground, but a few yards ahead, through some hazel trees and long grass, the outline of the wings could be seen, and on one of them a swastika gleamed blackly.

"I looked it up in a book," Masha broke the silence. "It's a Heinkel bomber. There were two modifications – one had a 30-millimetre cannon under the fuselage, the other had something else, I can't remember. Anyway, it doesn't matter."

"Did you open the cabin?" asked Tanya.

"No," said Masha, "I'd have been too scared on my own."

"Suppose there's nobody inside?"

"There is," said Masha. "The cabin's undamaged. Look."

She pushed aside the branches, and with her palm wiped away the layer of vegetable detritus built up over the years.

Tanya bent down and brought her face close to the glass. Behind it could be seen something dark and wet.

"How many of them were there?" she asked. "If it was a Heinkel, there ought to be a gunner as well, oughtn't there?"

"No idea," said Masha.

"All right," said Tanya. "Tuimi will find out. It's a pity the cabin's closed. If we could just have a lock of hair, or a bit of bone, how much easier it would be."

"You mean she can't do it without?"

"Oh yes, she can," said Tanya, "only it takes longer. It's getting dark. Come on, let's gather some branches for a fire."

"No, but, doesn't that hurt the quality?"

"What do you mean, 'quality'?" asked Tanya. "What sort of 'quality' are you expecting?"

The fire was burning well, and gave out more light than the evening sky, which was obscured by low clouds. Masha noticed her shadow dancing impatiently across the grass, and she felt odd – the shadow obviously felt so much surer of itself than she did. She felt stupid in her city dress, while Tuimi's costume, which people had been staring at all day, seemed in the flickering light of the fire the most fitting and natural dress for a human being.

"Now what?" asked Masha in a whisper, after a few moments of silence.

"Wait," replied Tanya in an equally low voice. "She'll start all on her own. We mustn't say anything to her now."

Masha sat on the ground beside her friend.

"I'm scared," she said, and rubbed the place on her windcheater which covered her heart. "How long do we have to wait?"

"I don't know. It's different every time. Last year, a couple of times..."

Masha started. The snap of the tambourine, alternating with the tinkling of many bells, sounded across the clearing. Tuimi was on her feet, bending forward, and looking into the bushes on the edge of the gully. Striking her tambourine one more time, she twice ran counter-clockwise round the clearing. Then, with amazing agility, she leapt over the wall of bushes and disappeared into the gully. From below came her plaintive cry, full of pain, and Masha thought she had broken her leg, but Tanya reassured her by closing her eyes.

From the gully rose frequent slaps on the tambourine and a rapid chattering. Then everything became still and Tuimi reappeared from the bushes. Now she moved slowly, ceremonially. Reaching the middle of the clearing, she halted and began rhythmically to tap the tambourine.

Masha closed her eyes, just in case.

A new sound was added to the tambourine. Masha was not aware of the precise moment when it started, and at first did not understand what it was. It seemed to her as though someone were playing on a stringed instrument, but then she realised that it was Tuimi's voice producing this piercing and sombre note.

It was as though the voice were emerging from some totally foreign space which the voice itself was producing, and through which it moved, colliding on the way with numerous objects whose nature was unclear, and each forcing Tuimi to utter disjointed, guttural cries. To Masha it suggested the image of a net being dragged across the bottom of a dark pool, gathering everything that fell into its path. Suddenly Tuimi's voice snagged on something. Masha felt she was trying to free herself from it but could not. Then her voice fell silent, and Masha opened her eyes.

Tuimi was standing not far from the campfire, and was trying to withdraw her hand from this space, this void. She pulled with all her strength, but the void would not let her go.

"Nilti doglong," cried Tuimi in a menacing voice. "Nilti dzhamai!"

Masha was quite convinced that the void before Tuimi was saying something in reply.

Tuimi laughed and shook her tambourine.

"Nein, Herr General," she said, "das hat mit Ihnen gar nichts zu tun. Ich bin hier wegen ganz anderer Angelegenheit." The void asked some question, and Tuimi shook her head in emphatic refusal.

"What's she doing, is she talking German?" asked Masha.

"When she's in a trance she can speak any language."

Tuimi tried to extricate her hand again.

"Heute ist schon zu spaet, Herr General. Verzeihung, ich hab' es sehr eilig," she said, angrily.

This time Masha felt a threat emerging from the void.

"Wozu?" cried Tuimi scornfully, and she tore from her shoulder the crepe ribbon with the two rusty nails, and swung it above her head. "Nilti dzhamai! Blya budulan!"

The void released her hand so quickly that Tuimi fell back on to the grass. As she fell, she laughed, turned to Tanya and Masha, and emphatically shook her head.

"What's the matter?" asked Masha.

"It doesn't look good," said Tanya. "There's no sign of your client in the underworld."

"Maybe she didn't look far enough?" asked Masha.

"What do you mean, far enough? There's no far or near down there. No beginning and no end either, for that matter."

"So what do we do now?"

"We can still try the upper world," said Tanya, "only the chances aren't good. We've never managed it so far, but of course, we can always try."

She turned towards Tuimi, who was sitting on the grass as before, and raised her finger. Tuimi nodded, went over to the tennis-bag lying by the tree, and took from it another tambourine.

The tambourine for the upper world sounded different, softer and somehow thoughtful. Tuimi's voice, on a long- drawn, plaintive note, was also changed, and instead of terror it aroused in Masha feelings of peace and a gentle melancholy. She repeated the same ritual as a few minutes earlier, only on this occasion the procedure was not sinister, at the same time exalted and yet unfitting. Why it was unfitting even Masha could understand. It was quite inappropriate to disturb those parts of the world to which Tuimi was now appealing, as she lifted her face to the dark sky between the branches, lightly tapping her tambourine.

Masha remembered an old cartoon film about the adventures of a little grey wolf in dense, dark, gloomy woods near Moscow. Every now and then in the cartoon all this would disappear and be magically replaced by a new scene of a road flooded in noonday sunlight, so overexposed as to be almost transparent, and along a washed out watercolour road a barely sketched wanderer was making his way.

Masha shook her head to bring herself back to her senses, and looked round. The objects surrounding her, the undergrowth, the trees, the grass and the dark clouds which had until now merged together into one mass, seemed now to be separating in response to the sounds from the tambourine, and in the gaps between them a strange, luminous, and unknown world momentarily opened out.

Tuimi's voice stumbled against some object, tried to go forward, then stayed on one insistent note, as though it had hit a concrete wall.

Tanya tugged Masha's hand.

"He's there," she said. "We've found him. Now she'll catch him."

Tuimi raised her arms, gave a piercing cry, and fell back on to the grass.

The distant drone of an aeroplane reached Masha's ears. It was impossible to tell from where it was coming and the sound continued for a long time, but when it ceased there came a whole series of noises from the gully. The crash of breaking glass, the rending of rusty metal, and the soft but clearly recognizable sound of a man's cough.

Tanya stood up, walked a few paces towards the gully, and then Masha saw a dark figure there at the edge of the clearing.

"Sprechen Sie Deutsch?" asked Tanya hoarsely.

The figure moved silently towards the fire.

"Sprechen Sie Deutsch?" cried Tanya, backing away. "Are you deaf or something?"

The reddish light of the fire fell on a strongly-built man of about forty, dressed in a leather jacket and flying-helmet. Coming up to them, he sat down in front of the giggling Tuimi, crossed his legs and raised his eyes towards Tanya.

"Sprechen sie Deutsch?" Tanya repeated her question.

"Oh, do give over," the man said quietly in Russian.

Tanya whistled in amazement.

"Who on earth are you?" she asked, sitting down.

"Me? I'm Major Zvyagintsev. Nikolay Ivanovich Zvyagintsev. And who might you be?"

Masha and Tanya looked at each other.

"I don't understand," said Tanya. "How can you be Major Zvyagintsev if that aeroplane is German?"

"The aeroplane was captured," said the major. "I was flying it to another airfield, and then..."

Major Zvyagintsev's face twisted in a grimace. Evidently he had remembered an extremely unpleasant experience.

"So you're what?" asked Tanya. "Soviet?"

"You could say that," replied Major Zvyagintsev. "I was Soviet, but now I don't know. It's all a bit different where we come from."

He raised his eyes to Masha. For some reason, she blushed and turned her face away.

"And what are you girls after here?" he asked. "After all, the ways of the living and the dead are not the same. Isn't that so?"

"Oh," said Tanya, "please forgive us. We're not out to disturb Russians. It's all because of the aeroplane. We thought there was a German inside."

"Whatever do you want a German for?"

Masha raised her eyes and looked intently at the major. He had a broad, placid face, with a slightly turned-up nose, and several days' stubble on his cheeks. Masha liked such faces – though it was true that the major's looks were rather spoiled by the bullet-hole in his left cheekbone. But Masha had already come to the conclusion that perfection doesn't exist in this world, and didn't seek it in people, least of all in their outward appearance.

"Well, you see," began Tanya. "Times are so hard today, everybody has to manage as best they can. So she and I..."

She nodded in the direction of the unconcerned Tuimi.

"In short, we're in a sort of business. You see, everybody's getting the hell out of Russia. To marry a foreigner costs four hundred bucks. We usually charge five hundred ourselves, on average."

"What, for corpses?" asked the major incredulously.

"Just think. The nationality's still there. We bring them back to life on the condition they get married. It's usually Germans. For a dead German we charge about the same as for a live Zimbabwean, or a Russian Jew without an exit visa. Best of all, of course, is a Spaniard from the "Blue Division", but they come expensive. And they're rare. Then, we get Italians, and Finns. But Rumanians and Hungarians we don't touch."

"Well, well, well," said the major. "And do they live long afterwards?"

"About three years," replied Tanya.

"That's not long," said the major. "Aren't you sorry for them?"

Tanya thought for a moment, and her pretty face grew serious. A deep furrow formed between her brows. There was silence, broken only by the crackling of the logs in the fire and the quiet whispering of the leaves.

"That's a hard question," she said finally. "Are you serious?"

"Absolutely."

Tanya thought a moment longer.

"Well, the way I heard," she began, "'is there's this one rule for earth and another one for heaven. Get the power of heaven going on earth and you set all creation astir and the invisible becomes visible. It has no substance of its own, being by nature but a fleeting condensation of darkness. That's why it doesn't stay long in the vortex of transformations. In fact really it's just a lot of emptiness, which is why I don't really feel sorry for them."

"That's just how it is," the major said. "You hit the nail on the head."

The furrow between Tanya's brows was smoothed away.

"Honestly, there's so much work you don't have time to think. We usually shift about ten a month, less in winter. Tuimi's got a two-year waiting list in Moscow."

"These people you bring back to life, do they all agree?"

"Practically all of them," Tanya replied. "It's desperately sad where they are. Dark, overcrowded, no grace. You grit your teeth and bear it there. Mind you, I don't know what it's like with you, we haven't had a client from the upper world before. Still, dead folk are all different in the underworld too. It was like that near Kharkov last year – terrifying. We got hold of this tank driver from the Death's Head Battalion. We dressed him, washed him, shaved him, explained everything to him. He agreed – I mean, we had a really good bride for him, Marina, from the Faculty of Journalism. We fixed her up later with a Japanese sailor... Lord, you should see them float up to the surface... I remember... What was I saying?"

"The tank driver," said the major.

"Oh yes. Well, to cut a long story short, we gave him some money to make him feel he'd got a life, and of course he started to drink; they all do at the beginning. Then at some private bar or other they wouldn't sell him a drop. They wanted roubles, and all he had was German occupation marks. So the first thing he did, he smashed their windows with his revolver, and that night he rolled up on his Tiger tank and flattened every last bar around the station. Ever since that they often see his tank at night driving around Kharkov, flattening all the private shops, but come daylight it disappears. Nobody knows where it goes."

"The world's a funny old place," the major said.

"Since then we've only worked with the Wehrmacht. We won't touch the SS. Their brains are all scrambled. Before you know it they'll seize a village soviet, or start singing in chorus. And anyway, they don't want to get married – it's against their regulations."

A blast of cold air swept across the clearing. Masha lifted her fascinated gaze from Major Zvyagintsev and saw three indistinct, ghostly figures emerging from behind three tree trunks at the edge of the clearing. Tuimi gave a squeal and hid behind Tanya.

"There," gulped Tanya, "it's beginning. Don't be afraid, you silly old thing, they won't touch you."

She rose and went to meet the ghostly figures, making calming gestures as she approached them, like a car driver stopped by the traffic police. Tuimi rolled herself into a ball, put her head between her knees, and began trembling quietly. Masha, just in case, moved closer to the fire, then suddenly felt with her whole body the full force of Major Zvyagintsev's eyes upon her. She looked up. The major smiled sadly.

"You're so beautiful, Masha," he said quietly. "You know, I was working in the garden when your Tuimi began calling me. She went on and on. It really got on my nerves. I wanted to chase you all off. I looked out and saw you there, Masha. There is no telling how much I liked you. There was a girl at school like you. Varya, her name was. She was so like you, the same freckled nose, but she wore her hair longer than you do. I was in love with her. Would I really have come if it hadn't been for you?"

"Have you got a garden there then?" Masha asked, blushing a little in embarrassment.

"Yes," replied the major.

"What's it called, this place where you live?"

"We don't have any names there," said the major. "That's why we live in peace and happiness."

"What's it like there, though?" Masha asked.

"It's all right," the major said, and his lips again parted in a smile.

"Do you have things, you know, possessions, like people here do?" asked Masha.

"How can I put it, Masha? On the one hand, we sort of do, but on the other, we sort of don't. Everything's a bit approximate, a bit blurred. But only when you think about it."

"Where do you live?" Masha asked.

"I've got a kind of cottage, and a bit of ground," said the major. "It's so quiet there, nice."

"Have you got a car?" Masha asked, and instantly drew back. It suddenly seemed such a stupid question.

"If you want one, you can have one," said the major. "Why not?"

"What sort?"

"It all depends," said the major. "You can have a microwave oven too, and a, what's it called, a washing machine. Only there's nothing to wash. And a colour television – mind you, there's only the one channel, but we get all your channels on it."

"Does it all depend, what kind of television you have too?"

"Well," said the major, "sometimes it's a Panasonic, sometimes a Shiwaki. But when you try to remember, it's not there any more, it's gone. There's just shimmering vapour there. I told you, it's all the same as here, except that nothing has a name there. Everything is nameless. And the closer you get to heaven, the more nameless everything becomes."

Masha could not think what else to ask him, so she fell silent, pondering the major's last words. Meanwhile, Tanya was making some very emphatic point to the three ghostly figures.

"How many times do I have to tell you, she uses thunder for her magic," her indignant voice could be heard saying. "It's all perfectly above board. She was struck by lightning as a child, and the spirit of the thunder gave her a piece of tin, to make herself a peak for her hat... Why should I produce it for you? She's under no obligation to carry it around with her. We've never had any problems of that sort... You should be ashamed of yourselves being so suspicious of an old woman. You'd be better employed going after the faith-healers in Moscow. It's positively scary living there now, and all you can do is pick on a poor old woman. I'll lodge a complaint and all..."

Masha felt the major's hand on her elbow.

"Masha," he said. "I'm going now. There's something I'd like to give you to remember me by."

Masha noticed a note of intimacy in his voice. She was pleased by it.

The Tambourine for the Upper World

"What's this," she asked.

"It's a reed pipe," said the major. "When you get tired of this life, come to my plane. Play on it and I'll come out to you."

"Could I come and visit you?" Masha asked.

"Certainly," the major replied. "Just wait till you taste my strawberries!"

He rose to his feet.

"You'll come then?" he asked. "I'll be waiting."

Masha gave an almost imperceptible nod.

"But what about you... Aren't you alive again now?" she asked.

The major shrugged, took a rusty TT revolver from the pocket of his leather flying-jacket, and put it to his ear.

A shot rang out.

Tanya turned and stared at the major in alarm. He staggered but kept his feet. Tuimi looked up and giggled. The cold wind came again, and Masha saw there were no longer any ghostly figures at the edge of the clearing.

"I'll be waiting," Major Zvyagintsev repeated, walking unsteadily towards the gully, over which a barely visible opalescence was hovering. A few steps more and his figure dissolved in the darkness, like a lump of sugar in a glass of hot tea.

Masha was looking out of the train window at the passing cottages with their vegetable gardens. She was weeping quietly.

"Don't, Masha. Don't be so upset," said Tanya, looking at her friend's weeping face. "Never mind, it just happens that way sometimes. Would you like to come to Arkhangelsk with the girls. There's an American B-29 Flying Fortress lying in a bog there. Eleven bodies. Enough for everybody. Why don't you come?"

"When are you thinking of going?" Masha asked.

"After the fifteenth. By the way, come and see us on the fifteenth, it's the Festival of the Pure Hearth. Tuimi's going to cook some wild mushrooms. We'll play on the tambourine for the upper world for you, as you like that so much. Hey, Tuimi, wouldn't it be good if Masha came to see us?"

Tuimi looked up and answered with a broad smile, displaying the brown stumps of her teeth which stuck out of her gums at odd angles. It was an unnerving smile because Tuimi's eyes were hidden behind the thongs of hide that hung down from her hat, which made it seem as if only her mouth were smiling, while her unseen gaze remained cold and attentive.

"Don't be frightened," said Tanya. "She's a good person."

Masha, however, was already looking out of the window, clasping in her pocket the reed pipe Major Zvyagintsev had given her, and thinking intently about something.

Published in Russian in *Oktyabr*, No. 2, 1993

This story will also appear in a collection of Victor Pelevin's short stories to be published by New Directions in New York.

Victor Pelevin (b.1962) has been widely published in many countries in the last few years. See also English translations of his stories in **Glas** 4 and 7.

Victor Pelevin
THE LIFE OF INSECTS
Harbord Publishing, 58 Harbord St. London SW6 6PJ, UK

After the success of his first novel, *Omon Ra*, Harbord publishes a second work by one of Russia's most talented young writers, "a natural story-teller with a wonderfully absurd imagination," as he was acclaimed by *The Observer*.

Set in a decaying resort on the Black Sea, *The Life of Insects* is Pelevin's laconic vision of late-Soviet grotesque, a Kafkaesque fantasy whose participants exist simultaneously as human beings and as insects, drifting through a world governed by greed and instinct. Alternately comic and philosophical, Pelevin's imagination is as rich and inventive as ever.

ALSO AVAILABLE FROM HARBORD PUBLISHING:
Victor PELEVIN's *Omon Ra*, 160 pp.

Vladimir Makanin
BAIZE-COVERED TABLE WITH DECANTER

Translated by Arch Tait
Readers International, London, UK, and Columbia, USA

WINNER OF THE RUSSIAN BOOKER PRIZE

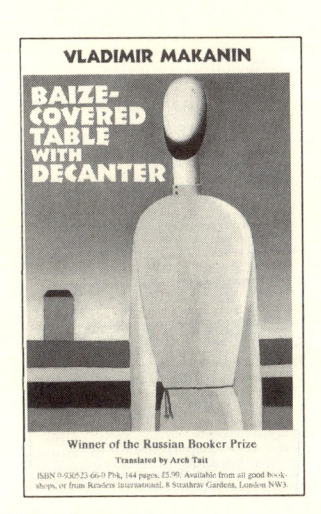

The hero of *Baize-covered Table* undergoes a searching bureaucratic investigation, that staple of the old Soviet and even older Russian police state. With the naked intensity of personal nightmare, the hero visits and returns to the stark scene of his inquisition: the bare room, the table, the ever-present decanter, and behind the table those recurring phantoms, "The Party Man", "The Young Wolf, "The Almost Pretty Woman", "The One Who Asks the Questions."

"It's the table that gives power to the people behind it," says Makanin. "Take it away and they're just ordinary folk, you and me, your best friends maybe. I've lived with these phantoms from childhood. Any Russian — it's an old Russian nightmare we're dealing with, not just a Soviet one — would recognize the situation. Having them rummage in your insides, being helpless, belittled. You needn't have done anything to realize your helplessness, your guilt."

"AN OUTSTANDING WORK OF RUSSIAN PROSE."
    — **Times Literary Supplement**
"Makanin has found a brilliant device
for giving his dystopian fantasy a human face."
    — **Sunday Telegraph**

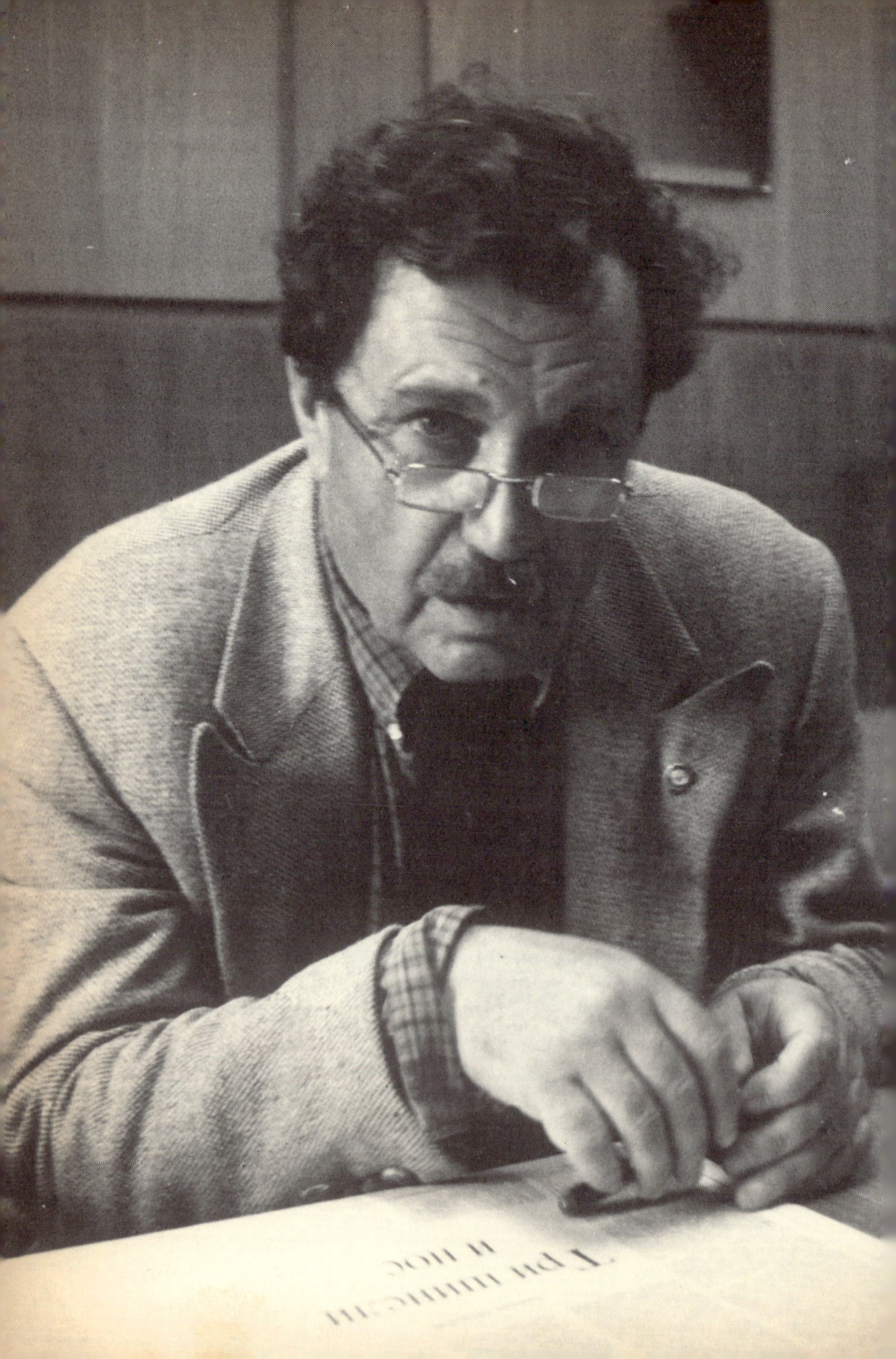

Vassily AKSYONOV

Palmer's First Flight
Palmer's Second Flight

Translated by Alla Zbinovsky

Vassily Aksyonov

Palmer's First Flight

The artist Modest Orlovich sat in his studio, located behind the old wall of Moscow's Kitai-gorod with windows looking out on the Bolshoi Theater. Outside, in December of 1991, Soviet communism was in its death throes. Meanwhile, in Orlovich's studio, something violet with crimson bruises was taking shape and a stormy blue with a lead underbelly was materializing – the new waves of an acrylic revolution.

In the dismal studio, the television was expressing itself with colorful flashes. That frightening fiend of a rock-star Kierkegorenko wailed predictably: "Red swine, get out of the Kremlin! Out of the Kremlin, the ground is groaning!" The smell of roasting turkey was wafting through the whole studio: Orlovich's girl friends Muse Borisovna and Hamayun Bird were preparing to receive guests on the occasion of the end of violet and the onset of blue.

The zinc-coated door began to shake, it was clearly being kicked. In former times, Orlovich would definitely have thought: "The vipers are here," although he had never given the "vipers" any special reason for coming, except for his famous leap into the trowel of the "Belarus" bulldozer, sent to plow down an unofficial outdoor art exhibition in the fall of 1974. His yellow-green scarf then flew over the dispersed modernist paintings, until it was thrown into a ditch along with everything else.

Now then, after all the events at the barricades during the August coup, the "comrades" won't be coming again, thought Orlovich. However, the door continued to shake as if being kicked by proletarian boots. With the help of his long levers, Orlovich climbed out of the crushed couch to open the door. Instead of a boot, a bare foot pushed its way into the studio. The proletarian turned out to be his declasse neighbor, Misha Chuvakin. "What are you locking yourself in for? What's happening, are you pigging out on sausage?" He made his way inside, spreading the disgusting smell of potato salad, akin to vomit.

Orlovich saw himself together with Chuvakin in the crookedly hung nineteenth-century mirror. "We deserve each other," he thought. "What vile slovenliness in our faces, our hair and clothing.

But you know, I've got two good suits, razors and eau-de-Cologne, to somehow set myself apart from Chuvakin."

"Does anything need fixing?" asked the neighbor, for some reason looking behind the mirror. Everyone in the apartment building knew that for all his appearance of a "Russian handyman", he could never fix anything and never intended to, and that his main business was – to penetrate a milieu so that he could get things from them, which was why he always appeared with proposals to fix something.

"Misha, what is it you need right now?" asked Orlovich.

"Some German woman is here, Modest. Maybe you could chat with her awhile," said Chuvakin.

"This is something new. Perhaps she's even an Englishwoman?" said the surprised artist.

Misha Chuvakin told this short story. In principle, he was sleeping already, having eaten some noodles in chicken broth. When this rock festival began, he shut himself off and even turned out the slutty Smaragda. "Modest, if you think I'm wiped out because of a hangover, then you're dead wrong! I'm just tired, working till dawn in the brigade dismantling the Kalinin monument, Mikhal-Vanych, the All-Union elder. Why so many details, Modest? What is there for people to talk about, if not the details?"

Casually pouring himself a glass of wheat vodka from an open bottle, and gulping it down as if it were beside the point, as if this were not the real reason he had come, Chuvakin continued. He had heard some sort of knocking through his dreams, somehow it seemed like an alien kind of knock, well you know, not the way the local police inspector knocks. The slutty Smaragda went to open the door and returned with a German woman. A young woman, not at all a slut. A slightly lame Englishwoman, as if a flower, well, a German. Trembling and holding out a baby in blue ribbons.

Here is a Dickensian story for you, with a Kitai-gorod twist to it, thought Orlovich. Christmas is coming, a lame German-Dutch woman with a blue-ribboned baby. Moscow, anarchy. "Chuvakin, aren't you twisting things just a bit, indulging in mythological thinking?"

Chuvakin was suddenly very offended. He addressed his neighbor in a friendly way, called him by his first name, Modest, and that one condescended by calling him by his surname Chuvakin.

"You're fucking around with me, Modest, you're not treating me like one of your own, as if I'm not your neighbor. I come to you for help, to translate what this single mother is saying, and you keep me at arm's length, as if I were a drunk." After splashing down another half-glass with the same casualness, as if he didn't attach the slghtest importance to the main liquid in his life, the declasse Chuvakin stomped to the door.

"What ribbons, you ask, what baby? See for yourself!"

Orlovich now saw with his own eyes an Englishwoman in the stairwell, or maybe a German or a Swede, in a black down coat and thick ear-muffs perched on the sides of her elongated head. She was wearing enormous down-filled gloves, with which she pressed a substantial package tied with blue string to her chest.

This was one Kimberly Palmer from the city of Strasburg, state of Virginia, USA (we beg you not to confuse it with the Strasbourger Torte found in the center of Western Europe). She was 29 years old. For some unknown reason, any mention of Russia, even as a small child, caused her throat muscles to spasm, and her tear ducts to well up. This strange emotional reaction brought her to the Russian program at Vanderbilt University, located in Nashville, Tennessee. She spent a whole semester in a state of agitation while taking courses in Russian geography and history; well, and in her Dostoyevsky class she lost all control. One night all her suite mates came running into her room, alarmed by the sobbing: Palmer was reading Dostoyevsky's "Netochka Nezvanova" in the Andrew MacAndrew translation. She would have made an excellent Slavicist, if she hadn't been forced to cut her education short. It so happened that her father, Mr Palmer, went mad from the endless life in the scenic Shenandoah Valley and cut his capers, completely in keeping with the spirit of Dostoyevsky's heroes. Without a word to his family, he re-mortgaged their house, took all the cash and went somewhere to the devil, maybe even to Las Vegas, for good. The mother, Mrs Palmer, collapsed under the weight of the monthly payments, the younger brothers went wild, and Kimberly, almost repeating the heroic act of Sonechka Marmeladova, sold herself to a bank called "Perpetual". And so, she got stuck there for some years in the car loan department behind an all-glass window with old-fashioned calligraphic lettering and a view of a Strasburg intersection: a traffic light, a competitor bank "First Virginia", Max's pharmacy and a shop called "Helen's Pottery".

She did well at the bank, that is to say, by the time she hit 27, she had been made section manager and was making $32,000 a year, which meant that even after making the monthly payments, she could afford a more or less up-to-date lifestyle. This whole time, she never stopped considering herself a student at a prestigious institution of higher learning and never forgot to renew the university sticker on her Chevrolet; over ice cream at Max's she often told Helen: "You know, at my university, Vanderbilt..." Twice a week she drove to Woodstock for anaerobics class. Naturally, all the pocket editions of the Russian classics were on her shelves, and at night they roamed all over her pillow. In the mornings, she ran three miles around the sleepy Strasburg, and sometimes in the evenings she ran three miles, and sometimes in the middle of the night she ran three miles, and sometimes she didn't feel like stopping at all, if it meant not having to return to the car loan department. Naturally, while running, a tape of Russian phrases or a Russian symphony played on her Walkman. "This Palmer returned from Tennessee a very different person," the locals said. Men did not dare ask her out on a date, and rightly so: none of them reminded her of Lermontov's Pechorin, nor of Chekhov's Gurov. By the way, in her literary celibacy she had begun to dry up a bit already, in spite of her vivid imagination.

It was Helen Hoggensoller who understood her the best. She was the owner of the popular local shop, which sold various types of pottery: pots and vases for your flowers, flamingos and marmots for your lawn, cherubs for your graves and, in general, objects of good taste, my dear. Three-hundred-pound Helen, in counterbalance to her obesity, had a light disposition, inquisitiveness, and even a degree of erudition. She managed to wear her oversized things with extravagance, including the ceramic necklaces that were constantly rattling on her breast, reflecting the centuries-old culture of a Shenandoah Indian tribe who called themselves "Moon Meditators". Our heroine could talk only with Helen about passion, about a faraway country which could not be understood with any computer, could not be measured with any calculator, in which you could only believe, believe... During Palmer's intense spasms, chest pressure and dampening eye sockets, Hoggensoller would press her hand and tell her that Sergeant Isaac Isaacson, a deputy sheriff from Front Royal, had again asked about her and sighed, just like, my honey, your Pushkin.

It was precisely at Helen's Pottery where the Strasburg women's club began to meet, about twelve of the better representatives of this settlement, founded back in the eighteenth century, with the overall number of souls exceeding a thousand. They gathered on Fridays among the ceramics and velvet poinsettias and demonstrated their capabilities, each in their own way: brownies or danish, or homemade raisin cookies, or a small bucket of pasta salad, and even celery and carrot sticks accompanied by a thick sauce which, in accordance with local tradition, was for dipping vegetables, thereby producing a pleasant moisturizing effect during the chewing process. If the conversation turned out to be good, they would wave away the high calories, and each chipped in two dollars for a cheesecake from Max's across the street. The conversations often turned out to be interesting, and the instigator almost always turned out to be Kimberly Palmer. The ladies sighed, listening to her stories about the suffering in Russia, and enjoyed repeating interesting words after her: "gorbachev","kremlin", "kaygeebee", "perestroika". They especially liked the word "glasnose": to them it sounded superior, in transparent opposition to the expression "hardnose", that is, dark dogmatism and blunt-nosedness.

So it was there, at Helen's Pottery, where the idea arose to contribute to the world's humanitarian aid effort to the all-suffering Russians. For Christmas, let's send them food packages, each of us will contribute our mite. We'll set an example for other Christians, other Americans, other women!

They began to collect money, that is, began fund-raising. The "Blue Ridge" newspaper reported on the initiative to the public at large. With increasing frequency, cars began to stop in front of the shop window filled with vases and pots. Some gave a dollar, some gave two. Deputy Sheriff Isaac Isaacson donated thirty bucks, that is, enough for the purchase of six six-packs.

Palmer got so carried away with this wonderful work that she now always ran out of her home with none other than a dazzling smile on her lips. Then suddenly, an unpleasant event transpired: her daddy returned, her sinful papa, in the flesh. He now looked like half the splendid man he had once been: second in the county in bowling and a salesman in the town's main enterprise, the "Antique Emporium". Apologizing to his family for causing so much trouble, this man of indeterminate age and a strange lightness clarified that the goal of his return was not the resumption of family life, but the restoration of his right of access to a state hospital, where he could die for free, or almost for free. Keep calm, boys and girls, don't panic! As a matter of fact, he had already registered in the hospital, he had only stopped by the old house to pick up his collection of baseball cards, so he could sort through them while dying.

Kimberly was stunned by the remarkable qualities of her almost unrecognizable daddy and attached herself to him for the remainder of his life, that is to say, for fifteen or so days. Papa suffered, but he never ceased smiling in expectation of pain-killers. Pharmacology submerged him into a state of almost total bliss. He took the hand of his eldest daughter and continued smiling, either from recollecting something not all that bad, or perhaps he was already travelling in some sort of extraterrestrial spheres. He died in a superior mood, even while sort of whistling something from the big-band era.

The stunned Kimberly now began running not three miles at a time, but all of six at once. Tchaikovsky's Fifth Symphony hovered over the sleeping Strasburg as it trailed after the runner. It seemed the night skies reflected the happy smile of her cast-off father. Isaac Isaacson frequently escorted her in his patrol car. While holding back tears, he told her about group therapy for the treatment of sexual sublimation, about family planning, about balancing budgets.

Once, just before dawn, the friendly hand of Helen Hoggensoller intercepted our runner. It turned out the Pottery Club at its latest meeting had decided to assign one of their members to accompany the humanitarian aid packages to Moscow. This representative, of course, was to be Palmer. After this, how can we still call our era the manifestation of mercantilism?

As a matter of fact, take a look at the arena of world events and you'll find all sorts of things there: gangsterism, sadomasochism, romantic cruelty, hypocrisy and compassion, a great deal of exalted idiocy, rather cheerful but also excruciatingly mean swindling, but you'll never find any displays of common sense associated with mercantilism. Million-strong crowds of people commit reckless acts, both individuals and governments live beyond their means; they are capable in three days of destroying socialism or throwing three ten dollar bills to the wind. It's only China that is systematically increasing its economic potential with no regrets for the students killed on the way to achieving this goal. However, that which applies to China does not apply to the rest of mankind.

And so, here was this 29-year-old girl called Palmer with the humanitarian aid package, mistaken for a baby bundle by the declasse worker of the USSR. She had thirty such packages in her luggage. Not quite enough to save a large country, but the most important thing was the initiative! If thirty packages came from every thousand Western Christians, then that would make seven and a half million from the USA alone! It goes without saying that our Russophile flew to Moscow in a state of exultation.

In the initial minutes of acquaintance, the longed-for city shocked Palmer by its smell. Possessing the keen nostrils of one who grew up among the relatively not-so-nasty smells of the Shenandoah Valley, Palmer immediately caught the essence: a mixture of urine and disinfectant. This basic smell, by the way, was constantly enriched depending on the presence of certain elements such as concentrated sweat, universal rottenness, chemical alcohol, exhaust fumes; in a word, the whole bouquet of communism's death agony. She caught herself with a strange sensation: it seemed to her in the presence of such a smell it was somehow awkward to conduct regular human activities. One should just stand and wait until the smell evaporated.

She had a room reserved for her in a huge hotel near the Kremlin. Masses of people constantly walked down the endless corridors. Out of her window, Palmer saw a narrow river with blackened ice and a monstrous building with six hellish smoke-stacks and mighty letters displayed on the facade. She had barely read the word "Lenin", when two fat women entered her room and began counting the towels, pillow-cases and quilt covers. Taking refuge in the corner of the room, Palmer looked at the flabby embodiments of "Russianness" in the coarse and wretched features of these two specimens.

"Where is your second towel?" asked one of them, but upon seeing the wide-eyed look of the new arrival, they brushed her aside: "Ay, this dummy doesn't know a word of Russian!" They looked at her more closely and added: "As far as money goes, I dare say the ugly dog doesn't have any. She's traveling on a shoestring!"

Palmer paced past the Kremlin with the first trial package of humanitarian aid. It was far better here, the smell was gone. The frost stung at her cheeks and nose. Seeing her reflection in the shop-window of GUM, she was astonished by her own beauty. A tall American woman with a humanitarian aid package. She was startled at the density of the throngs. People walked quickly, not paying any attention to the fairy tale architecture surrounding them. An adolescent girl stood on a corner with a sign, written in English: "We were deprived of all basic rights – please help my family to survive." Palmer extended 25 rubles to her. The girl motioned to a tin can with her chin and turned away contemptuously.

Endless lines of people stretched around the corner along the sidewalk. Palmer, shocked by the vast quantities of fur hats, attesting to the massive abuse of small animals, decided to begin a campaign against fur hats in the future! She tried to listen carefully to the Russian spoken around her. She frequently heard a Russian obscenity that sounded like Chinese, an unfamiliar hoarse exhalation on "khu". In general, the people standing in line were not talkative, it seemed they had exhausted all topics of conversation. One man had a small wooden board hanging on his chest with hard currency signs. She heard the word "kaufen" and dashed away to the side.

Suddenly, she found herself on the front steps of a building that looked as if it had been smashed by an earthquake. A baby stroller was being carried out of the door with a creaking sound. An apartment building. Palmer went inside. A cavelike entry way, permeated by the smell of cat freedom. Boards lay on top of a high stack of beat-up Dutch tiles. It was as if a Pennsylvania mine shaft gaped into the entrance of a long hallway. Of course, there are needy people living in these slums. The first Christmas present from Strasburg will be delivered right here, to the door labeled 7-a.

"Don't open it, don't you dare open it, you parasite!" someone howled from inside. The door opened. It seemed to Palmer that she had ended up in a New York ghetto, known to her only through the movies. This was all because the declasse Chuvakin, from his many years of drinking plonk, had turned substantially blue-grey, if not completely dark. His wife, Smaragda, was either Chuvash or one of those Lithuanian Karaites, so she could pass for a Puerto Rican. Palmer wanted to greet them in the normal Russian way, but from nervousness she said something totally senseless: "Zdravevichi" instead of the greeting "Zdrastvuite". Frightened, she began to poke at her package, as if entreating them not to suspect her of evil intentions. Then she noticed that the husband and wife were barefoot, and something was wrong with their oral cavities. She almost began to sob: these poor people, poor people!

"Take it!" she muttered. "Enjoy! Merry Christmas!"

"What a stupid cow," yawned Smaragda. "Whoa, look at her! She wants to abandon her goddamn baby!"

"You don't understand a fucking thing, you slutty Smaragda," said Chuvakin, scratching himself all over, from his ears to his toes. "She's a Swede, they are really frightening. I'll take her to the artist, he can speak their language. I've heard him myself."

"You're going to get smashed at the artist's again!" howled the wife. "Don't you dare come home, you bastard! I wish all you pricks would get smothered by a giant cunt!"

Chuvakin, with a diplomatic twist of his body, showed the way upstairs. They climbed up staircases. This house was once opulent, thought Palmer: in places you could make out marble, ornamental cast-iron and mosaic fragments. She recalled a lecture called "The World of Art" given by Kostanovich, a Vanderbilt professor. They climbed all the way to the top, just under the roof. This should be where the neediest roost. This self-sacrificing barefoot man didn't think of himself, but of others. Such depth to these characters. Some nice smells suddenly reached them from behind the zinc-coated door on the top landing. Smelled like home-cooking on Thanksgiving.

When the "Englishwoman" was led inside, Muse Borisovna and Hamayun Bird had already begun setting the table in the far corner of the cavernous studio. The Hungarian turkey legs stuck up to the cathedral ceiling like two mortars. The first fragrance of fish pie came from the oven. A soft mountain of caviar rose over the edges of a crystal bowl. This last substance was known to Palmer only from literature, and in its actual embodiment it remained unidentified by her until the very end of the story.

It was with great pleasure that the ladies continued their creative work around the table. By the way, both of them were Moscow celebrities, Ostankino mirages, as well as the "darlings" of the whole commercial and corrupted plebs. They didn't have any problem "using their faces", walking through any crowd into the office of a store manager and acquiring any hard-to-get item they pleased. And look – Modest has all the luck! Both prominent celebrities of different generations for some reason took it upon themselves to present the artist's studio as a "horn of plenty". Of course, this horn was constantly and obscenely being emptied by the crowd of motley bohemians, gathering at night in the loft, from where you could see the coachman's head and the back of the monument to Marxism's founder, and also, if you were to peer through the drunken gloom, the quadriga on top of the Bolshoi Theater.

Modest Orlovich knew one solid English interrogatory sentence, "Ver are you fram?" and in addition, a fairly good number of individual words, mostly nouns. This supply of nouns helped him to speak with foreigners in the mode of "telegraphic speech" created by the Italian futurist Marinetti, that is, without verbs. He usually presented himself as "paintor", patting himself on the chest with his hand. "Great paintor. My houz," followed by a circular gesture around the studio. "Guest goot. Frost, ah? Russia. Vinter. Ver are you fram?"

Meanwhile, Palmer looked with delight at the tall and gaunt painter – well, simply an incarnation of Prince Myshkin! Exclaiming in her own Virginian, occasionally adding sticky Russian words that sounded like caramelized popcorn. This is approximately what came out. "I'm from Strasburg, Virginia. We also have winterovs. No, no, I'm not afraid of Russian frostniks. I'm so gladski, many thanks! So you're a house painter, sir, and this is your friend, the barefoot gentleman, a plumber, right? That's just marvelous! Thanks for your gospitality!"

Orlovich replied quickly and boldly: "Good. Food. Vodka. Beer. Fuck. Table. Chair. Glass. Plate. Painting. Great. Voila!"

Chuvakin even dropped his jaw in admiration. An almost understandable conversation took place before him in a foreign language.

"Ask about the baby, Modest!"

Orlovich asked about the blue bundle with his two palms and chin. "Chaild? Child? Mazer? Fazer?"

Palmer didn't get a chance to answer. The zinc-coated door

flew open, never to close again that night. A drunken crowd with rosy cheeks burst into the apartment. Agitated, distorted faces and elegant clothing. Designer coats with capes fell into the heap, colorful scarves were unwrapped. A whole team of leggy tarts. Some fat Sicilians. A fine, large Russian fellow, a bare chest with a cross under a shaggy vest. Everyone talked at once, nobody listened to anyone.

"Where shall I put this humanitarian aid package?" asked Palmer, suddenly becoming timid. Nobody answered her. A rhapsody of kisses. The men sucked in parts of each other's badly-shaved cheeks. The women ground their groins into the host instead of shaking his hand. It was obvious they were all quite drunk already, and the table now held even more bottles, like pins in a bowling alley. "So you're all ripped already, my gang!" yelled Modest happily. "You need to catch up with us, our genius genie!" The Russian hunk grabbed the host by the beard and shoved a bottle of champagne into his mouth. Foam sprayed all around them. One heavy drop hit Palmer right in the forehead. Her head spun and made a wild circle around the vaults of the enormous loft. It was only now that Palmer realized that the walls glowed with paintings and glimmered with the deep gold of icons. Hamayun lightly shook Palmer out of her down coat and hugged her around the waist. "Put the child right here, under the icons, and have a seat at the table, the table!" A red mouth illustrated an invitation to the internationally intelligible "yum-yum." "Why, little mother, you've turned blue!" Muse Borisovna placed a bowl of hot broth before Palmer. "You need to boullionize yourself, my dear!" An amber slick of cholesterol covered the surface. The only thing that was still needed for total suicide was a glass of vodka, and here it was.

"Let's drink to Bruderschaft, my country schoolteacher!" yelled the Russian stud, Arkashka Grubiyanov into Palmer's ear. He sat on the arm of her chair, and when, after the vodka, he leaned over to kiss her according to Russian custom, he fell with his thick thigh between the Samaritan's two shapely extremities, accidentally pushing the palm of his hand into her crotch.

Her thin lips quivered under Arkashka's wet sausage lips. It's not his fault, this is tradition, such sincere national character, Russian-ness, this man is not to blame, one shouldn't pick on him. What passion, what freshness of feeling, even though he does reek of something sickening.

Grubiyanov shoved a tablespoon of caviar into her mouth. "You must have it, eat our treasure, the last caviar of a dying Russia! You can't swallow it? Hey everyone, she takes it in her mouth, and then she can't swallow it!" Muse Borisovna cut off Grubiyanov's boorishness with a dramatic gesture. "Stop your swinish antics, Arkashka!" Then someone at the table began playing *Eine Kleine Nacht Musik* on the violin. A group of European and Russian menfolk dressed in fancy suits got up at the far end of the table, drinking some sort of separate toast to a joint venture. Arkashka had already forgotten about Palmer, and was grabbing a big-headed critic by the chest. "You just don't get the Russian idea, you jerk! You still don't comprehend Rozanov!" One more big-headed man crawled up to Palmer from her other side. "Je vous voudrais de ride on a Russian troika!" The leggy girls wouldn't sit at the table, they kept getting up, as if trying to slip out of their tiny dresses, and then they would pull them down with rather enigmatic smiles. Suddenly, the whole company, no less than thirty mouths, all sang at once: "Let's take each others' hands, our friends, so we don't perish one by one."

The candles were already burning. Palmer, dumbfounded, looked at all the faces lit up with inspiration. The slightest puffiness in the cheeks or under the eyes appeared exaggerated, any sunken spaces sunk in twofold. A living sculpture of a suffering people. Pouring herself some vodka from the octagonal carafe, the girl Palmer rose with a toast.

"Gospodin i gospodan!" she said, meaning to say "Ladies and gentlemen". And she went on in Virginian: "I have the distinctski privilege of sending you heart-felt and warm regardovs from the peopleniks of the Shenandoah valley, particularly from Mrs. Hoggensoller's Pottery Clubchik. Let me emphasize that this humble donation reflects just a small part of a great sympathy for a large people at a very, very important crossroads in historich!"

The women looked at her with great surprise, as if they had just noticed her. The men leaned out of their chairs, trying to check out her backside. Even those sexually satisfied or with poor appetites considered it necessary to demonstrate their libidos were not asleep. Only Arkashka Grubiyanov for some reason right at this moment became gloomy. Somehow it was during the toast made by this goggle-eyed sort-of Swede he thought of his KGB basement, which because of the disintegration of the USSR, might suddenly be opened only to expose a stunning stench.

Palmer pointed out the blue bundle under the glimmering icon to everyone. The declasse Chuvakin sat next to the bundle, his feet no longer bare, but sporting Muse Borisovna's large steel-spiked Italian boots. He took the bundle and passed it to the host, Modest Orlovich, who took it in his arms somewhat tenderly. "What's his name?" he asked the guest in Russian. "Nom? Navn? Name?" Rocking the bundle, himself swaying over the table, a perfect papa. Warm feelings streamed out of the artist's childish, if not donkey eyes. The menfolk laughed, not very maliciously. "Fess up, Modest, you knocked up the Swede! Now take the baby for upbringing."

Palmer quickly de-diapered the bundle right on the table next to the octagonal decanter of Czarist vodka, the crystal slavic bowl, still heaped with Caspian caviar, the half-gnawed turkey leg from the Hungarian plains, a scattering of cigarettes of the more prestigious brands at that troubled time in the Russian winter, that is Marlboro and Dunhill, and also items of Western preserved delights, which had already struck an irreparable blow to Soviet Marxism, well, so as to not bumble around this disgraceful phrase any longer, next to some cans of beer. The assortment, so painstakingly collected by the Pottery Club ladies, now appeared before the gathering: two boxes of Uncle Ben's quick-cooking enriched rice, a packet of thick mushroom sauce, a big box of oatmeal cereal called Common Sense (which as we can see, is still available in the context of today's civilization) – a goldmine of beneficial fiber with good vitamin combinations, including riboflavin, magnesium, zinc and even an optimal quantity of copper, moreover, with the full absence of saturated fat and cholesterol, two packages of Town House spaghetti, and two necessary ingredients to go with it – a tube of ketchup and bottles of powdered Parmesan, three boxes with an ideal supply of protein, that is, tuna fish in spring water, so that every mouth, if just for a while, could feel like a sponger, Wiler bouillon cubes, the obligatory three cans of Andy Warhol's Campbell Soup, well, a package of Lipton Tea, (drink 100 strong cups, or 200 moderate cups, or 300 sensible cups), and a jar of Maxwell House instant coffee, whose last drop was evaluated even by Mayakovsky, while refusing to remove his cap from his head, well, a packet of pseudo-cream to go with the coffee, so that the hungry people would still not gain eight, hot cocoa mix, a mixture of McCormick spices consisting of ground parsley, celery and sweet basil (note the indubitable good taste of Helen Hoggensoller), well, Head and Shoulders shampoo, Crest toothpaste, a selection of miniature Proxa Brushes, to purge the Russian interdental spaces of the remains of American food, a jar of Geritol vitamins, Bayer aspirin and Preparation-H suppositories for the successful outcome of everything listed above, well, and finally, some delicacies for children - crunchy chocolates, Danish cookies, gummy jellybeans, and also, in conclusion, something for the soul, an American Father Frost – a Santa Claus figurine.

"That's all of it!" exclaimed Palmer, her voice ringing with joy. "Alas, not a lot, but from the very bottom of our heartniks!"

"Foreign grub!" howled Chuvakin, throwing himself on the unwrapped package and fishing out the life-giving contents. As Grubiyanov pulled the package toward himself, it all spilled out on him. Everything whirled around in a cheerful greedy mess. Her lavender eyes blazing, Hamayun Bird flew by with some Chicken of the Sea cans. The other girls were powdering themselves all over with the Parmesan cheese. Even the joint venture businessmen did not refuse the gifts, although they had the same goodies, in the Italian version, stored away in the event of a many months street battle in the Soviet capital. Even the Slavophile critics, a very proud bunch, didn't mind helping themselves to a packet of mushroom sauce each. In the midst of all this bedlam, only the violinist didn't allow himself to be distracted. Biting a small tube of macaroni, he tediously forced out the melody "Yesterday". And Muse Borisovna, unexpectedly smitten with wet nostalgia, cried without any sadness, while holding up her still-lovely breasts. Between them lay a set of dried McCormick spices, giving a special meaning to the fleeting moment.

It seemed that the host, the future Sotheby's exhibitor, Modest Poligamenovich Orlovich, was the only one left without a souvenir, which was soon found for him. Looking over the ripped package at the illegitimate baby's narrow-shouldered mama, he suddenly decided that this was exactly what was left for him: a symbol of motherhood, a model for a new acrylic "World of Art" in blue.

"Mazer! Chaild! Painting! Je vous aime! Lav! Seance!" He seized Palmer by her trembling wrists, her pulse beating like large grasshoppers, and brought her through the labyrinth of partitions, into the holy of holies, where the stretched canvas stood, where Russian history dimly shone through the window: a granite statue with a coachman's mane, very high spotlights which knew the better days of socialism, and the imperial yellow yolk of the Malyi Theater was mixed with the sinister tar of the rows of empty shops, and the classicism of the Bolshoi Theater, out of place in 1991, with its completely other-worldly chariot.

The half-raped Palmer was placed on the window ledge to pose in her ripped-apart form. "He didn't even notice he popped my cherry," she thought with some tenderness, gazing, as it was said, "into the murk of this goddamned Byzantium", and only slightly trembled in her stupor. The artist was in the middle of a burst of inspiration, or as they said in a circle of jazz musicians, he "grooved" at his canvas. From time to time, through his wiry beard littered with caviar, chocolate and lipstick, nouns would break through: "Solitude. Alienation. Engagement. Weltgeist!" From behind the partition, the noise of the party's intensifying wildness reached them.

Two hours passed like this, after which two small explosions reached them from the square still carrying the name of the humble Bolshevik, Yakov Sverdlov. The lights went out everywhere. The dreary gloom was filled with smoke.

The session lasted still another whole hour. Palmer's silhouette was now reflected in the enamel basin stuck to the wall. "Thanks to jogging," she thought, "I managed until age 29 to preserve myself in the form of the Dream Princess." A whole series of loud sounds reached them from the refectory. From various directions, no less than a dozen mugs flooded with wild happiness thrust themselves into the creative corner. "Ride, ride! Let's go riding on horses!" Modest threw away his brushes. "Ay da, Kimberlylulochka!" Carnival masks were raving around them. "The horses are shaking their manes out there!" Palmer quickly but carefully packed up her small breasts.

"Troika?!" she said, suddenly recalling the word. "Troika russki?!" Grubiyanov grabbed her, intent on hoisting all of her one hundred and ten little pounds on his shoulders. A crowd of guests poured down from the top floor like a giant wave. They leapt out to freedom, which was still called 25th October Street, although right on the verge of throwing up all of its Communist past.

The carriage was already waiting. Ordered through the armed company "Alex". Safety fully guaranteed. The troika turned out to be superluxurious, not even a troika, but a quadriga, cast according to the finest traditions of the imperial designer Baron Klodt. The stomping hooves struck many sparks and crumbled the old asphalt. The stability of Russia's fundamental core was guaranteed by the enormous, broad peasant back of the coachman. Palmer pressed her cheek to this roughly chiseled Russian monolith. An inorganic cosmos, isn't it? Could it be a flight to bumpy celestial roads?

April 1993

Palmer's Second Flight

Kimberly Palmer spent almost all of 1992 in Russia, but by autumn she returned to her hometown of Strasburg, in the state of Virginia. "Palmer came back from Russia a very different person," said the pharmacist Ernest Max VIII, at the forefront of the current generation of Strasburg milkshake beaters, who although they didn't get monstrously rich from this popular food-stuff, had never once gone bust since the last quarter of the 19th century, preserving their enterprise as the leading attraction on Main Street and introducing the best life had to offer into the lives of eight generations of local German cherubs; oo-oops, someone dropped a glass with a pink shake while staring at the "adventuress Palmer" crossing Main Street. "Never mind," exclaimed Ernest, "did you notice that she even has a different walk now!"

"She obviously lost her innocence over there," some well-wisher whispered to Sergeant Isaac Isaacson, almost deserving a bullet in the forehead, which he would have gotten, if the sergeant's sense of duty hadn't prevailed over his personal emotions. Meanwhile, Palmer, wrapped in a multipurpose Slava Zaitsev cape, crossed the street heading toward Helen Hoggensoller's Pottery Club, where ladies were already hopping around outside waiting to envelop her in their embraces.

"It feels weird to see you all, dear friends," said Palmer at an extended meeting of the club, where canaries twittered among the refined ceramic objects, and Helen shone proudly in her oversized Russian double-headed eagle T-shirt while she brought the guests miniature cups of coffee – ! – espresso! "Oh, how strange it is, friends, to return to my homeland, to this quiet town, after ten months in that incredible country!" Then she was silent, and her eyes opened wide as if she had completely forgotten about what was around her at that given moment. And the awestruck ladies also widened their eyes.

Now, in the quiet of the Shenandoah Valley, this ten- month "Russian film" turned itself on in Palmer's consciousness like virtual reality, in absurdly scrambled pieces, sometimes at night on her pillow, sometimes at the wheel of her Toyota, then in the supermarket, at times while running, then while watching television, sometimes while smoking – this harmful habit, acquired in Russia, somehow seemed like an infectious disease among the enlightened inhabitants of Virginia – and the "film" even surpassed the blazing Indian summer, fleetingly glimpsed squirrels, the marching of the school orchestra, the usual TV series, which one should say she really had missed while in Russia, while they were still in her mind.

She would suddenly have visions of the giant commercial strife of Moscow, dirty slush underfoot, and overhead, crows crazed from all the wild capitalism, women's blouses hanging next to bunches of dried fish, stalls of tinned goods lying in a mess next to doorknobs, bottles of vodka, lipstick, books by Sigmund Freud and Elena Blavatskaya. In her deepest sleep she saw glimpses of Russia, containing something more than feelings or thoughts, imprinting themselves into the darkness, like images of her own agony. The Mesozoic plate under the Russian continent stirred like a sluggish toad, a meter every millennium.

Shaking herself awake, she smoked in the bedroom – only Marlboros, which for some reason were considered to be the hippest brand in Moscow – and again watched her fragmented "film": Vietnamese merchants fighting on the train from Saratov to Volgograd, tiny and ferocious in their denim "Army USA" shirts, spraying each other in the face with poisonous atomizers and dragging about some sort of bales; distribution of humanitarian aid to the children at the orphanage near Elista, where she had traveled during a joint effort of the British Red Cross and a German group called "Redemption"; hanging out in Moscow's bohemian attics and basements, and the men, a plenitude of them, not always strong, but always insolent, smelling of sweat no perfume could eradicate, cursing coarsely or soaring to the heavens; dragging her into a corner, shoving vodka at her, and immediately letting down their flies, as if feminist ideas had never spent the night in this country.

Sometimes she cried out in horror: could it be that she subconsciously anticipated such SOBs when she thought about Russia? No, no, there was also something else which matched her youthful ecstasy: violin concerts, poetry readings, and spontaneous rushes of mass inspiration – a crowd suddenly waltzing to the flute, tuba and accordion in the spit-filled passageway under Pushkin's statue – "The Blue Danube!" After the waltz, however, everyone ran off like a herd of jackals, with the accordionist howling after them: "Sons of bitches! Motherfuckers! And who's going to pay, Pushkin?!" Left alone in the void, he closed his eyes and played "Yesterday".

There was so much of everything, and still, Kimberly Palmer, admit it, your main discovery in Russia turned out to be men. At first she met with them as if prompted by some sort of tearfulness, a motherly atavism, and then, the truth is, something exclusively physiological appeared, a kind of bitch in heat, ma'am. It was likely that in the Kitai-gorod art studio there wasn't one regular who didn't get to know the "Englishwoman" intimately, or, as she was called after that memorable night in December 1991, when the humanitarian aid package was mistaken for a baby, "single mother". It got to the point that something that she didn't quite understand was said about her: "the broad's out of control".

The most horrific memories were connected with the Sokolniki abortion clinic, where Orlovich brought her to a doctor he knew. In sterile, clean Virginia one couldn't even begin to imagine comparable medical care, orderlies and nurses, not to mention the patients. Palmer was sure she wouldn't get out of there alive, and it was even more amazing that everything turned out well, leaving nothing but pride like the kind that remains with hostages after an ordeal in Beirut.

The stunned Sergeant Isaac Isaacson, who got from her on the first night of her return that what he had wished for during many years of Tantalus torments, muttered with a touch of tragic sarcasm: "I can see you must have gone through group therapy for overcoming sexual sublimation, am I right?" "I wonder if it wasn't group surgery," smirked Palmer.

Sergeant Isaacson, in the course of duty, often came across displays of madness; however, up until recently, he hadn't really understood where it came from in human nature. Now, when he himself had to sometimes suppress his own outbursts of madness, his views on human nature broadened significantly. And even kind of deepened. Yes, exactly, sometimes he said to himself while off-duty, sitting in front of a grunting television with a six-pack of beer, now I somehow look at all those swine in a deeper way.

He proposed marriage to Palmer, and she unexpectedly consented, which again shook his conceptions about human nature; in which direction, he couldn't quite tell yet. Now they appeared together in public, sometimes at the Ascot bowling alley, as an engaged couple.

Things settled down into normal routines. Of course, another Kimberly Palmer sat in the car loan division of the "Perpetual" Bank, if that could be said about a sloppy broad from West Virginia perpetually chewing on something. However, the competitor bank quickly hired the local celebrity who had fulfilled her Christian duty in a very faraway and dangerous country, thereby attracting new clients to their financial sources. On the streets of Strasburg, enormous maples, poplars and chestnut trees accepted the prodigal runner under their boughs with tranquilizing rustles. Nobody in Moscow responded to Palmer's letters, and Russia again began to fade into an academic abstraction from a university curriculum. At best, it was still associated with Tchaikovsky's "Sixth Symphony", which Palmer listened to during her five-mile run; violins and brass, piercing flights of the small pipes... and this is Russia?... the object of inspiration and the product of inspiration existed in different planes that never merged. The music was in frightening contrast to the olfactory matters.

"Even if you really love all that rubbish, that doesn't mean you have to go there. Go back to the university and learn about 'em all," the reasonable Isaac would say. He began applying for a vacancy in the law-enforcement agencies near Vanderbilt University in

Nashville, Tennessee. He had some savings from his temperate bachelorhood which would allow him to hold out for two to three years until our girl received her Master of Arts.

Things flowed along for almost a year in this undemanding way, precisely until the end of September 1993, when an extracurricular phone call resounded in Palmer's home at three o'clock in the morning. It was Arkashka Grubiyanov. Well, to put it in the old-fashioned way, he was "on the line". In the reality of the night, the frightened Palmer thought she heard a cosmic echo in this fateful call from the eternal Moscow playboy, "user" and "boozer." "Hi, old girl," he said according to the rules of Moscow jargon, which not all that long ago elated the humanitarian aid pioneer, but now evoked only a feeling of slight nausea. "I hope you haven't forgotten those fiery nights yet? I'm calling you from your capital. No, not from ours, but from yours, from your-not-our Washington-not-Russianton, you get it? Insomnia, old lady, Homer, tight sails, a list of ships, well, I read it halfway through and thought: why not call good ol' Palmer, it's great to have a chick across the ocean, isn't it? No, I didn't emigrate, why should I emigrate when things are fine at home too. Business, of course, not private, but state. You can't measure us with ordinary yardsticks, mama, I'm just here on an official state visit."

From the reckless Grubiyanov's faraway chatter, sometimes lazy and sort of slurping, then tongue-twisting and sort of choking, Palmer understood, that he had recently become a member of the government, namely the Minister of Cultural Communication – not to be confused with the Minister of Culture – of the Russian Federation, and now here he was in Washington, heading a delegation. "We're having negotiations, old girl, five, fifteen negotiations a day, five thousand negotiations in all! Ten thousand agreements are being signed! Couriers are flying here and there, thirty thousand couriers! Faxes, modems, things are really cooking! I'm already getting hot as well, that's why I'm calling you! Come on over to the Ritz-Carlton, and ask for Minister Grubiyanov!"

Palmer could only assume this nocturnal outburst was none other than a ridiculous joke by a Moscow buffoon in the role of a "hero-lover." He was even now almost totally plastered while talking rubbish with his mighty, but not very obedient tongue about a government fitness center, where he swam daily with Rubleskauskas himself and jumped off the diving board into the water after Pel'meshko himself, prone, on his belly, a fountain coming out of his ass, and where he was offered, among splashes of champagne, a ministerial seat. Palmer didn't really understand the specifics of the revolutionary situation and that was why it was difficult for her to imagine how some mostly-mad actor could become a minister, and in addition, that a ministry could be created for him right at the edge of a swimming pool. "I'll send a car for you, if you want! With a bodyguard! Five bodyguards! Ten!"

"Listen, Ark, I'm in no position to go see you at three o'clock in the morning," Palmer finally formulated. "Now then, you're talking in Finnish again," sighed the minister distressingly, and then he completely stunned her by saying that in that case Mohammed would come to the mountain himself, that the next evening he would be ten miles away from her in "what's-its-name-Strasburg," namely at Korbut Place, well yes, at those same Korbuts, who are throwing a dinner in his honor, and he was inviting her in his capacity as minister. "Come on over, no fucking excuses! You know that Stanley Korbut – he's a normal guy, one of us, a great guy, hung up on Russian Art, Hamayun has turned him into a horny beast!" Korbut Place! Even if this estate was located ten miles from Strasburg, the local inhabitants could see its rooftops only from a scenic stop high up in the Blue Ridge, thirty miles away. All the approaches to this wooded territory, the size of which did not concede to the dwarf kingdoms of Europe, such as Andorra or Liechtenstein, were closed off by roadblocks. For a local girl, an invitation to the castle of the kings of the meat-milk business was equivalent to some Oprah-Ivanna-Vannaesque fulfillment of her dreams. Palmer was already not quite a local, but she went anyway. For some unknown reason, she wanted to see Arkasha Grubiyanov's full red lips again. And about feeling timid in front of the meat-milk aristocracy, Palmer, after hanging out with the bohemian crowd for almost a year, or as they said then, the "free-buffet gang", had learned one cardinal directive: "go fuck yourself" or, in indirect translation, "no problem!"

Without saying anything to her sergeant, she took off in her Toyota. Maybe, Arkasha had made it all up, but why not take a chance? At the first barrier, some large men from the Korbut Guard were on duty. Upon learning that she was there on the invitation of Minister Grubiyanov, they respectfully showed her the way with their beefy hands. Right after the checkpoint, the forest turned into a park. Beyond the avenue of tall trees, you could see hills rolled smooth with an ideal cut, antique sculptures, terraced Versailles-style gardens descending into a pond with a fountain. The chateau windows reflected the Shenandoah sunset in all its grandeur, and even surpassed this phenomenon of nature by adding an architectural symmetry to it. "During my whole life I've lost my senses in these sunsets," thought Palmer, entering the castle. Only after crossing the threshold did she realize that a footman in tights and gloves had opened the door for her.

The guests, no less than two dozen in number, sat in an oak-carved dining room, which had enough oak-carved sidings for a frigate squadron. It was as if the naked shoulders of the women widened the scale of the lavish spread. Palmer removed her antique Russian scarf: her shoulders were not the worst parts of her equipment. "I slept with these shoulders, I lived with them," recalled Minister Grubiyanov. He was the embodiment of etiquette. Instead of his usual ragged sweater with rolled up sleeves, he had on a complete black tie outfit, rented through the service bureau of the hotel. With a gracious smile he showed Palmer to a free seat, a few places to the right of him. An even more ceremonial peculiarity appeared to be Madam Vetushitikova, a maiden with lilac peacock rings around the eyes, known in certain circles of the Russian Federation as Hamayun Bird, currently the head of a youth exchange division. From afar, she sent Palmer an air kiss, barely moving her lips. I can just imagine what will happen when they all get drunk, thought the kiss's addressee.

A lively conversation was taking place at the table, naturally, it was about Russia. Leonid Brezhnev was a real leader, gentlemen, and then there was his daughter – the picture of femininity. I'm in complete agreement, I knew both of them. Leonid was tough, but his daughter Brezhnev turned out to be utterly charming! An old woman with bluish-grey curls was gradually taking over the floor, a certain wealthy, well-known half-mad enthusiast type, who came up with a new pet project every year: either giving Winnie Mandela an award for "moral heroism", or flying some overfed poets to Portugal on her personal jet, or setting up a visit to Disneyland for hoods, to distract them from guns and crack. Currently, the old lady was engaging herself with dollar infusions into the Ministry of Cultural Communications, MCCRF, and this is why everyone listened to her with great attention. Naturally, this woman was called "Jane", and she explained:

"Colossal impressions, folks, indelible! We visited the house of a great Russian poet near Moscow, whose name starts with the letter 'P', I'll think of it in a moment, oh yes, Potemkin's house!"

The minister and the members of the delegation respectfully nodded their heads. Nobody interpreted for them, and they of course didn't understand a thing. Upon the word "Potemkin" someone laughed inappropriately. "The poet Potemkin?" asked Palmer, to make sure she had heard correctly. From her early studies at Vanderbilt University, this name was connected with something not quite poetic, but something from 19th-century secret wars, the assault on Turkey: a scepter with a diamond bulb on top, a glass eye, the Onassis yacht, no, that's already from a different story altogether.

"Not just a poet, but a great poet," Jane said, frowning sternly, looking as if she herself was from the Potemkin epoch with her bluish wavy hairdo. "He lived in the town of Peredelkino," unexpectedly pronouncing the name almost in Russian.

"Pasternak!" Palmer then exclaimed, and Grubiyanov roared with laughter, almost splitting at the seams. "Where?" asked the billionairess, quickly looking around, and then it dawned on her. "Well, of course, I mixed it up a little, it's Doctor Pasternak!"

Palmer trembled as she began to cut up something that resembled a pacific atoll served on a porcelain plate. "The son of the great Doctor Pasternak showed us the house," continued Jane. "Poor, poor man, how he lived! Listen, I said to the son, please, would you mind if I took a picture of you at your father's desk? Oh, boy, the son became so indignant! He yelled and waved his arms, rejecting my modest proposal! I never imagined that the father and son had such a tense relationship!" "Oh, boy!" exclaimed the Cinderella of the evening, who nobody knew, except for a few Russians. "Don't you see, dear Mrs. Caterpillar, that your proposal was sacrilege to this man?"

"Sacrilege?!" the lavish old lady proudly placed her arms akimbo on the background of the carved oak, just like Admiral Nelson. Then

Grubiyanov burst out laughing, despite his ministerial title. It appeared that someone interpreted a part of the women's dialogue, and he bellowed across the philanthropic Russian cultural communication table: "Why Jane, old girl! Don't you see that your proposal was like asking to try on the shroud of Christ in the Cathedral at Turin! Don't you see that Pasternak is a saint for us, and his house a shrine! Hey, someone please interpret something for her!"

Nobody of course interpreted anything, but everyone began to laugh, looking at the Russian minister who it seemed would at any moment burst out of his tight tuxedo with an abundance of emotion. The first one to get drunk, however, was not the minister, but the host, Stanley Korbut, the slender business veteran, constantly occupied with golf, sex and champagne. This last thing, it appeared, didn't completely disappear into the depths of his body, but partially settled into the turkey bags under his chin, which made him a walking symbol of negligent and don't-give-a-damn capitalism, the kind that had already lost all interest in profit. "Dancing!" he howled. "Let's waltz!" He grabbed Madam Vetushitikova by the arm and twirled her around in the direction of his bedroom.

Then again, we didn't have to wait long for the guest of honor to follow suit. With no less spontaneity, he shoved a pair of cigars from the cigar table into his breast pocket and a bottle of "Glenmorangie" from the cocktail table into the deep wings of his trousers, after which he decisively led his girlfriend Palmer to the exit. The reciprocity principle in action. Russians don't surrender, they just become allies! All our prophetic birds, Alkonost, Siren, Hamayun, real, not tarts, soar in space, but the all-important Phoenix rises from the red ashes, matures with both heads, and demands a double ration! We're still to see the sky in diamonds! A man is not a flea! The Russian Federation is vast, but there is nowhere to retreat!

When he calmed down and fell asleep on the sofa bed, Palmer went out under the plentiful moon and sat on a heavy cast-iron chair, the best item from her grandmother's inheritance. A human shadow crossed the meadow, moving out into a forward position. It was Sergeant Isaacson with his full hip collection: a stick, pistol, walkie-talkie, handcuffs. "I guess this here is one of your Russians?" he said with sufficient inflection. Palmer nodded thoughtfully. "You know, these Russians today aren't really quite Russian. That one, sleeping over there now, a minister, is less Russian than I am British, or you are Swedish. Alas, the age of literature is no longer." "I'll still shoot him before sunrise," surmised the sergeant.

"No, you won't," she resonated, not in the sense of echoing, but because she put forth a reason to restrain him from using force. "Why? At least because you respect me and look upon me as more than just a vagina!" Steel objects shook on the sergeant's hips. To be honest, he wasn't capable even of imagining a comparable reason, and so now he shuddered. As she rose the moon enveloped her with its light, around the body of a future Boston marathon champion. "Well then, let's go to the garage, Isaac."

In the morning, over breakfast, Minister Grubiyanov, still in his rented tuxedo, gave Palmer's nephew Fritz Germenstadt a Tissot watch on a bracelet, and to the boy's mama, Rosalyn, he gave two bills, from a stack of hundreds rumpled inside his bosom. Having eaten a fairly substantial mountain of Virginia buckwheat pancakes with maple syrup, he asked if he could switch on CNN. It appeared that in Moscow a "Second October Revolution" was developing in full force, to use the expression of the new president, Sasha Rutskoi.

From that moment on, the whole weekend went by under Atlanta's eye, if one could say it that way for the sake of beauty, having in mind the CNN cameras, swooping over the assembly of Moscow buildings, including Grubiyanov's own ministerial mansion. In the end, the tuxedo ripped at the seams. The unshaven minister smoked a stolen cigar in a deep chair in front of the telly and gurgled Glenmorangie malt whiskey. Meanwhile, newly maddened Bolsheviks swept by the screen in waves. Bonfires made of rubber tires burned along the Garden Ring Road. A mob with pounding hammers, swishing sickles and rolled swastika chariots settled scores with the police. Along with the big, raging fellows with Lenin and Stalin profiles in their hands, the komsomol girls from the forties and fifties flew with the mob as old valkyries. Shock-workers tightened nooses made of bicycle chains on the cops' necks, old women completed the affair with banner poles.

Grubiyanov punched his hand with his fist, laughing a bit, wildly turning to Palmer as if looking for confirmation of his unspoken thoughts. Everyone around him walked on their tiptoes, pressing their fingers to their lips. It seemed to the members of the household that a typhoid-ridden man or alcoholic had moved into their living room.

The hours went by like this, the minister's stubble grew, in Moscow the Reds were winning. The siege was broken! Sub-machine gunners in camouflage came out in a line formation from the enormous building, as if fittingly constructed in the style of a socialist apotheosis. On a roll, they hacked their way through the neighboring skyscraper with heavy trucks, threw out tri-color rags, raised the triumphant red calico. The glass walls of capitalism were coming down. "Oh, now they've done it! Oh, good job! Go on, Sasha, go ahead!" yelled Grubiyanov, all carried away. From the huge balcony, the head of the Moscow uprising, no less swollen than the Virginia viewer, proclaimed victory and sent the proletariat to the TV tower at Ostankino and to the Kremlin!

Not long afterwards, close-ups of the carnage appeared at the television station: American television covered the demise of Russian television. A general with a hyena's face and a beret pulled down over his ears directed the assault. "When comrade Stalin will send us into battle and Makashov will lead us into battle," wailed the masters of tomorrow's executions. A rocket grenade flew past the central entrance with a roar. Glass flew and concrete collapsed. "Oh wow! Oh wow!" laughed the minister of the overthrown government into the Virginia night.

"My God, what's with him," whispered Palmer. "It's all intertwined here, Stavrogin and Svidrigailov mixed in with all this modern filth! Who is he, if not a fiend from Russian literature?" She dozed off a bit in the corner of the century-old Palmer sitting room and woke up when the television began to rattle at higher speeds and when something in Moscow toppled over with a thundering crash, prompting a new burst of laughter from Grubiyanov. History was turning backwards, and the fiend was laughing!

However, history, turning back, really only stomped around in place, and then spun around and drove the red- bellies back, under the protection of the Soviet constitution. Minister Grubiyanov continued to enjoy the spectacle. Kantemirov tanks began to flog the headquarters of the "Second October Revolution," and he laughed with the same delight: "Oh, they're giving it to them! That was great! Forward,

Pasha!" The leaders went to surrender, and then he laughed until he began to hiccup: "Far-out!"

When the next day began over an innocent Virginia, and evening began in a putrid Moscow under falling ashes, the minister fell with a crash to his knees, embracing Palmer's legs as if embracing all of mankind, and began to wail rapidly in a theatrical manner, sometimes plunging his nose into the edge of her female grove, a bit prickly even through the jogging bottoms: "Take me, my cursed Kimberlylulochka, single-mother, I am your only humanitarian aid package! Nobody, nobody knows what I'm really like, and if anyone ever finds out, they won't believe it! Take me away, away from myself with all of my dollars all stuck together! I still dream of a good life, beyond the meanest horizons! In Trinidad, or Tobago, let me find myself in the tropic of feelings, cleanse myself in a waterfall of confession! Don't leave me, Maiden, in the apotheosis of my desire for world-wide democracy! Lady of kindness, only in your bosom do I see universal grace, trust my fucking words, angel of humanity!"

Palmer lifted her head up to the ceiling and waited for the outpouring to cease. The question of kindness was a tortuous one for her. In her early youth, when she looked in the mirror at her face and caught an expression of kindliness in it, she would think masochistically: "With my looks, kindness is the only thing I can rely on." These thoughts tortured her. "What people and particularly men perceive as kindness is really a self-inflicted mask, but it's possible that deep down I'm sly and evil." The trip to Russia intensified this contradiction. The mask, it seemed, had fastened itself too tightly to her lips and to the creases between her nose and lips. Everyone around her drank to her kindness. "I'm insincere," she tortured herself, "I'm doing tricks with my kindness, and all because of these cursed men."

"Elevez-toi, Arkasha, s'il te plait!" she said neither in English, because of her confusion over the next twist of fate, nor in Russian. The French language program from school suddenly splashed out from her depths, yet another springy fountain of mercy.

A hundred-mile-long tourist highway called Skyline Drive weaves south along the very crest of the Blue Ridge over the Shenandoah

Valley. Stunning sunsets unfold from the right, beneficial sunrises from the left. Depending on the time of day or night, of course, though if you're in flight in the heat of a humanitarian action, it might seem to you that the sky is blazing from both sides simultaneously.

Palmer instinctively chose this road, and only later understood that she was trying to get away from the law enforcement authorities. She drove her car, trying to rid herself of any hints of kindness in her face. The body of the minister, his tux split open at the seams, settled into a heap next to her. Not seeing any manifestations in the skies, he snored unconsciously, still jerking occasionally and clearly answering some unheard questions: "Never joined! Wasn't there! Didn't sign! Didn't inform! Didn't take it!" Once his body suddenly distended, and he muttered: "Lord have mercy, Lord have mercy, Lord have mercy, forgive and protect me!" – and again he crashed.

After half an hour, Palmer glanced in the mirror and saw a Chevrolet with a red crossbeam on top following her steadily. The Viking mask behind the windshield was missing just two horns on the sides of the head. Well now, Sergeant Isaacson, now your true character will be put to the test!

November 1993

Vassily Aksyonov was born in 1932 in Kazan (Tatarstan) and trained as a doctor in which capacity he worked for many years, first in the provinces and then in Moscow, while writing short stories which won him a reputation as one of the most original talents in Russian literature. He has an ear for the slangy racy Russian of students, bohemians, and common people, and an eye for urban landscape and street scenes. His heroes are in constant search of their identity and refuse to settle down spiritually or physically. Aksyonov was forced to emigrate from Russia in 1980 and settled in the USA. He teaches Russian literature at George Mason University in Virginia and lives in Washington DC.

Aksyonov has been widely published in the West. All his major novels are available in English translation: **Generations of Winter, In Search of Melancholy Baby, The Island of Crimea, The Burn**, to name a few.

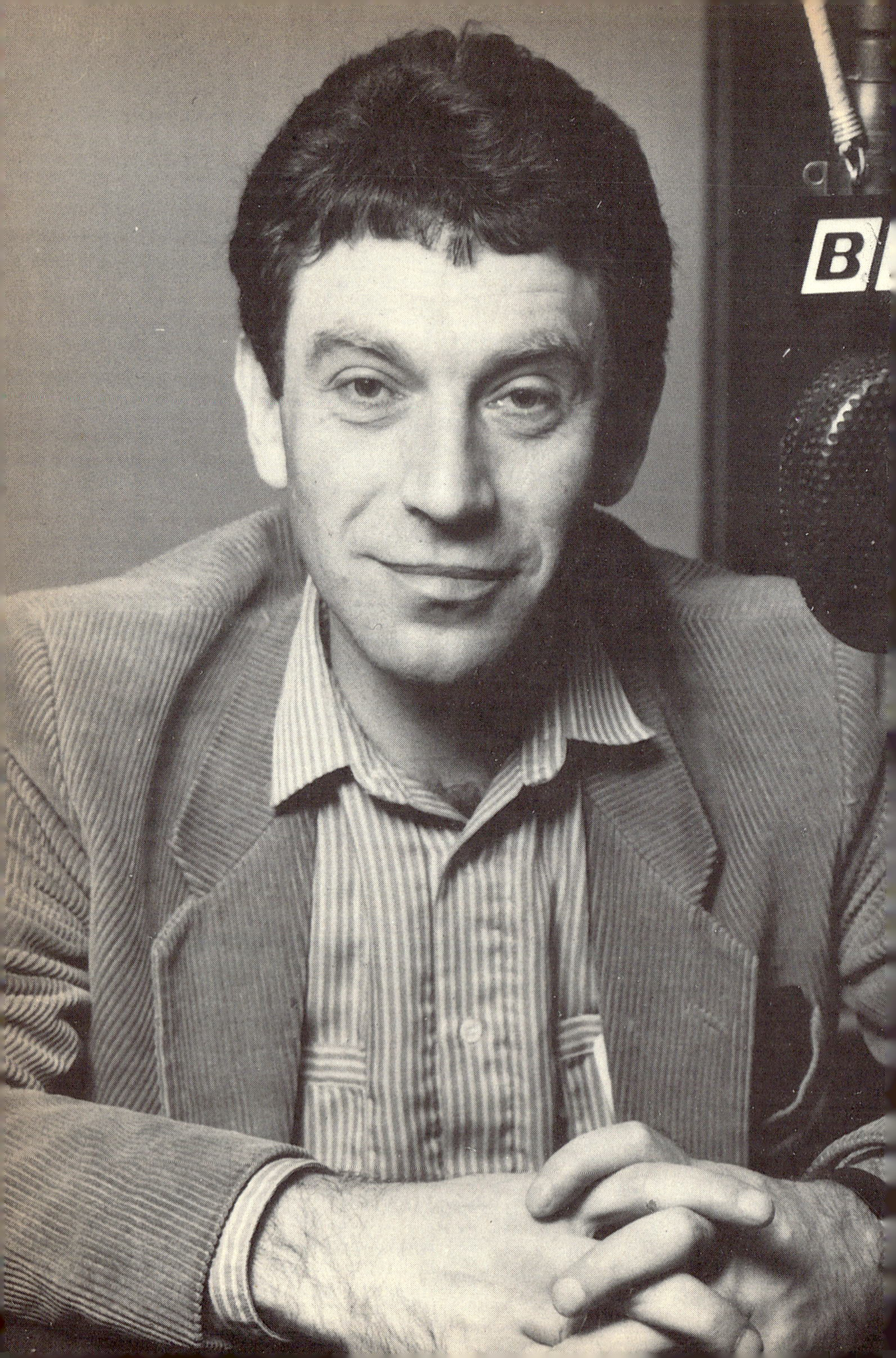

Zinovy ZINIK
The Moth
Translated by Bernard Meares

They say in Russia that the theatre begins with the cloakroom. And Lena's English sheepskin coat was stolen from a theatre cloakroom on the first night of the show, just a week after she arrived in Moscow from London. It was an avant-garde production of Richard III, in which the hunchback king represented Stalin with his withered hand; while Buckingham, Rivers, Dorset, Hastings et al. symbolized Trotsky, Bukharin, Kamenev, Zinoviev, etc. It was an interpretation in which everything between the lines had been turned to metaphor. What else could you expect from a country where there are too few things and too many ideas?

No-one was surprised at the theft: for only a fool would leave an English sheepskin coat in a Soviet cloakroom. The attendant stared at the English girl through transparent eyes pickled in alcohol. He swore blind he'd not seen hair nor hide of any sheepskin; and true, with eyes like those he would have been hard put to see anything. Yet before the show, he'd raced across the foyer and had planted himself in front of her. "Where are you going in that coat, lady? Coats are not permitted in the auditorium." As Lena was not only a foreigner but also the director's best friend, she'd been allowed to jump the queue. How could she have known that in a Soviet theatre overcoats had to be left at the cloakroom?

Her friends mumbled something about the need for cloakrooms in Russia because of the bitter winter weather outside and overheated buildings, and about the difference between inner and outer freedom.

In any case, then and there a new overcoat was found for her. That is, neither new nor a sheepskin, but rather its complete opposite. In her luxurious theatre dressing room with its mirrors and plush armchairs, Ludmila, cast as Lady Anne, flung open the oak doors of her wardrobe and said: "Take whatever you fancy." She said she had inherited the dressing room of the theatre's renowned former leading actor, a sometime Honoured Pensioner of the Soviet Union, now gone to a better world. "He was a dreadful old man, they say, but he obviously loved to snob around." She continued to fish through powdered wigs, false noses and old jars of congealed make-up looking at herself from time to time in the cracked mirror with its elegant gilt frame. The room was cluttered with rubbish from its former occupant, although everything seemed suitably faded and the very dust had taken on a patina of time: the vanished eras of Stalin and Brezhnev seemed just part of a harmless old museum past. The dressing room had remained locked for years; despite the temptation to do something with such elegant quarters nobody had wanted it. Strange rumours circulated about its long- gone tenant. But Ludmila, a young woman with no religious scruples or political rancour, had moved in as soon as the theatre management changed and her Sergei was made artistic director. Exotic clothing and theatre costumes that had outlived their time were piled in a heap on the floor and in the wardrobe were hanging brightly decorated Tartar caftans and Roman togas.

"For you people over there this stuff's all the rage," said Ludmila with a sardonic grimace. Ever since her first and so far only visit to London, where she and Sergei stayed with Lena, she had become an incontrovertible self- appointed expert on London folk ways. No matter how those Tartar and Roman clothes glistened with imitation jewelry Lena's gaze was arrested by something completely different in the props wardrobe: a heavy winter overcoat of awe- inspiring dimensions with an astrakhan collar. When she touched the heavy nap her fingers trembled with strange excitement, as though her very touch had made that long-dead product of Stalinist tailoring come alive and its sleeves shiver. The almost imperceptible movement gave her butterflies in the pit of her stomach. These days she had been subject to bouts of exaltation, at such moments her blue eyes widened and the objects around her began to be reflected in them, so that she seemed to be blind.

Now her eyes darkened, and nothing was reflected in them but that exotic winter overcoat. It was made of thick black cloth with heavy padding and a silk lining. Gigantic and reaching almost to the floor, it was like a knight's armour, a brontosaurus skin or an upended armoured truck. It was cladding and defence against the ubiquitous enemy, the winter outside. Its astrakhan curls shone at her out of the semi-darkness of the wardrobe, making it look like some wild animal lying in ambush. Simply taking it off its hanger and pulling it out of the wardrobe was an enterprise in itself, but when she tried it on, looking at herself in the cracked old-fashioned looking-glass she gasped. The coat enclosed her from head to toe, wrapping her in its wide and generous grasp, almost bedding her in its embrace. It gave her immediate strength, independence and unshakable confidence, though she knew not quite why; whether it was confidence in what the next day would bring her, or belief in mankind's radiant future. It was an inspiring mixture of terror, sweetness and freedom, as in childhood when a tooth is extracted and there is still blood in your mouth and horror in your eyes but you no longer remember the pain and you are light of heart. All her past cares and present Moscow fears seemed to retreat before that Stalinist chain-mail of heavy cloth. The mirror showed her a maid in armour, a damsel squire, a girl hussar. "What's so dreadful about the coat in any case? It's just very nice, very nice indeed," she muttered in a voice strained from delight like an excited schoolgirl, as if excusing her unjustified enthusiasm before Ludmila's ironic gaze. She immediately recognized her mistake: you should never be too enthusiastic in such circumstances, so as not to put too great a price on the unexpected gift. So she said with feigned indifference: "But the collar is pretty moth-eaten, isn't it?" And immediately choked on her words. The collar gleamed like a dragon's scales. The buttons shone like baleful eyes. And Lena's eyes shone back at it.

"On my Young Pioneer's honour", she told Ludmila, adopting a widely used parody of Soviet officialese, "when you next visit London I shall be on the official welcoming committee in this very coat; it's straight out of Gogol." Though Gogol had nothing to do with the matter. For the overcoat was not like Gogol's but was outright Stalinist kitsch; women readers of the London Tattler or their friends, the regulars of the Groucho Club, would have burst of envy, given the recent craze for Sots-Art, though she would never have had anything to do with that crowd. She had never been particularly interested in clothes either. But in Moscow, a mysterious force seized her and drove her round the most dreadful sales-counters, whispering in her ear all the time: "Have a look at this, take a glance at that." Moscow's pawnshops and regular stores were flooded with museum pieces from the Stalin era: all those 1950s gabardine raincoats and velour hats, shoes fit for hippos, and double-breasted jackets.

She would buy them up unbeknown to her Moscow friends, paying for them in rouble notes that were meaningless to her, and her hands trembled with excitement. She was afraid it would all disappear like an early-morning dream just before you wake. They were fetishes from another past, from her parents' generation, things surfacing from someone else's childhood and materializing before her eyes. She was afraid they would all vanish in that half-waking dream. Moscow, too, was like a dream of a seven-year-old schoolgirl about the 1970s, stranded in her memory through her parents' stories about the 1950s. Unlike her new friends in Moscow, her nostalgia was threefold. The winter overcoat took her back into her parents' past but she herself was homesick for her London present rooted in her own Soviet past. The overcoat was a triple masquerade in that Moscow carnival unfolding before her eyes.

The theatre began with the cloakroom and continued in the street: the streetlamps were the footlights. The icy cold pinched her cheeks with the brazen familiarity of the boy next door; as if trying to undress her, fondle her, fool with her. In that overcoat there was no room in her soul for regret, either for her London sheepskin or for London itself. After all, she had bought the sheepskin solely with a view to her Moscow trip, it had cost her next to nothing at the Oxfam thrift shop, and before leaving Moscow she intended to give it to someone whose need was greater than hers. You did not have to look far to find people in need. That cloakroom attendant, for example: the wretched crook must be as poverty-stricken as any upstanding dissident. She was aware of her own moral superiority, with people in the street seeming to gaze at her in admiration. And indeed, she did find glances dwelling on her, because foreigners in Russia can be spotted a mile off; not so much because of their clothing as expression on their face and a kind of upright carriage.

People would stare as she strode by in that coffin-like garment that seemed cast in pig iron. Despite her Soviet childhood and for all her emigre parents' kitchen talk etched in her memory, Lena had succeeded in her years of London schooling in becoming infected by that peculiarly English tendency to take pleasure in the very act of overcoming difficulties, irrespective of the reason for them, provided the circumstances were far enough removed from the routines of daily life. It was an attitude toward life not too different from that of the jockey or even the racehorse unleashed by its rider and joining in the spirit of the race foaming at the mouth as it takes its fences in a steeplechase. She had no regrets about her decision to take Ludmila and Sergei up on their invitation.

"Lena, darling, what are you doing all alone on this old island?" the ever tipsy Ludmila would exclaim in London. From the very first time they met, they had been close, and it was rare moments when they managed to sober up. Conversations lasted long into the night. "Why wither away over here, you Britain's bastard daughter? Come to Moscow and we'll find you a feller. What are you waiting for?" And giggling with excessive familiarity, she added in completely different tones, lyrically, squeezing Lena's palms intimately in her hands with nails painted in scarlet and pearl: "I feel I've known you all my life, forever." And straightaway proposed toasts to friends, the arts, and the other side of paradise. After racing about the city and gatecrashing parties, she and Ludmila would sit up till dawn, telling one another all they knew about everything, drunk with talk. But it was really Ludmila who had most things to reveal in the true confessions she made as she sat chain-smoking in a state of undress with her make-up half- removed, as if she had just left her theatre dressing room.

In great detail she would recount Sergei's sexual foibles, good points and failings, would talk about the role of women on the Russian stage, about the theatre's role in Russian history, about the stupid behaviour of foreigners in Moscow and about the best ways of avoiding pregnancy over there. Lena was agog at what she heard and didn't know how to reciprocate, having nothing to confess about her life in London: whether she should begin with the loony behaviour of the Labour Party group in the local borough council or the mice breeding like rabbits behind her walls.

Even in such intensely personal exchanges, however, Lena never forgot her role as an interpreter of London life into Soviet categories. Sergei's theatre company had come on tour to London after the Edinburgh Festival, and so from the very outset Lena's relationship with the couple had taken place in the glare of the footlights, backstage intrigue, the intimate aura of theatre boudoirs and the hullabaloo of the make-up room, and the tension across the divide between the stage and the auditorium. All three were in a constant exaltation as if hearing unending applause at a premiere. It was Ludmila and Sergei's first trip to the West, and Lena's first meeting with people from her own Soviet childhood background and age. She and Ludmila might even have been in the same class at school. Lena had been at primary school when her parents took her away to Europe. All three of them were constantly searching in one another for things they had in common and which would provide reasons or excuses for that carefree wish to be together, feel one another, and bare their souls to one another in that tourist dance round pubs, theatres, museums, cocktail parties and social visits. Quite possibly they had nothing in common and that was why their so very Russian feverish first meeting was so long-lasting and accompanied by embraces, squeals of delight, kisses and drinking one another's health.

Lena showed her Moscow visitors all these Westminsters and Big Bens, Towers of London and Nelson's Columns, as if there weren't enough of her own words, gestures or emotions to tell them about her life spent outside Russia, at once so delightful for them in its mysteriousness and so frightening. Every Soviet citizen is either secretly or openly convinced that a Russian living outside his country is as good as done for, is actually only pretending to be alive. After passing all her conscious life in London, Lena for her part treated Russia as some kind of phantom world out of her parents' conversations, populated by ghosts of her childhood. Thus, it was a meeting of zombies and ghosts. Lena on the one hand, and Sergei and Ludmila on the other with the itchiness of curiosity, now and then tried to reach out and touch one another, if only to find out whether they really existed.

"Truly, why don't you come over?" Ludmila urged her almost girlishly. "It's difficult back home, but it's really fascinating."

"Fascinating?" questioned Lena with ironic skepticism, frowning a little. "Really?"

"Fascinating, of course. Frightening too, naturally. Sometimes really frightening", added Ludmila and lowered her eyes.

"Very frightening?" asked Lena hanging on her hand as if Ludmila was her nurse, like someone anticipating the dreadful ending of a fairy-tale. "Fear" had been a constant theme of her father, in those long epistles that came thudding into her letter box as soon as he heard of her intended visit to Moscow. In his telephone conversations with her from across the Atlantic (he was working for Radio Liberty in New York) he would shout at her that she was completely stupid and didn't know what she was talking about, that Russia was a country of monsters and freaks, hunchbacks, cripples and deaf-mutes. "So what? What about your old writers like Soul Zhinitsyn and Sin Yavsky?" she would retort mercilessly. All that came back from over the oceanic sighing waves of the ether were the heavy sighs of her father's civic conscience.

"You think it's all literature?" he shouted at last: "You think it's all a big game, a laughing matter? It may be literature, but it's all mixed up with blood and guts. So that's okay if you want a job as a vampire. You'll be able to get fresh blood over there alright. If that's your drink." In reply, Lena clenched her teeth and the phone more tightly still. "It's not blood I want," she said carefully enunciating each syllable into the phone and swearing to herself. "I am simply planning to visit the place. Travelling to Moscow, that's all." From the far side of the Atlantic her father seemed to give in, sighing defeatedly: "I can't tell you what it's like. It's just awful. It's treachery if you go. What was the point of emigrating then? Where are your principles? You don't understand anything," he finally finished on the same impotent note, a hysterical howling in the telephone wilderness. She failed to understand. But of course. In the past few years she had often been unable to sleep nights, thinking she had committed some fatal error when her parents left London for New York by not going with them. Every time she spoke to her father over the phone strengthened her conviction that she'd been right to decide to stay in London all those years ago. But now that she had reached Moscow she began again to doubt the wisdom of the path in life she had mapped out for herself.

At some point she began to sense that Sergei's and Ludmila's invitation was an obligatory gesture of sham gratitude for her London hospitality: the only way they could repay her was with a return invitation, or rather a mere show of readiness to provide hospitality. Who could ever have imagined that Lena would take them up on their hasty invitation? All the way from the airport Ludmila hadn't tired of wondering why Lena had decided to come to visit a barbaric country like Russia. On the other hand Sergei appeared willing to try her as an adviser, an idea first raised at the height of their orgiastic rounds of London. It had been mooted in connection with the stage adaptation of the then fashionable emigre novel "The Rousseauphobe and the Fungophile", a macabre love story between a left-wing Englishwoman crazy about Jean-Jacques Rousseau and a Russian crank hooked on cooking. The heroine, contemptuous of her native England, falls in love with this Soviet monster, apparently an imbecile but a Stalinist at heart; he marries her solely to get a visa to go abroad but all the while is sleeping with her best friend, and when she finally finds out she nearly commits suicide. The text was flooded with Anglicisms, the way Russian is spoken by foreigners in Moscow, and by Russicisms, the kind of English spoken by the Russian characters of the novel in London. Sergei, a husky young theatre type with a curly beard, infantile yet fanatical about truth in art, had convinced himself in London that the theatre absolutely had to take on Lena as a bi-lingual consultant. During their long nightly conversations in London, Sergei had been collecting the Anglicisms in her Russian, the way she could call a teapot a teachest, for example, or a coffee machine a coffer. When Ludmila heard her malapropisms, she howled with laughter, rolling about on her pillow or planting ruby lipstick kisses on Lena's cheeks. Ludmila was to play the radical English girl, and Lena's tuition was intended to teach the cast a series of properly pronounced English obscenities. This power she had over pronunciation, particularly of foreign words, lent her an aura of exclusiveness from the day of her arrival in Moscow (not to mention her foreign passport and appearance, and her hard currency); her foreign accent and that odd language she spoke seemed to have also influenced the way she saw things: she observed Moscow and listened to its speech as an outsider, as if she were an onlooker carried away by her shameless curiosity.

That depressing, caravanserai lifestyle, all those concrete buildings, bureaucratic restructuring and mafioso privatization were for her exciting, exotic. A state of ambivalent proximity, of unhealthy curiosity about the embarrassment of others caught in a casual embrace with someone unlikely. Or the other way round, as when former lovers meet but feel too guilty to resume their relationships. Her very walk down the vaguely familiar streets was almost sexually arousing. It was an arousal to be concealed, it was not nice, particularly for a foreign girl. Despite her Soviet childhood, with an emigre's homesickness learned subconsciously at her parents' knees, it was only in Moscow that she finally felt British. But among Russians she had to pretend she was Russian and behave as if she really were one of them. Often when she clearly could not remember a thing she was obliged to fake total recall. She was terrified lest she be caught out in subterfuge. Through the fact that she'd been born in Moscow she had earned the right of return, but the route she was taking to get there was in no way guaranteed.

Still, her feet remembered the way home. When she was given instructions how to find an address she nodded and pretended to know the way. Of course she got lost at the third turning after leaving the Metro and wandered for hours down totally unfamiliar streets and interconnecting courtyards. However, just when she was finally completely off course, some rudimentary, primordial intuition prompted her, and at some strange crossroads she'd suddenly know how to get there as if she had left only the day before. Such tiny victories stunned her with a forgotten sensation of belonging. It was a feeling of both belonging and bastardy that made her plunge deeper and deeper into the bruising whirlpool that was the city in those squabbling times. How often did she find herself on Manege Square, staring with those dilated blue eyes of hers at the stubby Kremlin towers beyond their dragon-tooth battlements, looking almost like human heads mirrored in the wet asphalt of the square where faces, placards and megaphones all merged together in a single cry "Down with the Communist Party! Commies out!" She too shouted out those slogans against Bolsheviks and nationalists until she caught sight of Ludmila staring at her. A blend of irony, curiosity and even revulsion. Or was it her imagination?

Her imagination had undoubtedly been working overtime of late. To her London mind, Moscow had always been the crossroads where all the feverish and disorganized emigre disputes went on in her father's flat. It had been associated with KGB provocations, samizdat, friends around the kitchen table drinking "to the success of our hopeless cause" and, under the watchful eye of the State security authorities, composing appeals to enlightened humanity. That Moscow had been a world of separations and friendships, farewells and forgiveness, prison and poverty, elitism and existential choice, sincerity and self-serving zealotry. The post-perestroika Moscow was like an upset ant-heap where crowds of angry and tormented people shoved and cursed, caught in the time of primitive accumulation, they raced between market and bazaar, from big-store to bring-and-buy, and spoke a language full of Russified Americanisms. That

The Moth

nostalgic Sots-art in the form of portraits of Politburo members and Party slogans had disappeared and the few remaining Lenin monuments stood lonely and miserable on street-corners and squares, looking around them with an air of self-doubt.

In just the same way a dwarf statue of Lenin tood in the shop window, called "Schoolboy", gazing out at the scurrying crowds with an amazed short-sighted frown. Lena haggled over it with the sales clerk for an American dollar and when she got home she hid it in her suitcase. For this idol of the Revolution the only way left was back into exile. From monuments to a victorious present these idols had turned into pitiful school aids for future lessons of the past: dusty and unneeded by anyone in this new and still undiscovered country. The former Motherland was vanishing visibly and the monuments of the former Soviet Union, together with its population, themselves felt like White emigres, as if the streets of Moscow were trodden now by a nation of changelings, a completely different people.

Sergei and Ludmila did not seem to be themselves either. She could not say what she had expected their Moscow life to be. The reality belied any expectations. On the evening of her arrival and on the occasion of the premiere of Richard the Third, when everything had been prepared weeks ahead, carefully thought-out and calculated, their petty-bourgeois pretentiousness and grand airs sprang to the fore.

What had happened to their bohemian attitudes in London and their scorn for bourgeois appearances? Lena's eyes, merciless after her sheepskin was stolen, noticed the long English bolsters, in place of square Russian pillows, spread out on a Japanese futon rather than the usual ancient Russian divan, and the cheap, in English terms, but exotic paper lampshade, full of snob-value for Muscovites. The living room was stuffed to the brim with electronic goods and video sets, and even the wretched beer-mats stolen from some London pub were proudly displayed on a lacquer table. As they arrived, guests were administered careful measures of whisky, purchased at so-called commercial prices, i.e. the equivalent of an average citizen's monthly wage-packet. When, with much pomp, a couple of lumps of ice were dropped into each glass Lena said pointedly that whisky and ice was an American habit whereas the English added only plain water (if they did all), not even soda, also an American habit, she added when she saw Sergei helping himself to tonic. She addressed the two of them in as penetrating a voice as possible so that everyone could hear: a pair of Moscow snobs shouldn't be allowed to pass themselves off as Londoners.

The guests, and the hosts more particularly, showed off their leather and tee-shirts. The taste for imitation leather was something she had long ago described as a subconscious Freudian urge on the part of Soviet man to change his skin, tear it off. Lena smiled to herself again remembering how successfully she had swapped her sheepskin for the stylish cloth of the Stalin era. In the hallway the guests raised their eyebrows at her overcoat: Lena knew they were smirking at her too behind her back. Even her linen blouse from Bond Street earned a scornful snicker, as if to say she might have ironed it before going to a party. The trend here was for tee-shirts purchased at mark-down prices in the dime-stores of all the capitals of the West, and were flashy with the pop slogans and phoney graffiti beloved of working-class London youth. Lena might just as well have stayed behind in Lewisham and hung out in the saloon bar of "The White Horse" where kids with the same greasy long hair and similar tee-shirts spent their time playing snooker or throwing darts. The party atmosphere reminded her of the sweaty crush of those working-class pubs.

"Life is all a vicious circus," she said in her emigre Russian, making her way through the crowd in the living room, filled with alcohol fumes and cigarette smoke like a smoking compartment in a London suburban train.

"It's all a vicious circus, is it?" groaned Sergei, almost singing the words, shaking his head and rolling about in happy laughter. He strode about the room, combing his curly hair with his five fingers, repeating "Did you hear that? It's all a vicious circus, is it, eh, Ludmila? That's marvellous. We'll stick it in the play, shall we?" Such statements, along with Lena's other fantastic neologisms elicited only weak smiles among the others. Moreover, Lena noted sympathetic looks among other guests, as if they were in the presence of someone severely ill. Lena did not like what was going on. She was used to being treated as someone special. In London her Russian origins had given her an air of exclusiveness and she expected that in Moscow her Anglicisms would create the same aura of someone special, someone chosen. But instead, they looked at her askance as if she were some eccentric in the local bar of a provincial English town, where they have their own notions of who's special. But of course here she was immediately given to understand that nowhere else on Earth was life as bad as in Russia. So being among the chosen, according to this half-baked theology, was intimately bound up with the idea of martyrdom. Lena smiled back condescendingly.

However almost from the doorstep she could see in all that martyrdom of a chosen people, that same old Russian simpering of hangers-on that you would have in any other intellectual gathering, parasites preying off their own wretchedness. That same old idle slovenliness. They complained that their kids didn't get enough greens or the adults enough meat, yet they were willing to spend money on vodka and refused to use the private market even for the most urgent necessities. "For that crap? How dare they charge that much? Just speculation and profiteering! Why should I? What the hell is the government doing?" And so on. It was always the government's fault. It was always either the government, religion, the authorities, or the cosmos that was at fault. The foolish chatter irritated her, with its cheap philosophy, that intellectual masturbation, that flippant sneering at social duty and personal lifestyles. It was time they learned something about collective discipline, she thought. They had to get used to the idea that there were bound to be temporary sacrifices and losers. They were incapable of foregoing anything: their vodka, their books, their kitchen chatter about what the world was coming to. It was easy to talk about someone else's comforts and parliamentary democracies a thousand leagues away. They probably thought that in London things were free, that it cost nothing. During the war the Londoners had dug up all the royal parks and planted potatoes in them. They would have to learn to count every penny. Lena flushed: she was ready to boil over from self-righteous indignation.

"But Lena, sweetheart, you must understand that if my husband's socks have holes in them, there's no thread to darn them with, because, my dear English lady, thread cannot be found for love or money," squeaked Ludmila after a long pause for smirking, smiles and winks.

"Nothing to darn them with? What? Really? Well go without socks. Like in California," Lena persisted.

"But Lena, child, this isn't California. Here we have temperatures of forty below, vodka is forty degrees too, only there is often just frost but no vodka. Often nothing at all. Nothing to warm yourself up with, that is."

Lena tried not to take all this irony personally, though her situation was somewhat ambivalent; since she was from Russia, any complaints against the West ostensibly had nothing to do with her, and if she had not been there as an English visitor in Moscow no-one would give a thought about the West. But Lena was not getting muddled up. After all, the main thing in life was creativity, the artistic spirit. An artist is even prepared to walk naked in the snow, as a yogi walks on burning coals. Everyone should be an artist at heart. She said all this with the gleaming eyes of a rebellious teenager, plunging in at the deep end of the argument without a moment's hesitation. Lena noticed that Sergei liked it all: her fire, her defence of spiritual values, in that atmosphere of general sneering and pessimism. As a theatre director he appreciated the unquenchable charm of her paradoxical optimism. Her words would please the audience weary of intellectuals digging around in the grave-vaults of the social conscience. Ludmila, as a Russian woman scorned, did not like what was going on. She was again drinking too much and behaving like Lady Anne to Richard the Third: bile and hatred switching suddenly to pliable lasciviousness. Lena looked at her puffy pale face swollen from the vodka she had drunk.

If she drank and ate less, there would be more on the shelves in liquor stores and bakeries, she thought. Lena was stupid enough to mutter something about the Greek stoics, to the effect that "If you can't eat your fill, then live off what you've got."

"But if you haven't got anything, what do you live off?" said Ludmila angrily, washing down a pickled cucumber with her next glass of vodka. Lena felt the gap between her and coarse-voiced Ludmila growing wider with every glass, as if her crooked vision, all the more blurred by alcohol, were also drastically changing her view of their relations. Raising her plucked eyebrows, Ludmila muttered through set teeth: "Sweetheart, illegitimate daughter of Albion, surely it has penetrated your thick English head that here in the Soviet Onion the

The Moth

Bolshevik terror and its Dirty Tricks Department do their filthy deeds on food and everyday necessities. Or haven't you noticed?" And leaning across the table, her mouth broadened in a malicious smile, "We haven't had cheese in this city for more than a year. Haven't you found out back in Britain that they are trying to starve us to death over here; they're trying to slaughter us like rats."

"You can live without cheese", said Lena shrugging her shoulders. "Cheese is bad for you, anyway," she said more or less mechanically, with the English social insouciance in her reply, because the word "rats" had carried her back to London.

She recalled her sleepless nights in London the previous winter, when she had practically no work; or rather no desire to work. No-one appeared to have any particular desire to work; the local Labour borough council, scared of strikes and afraid of losing votes from its out-of-work supporters, paid no attention to the idle garbage collectors or the pavement before her house in Lewisham which sprouted thick heaps of garbage the way Moscow grew piles of snow each winter. She had been unable to get to sleep before three or four in the morning, reading over and over again her beloved Chekhov until she felt completely stupid and exhausted, and when she finally sank into a restless sleep she imagined she was still turning the pages. On one occasion, what she had taken for a monotonous rustling of pages in her sleep turned out to be a careful but insistent scrabbling from behind the wall. Stirring from sleep, at first she thought it was the rustling and shivering of branches in the garden beyond the window. But the frozen garden in that chilly dry snowless winter was cramped from the cold and still. She got up to calm down and have a cup of tea, and went to look for some biscuits in the cupboard, only to discover that there were only crumbs. Hungry and irritated she went back to bed, but again heard that rustling behind the wall. Strange neighbours. English sexual perversions were amazing. It was only the next day when she found on the table a lump of cheese that had seemed etched by the fine lines of sharp teeth that she understood it was mice. Mice had bred in the wainscot, and she could not work out how to deal with them. Alec, also a third-wave emigre, her adviser in all matters English and one-time lover, though old enough to be her father, recommended she put mouse traps around the house. "Mousetraps!" she howled, "I could catch my fingers in them and break my extremes." "Extremities," muttered Alec, "not extremes." But finally he spread those "extremities" wide in a gesture of helplessness. At his proposal to call in rat-catchers, she burst out: "Rat-catchers? What have rats got to do with it? I have mice, not rats. And those mice catchers will spread poison everywhere. There will be corpses all over the place. You want me to walk about on their corpses? Wasn't the Soviet experiment enough for you?" That was when she decided to go to Moscow, recalling the lyrical summer chats with Ludmila and Sergei.

Friendships travel as poorly as local wines. They had invited her to Moscow during the sustained and noisy binge that was their stay in London. Afterwards, in Moscow, they behaved as if they had a hangover. Sergei walked around like a caged and angry genius, swearing and tearing at his hair (he was having trouble developing his ideas). Everything was much simpler, so far as Ludmila was concerned. She could not stand Lena as chief adviser on foreign affairs. Actors do not like it (who does, in any case?) when aspersions are cast on their skills, and no matter how Lena pretended to be just an ordinary pronunciation coach and not get involved in what her charge did on stage, Ludmila took the slightest comment on her accent as if she were being panned by the critics, and as if her acting abilities were being questioned. Lena, however, was irritated not so much by Ludmila's lack of linguistic talent as by her demonstrative psychological rigidity, intellectual pedantry and an almost ill-intentioned obtuseness. The Russian disrespect for phonetics notwithsdtanding, it was still hard to see why she felt compelled to confuse words "fag" and "fuck". A sickened grimace twisted Lena's features each time Ludmila proffered her a cigarette with the words: "Would you like to have a fuck?"

"Why should I twist my tongue around your stupid sillaballs?" Ludmila flared up at Lena's mild reproof. Every such outburst was met by a condescending ironic smile from Lena, but her air of superiority irritated Ludmila still further. The more Lena resembled Professor Higgins, the less Ludmila resembled Eliza Doolittle.

Sergei nervously chewed his nails and sank deeper into his director's chair, watching Lena's stubbornly clenched fists as she pressed on with her coaching. When for the umpteenth time Ludmila threw a tantrum and walked off-stage, Lena exchanged glances with

Sergei and caught his smile of sympathy. Their eyes met and she instinctively shrugged; it was like two adults witnessing the misbehaviour of a child. Sergei seriously began to worry about the show's chances and meanwhile the stakes had risen: thanks to Lena's London contacts there was a chance of putting it on over there. Sergei began to wonder whether it might not be possible to stage the play in English, with Lena coaching all roles in translation from beginning to end. That led to bitter ideological squabbles with Ludmila. She was against foreign tours at a time "when our country is at a turning point and the future of Russian art is being decided." Sergei made fun of her "small-beer patriotism," arguing that the "aim of the arts, like that of the Jews, is self-preservation." The next time she burst out with the remark: "Why should I go in for all this foreign tongue-twisting?" Sergei replied quietly but clearly: "You don't need to, Ludmila. You can leave. Go on, go home." He asked Lena if she wanted the part. At first Lena turned down the idea categorically, and yet it was obvious that the show might fold. Ludmila retired to bed, with either an alcohol-induced liver condition or depression-induced heart pains. At all events, she had been unable to move her part forward at all, and there was only a week left before opening night. So Lena agreed. After all, art means self-sacrifice.

What a week it was. Lena threw herself whole-heartedly into her new role, with all the enthusiasm of a star pupil at school; she began acting it out not only on stage but in real life too. That was theatre indeed. It was fascinating to turn into a left-wing English woman onstage, smitten by the Russian revolutionary idea, while offstage she was an exiled young Russian dissident raised on English conservative ideals. In arguments that sputtered on for hours they worked out the philosophical aspects of her role: that Rousseau-esque disgust with self, with near and dear ones and with one's country; and the sense of guilt born of that feeling which in turn bred adoration of one's sworn enemy, neatly binding her to a monster. During rehearsals they hardly noticed time and would come back to earth only in the small hours, realizing that there was no sense in going home. On one occasion after staying up so late, she was too tired even to go to the theatre dressing-room, so she spread her Stalinist overcoat out in a corner of the wings. In a half-doze with her eyes half-closed she saw Sergei striding up and down in front of the theatre's back-drop, smoking. The velvet drapes of the wings hung overhead like threatening storm clouds in an alien sky, and all of a sudden she felt so lonely and far from home in this foreign land that she was overcome by a sudden and desperate need for protection and tenderness. Art meant self-sacrifice. And feeling the urgent trembling of his hand on her shoulder she let out no sound but slipped silently out of her dress. Aware of her own body awakening in a responding tremor she just had time to slip a piece of curtain beneath her so that the overcoat's silk lining did not get stained.

However, a stain did appear, and an impressive one at that, a stain of quite a suspect shade: only at the last moment she noticed that her period had begun. She tried to wash the stain off under the tap but it simply spread, spoiling once and for all the museum reputation of that work of some forgotten Stalinist tailor. Lena lost her peace of mind; because of the obviously shameful stain on her coat that she had until then so readily displayed to everybody on every possible occasion, she now began to shut it away from prying eyes in closets and dark corners wherever she went.

One day, she decided simply to leave the overcoat at home, donning instead a leather jacket from the "Beryozka" hard-currency store, but the idea of the overcoat hanging in the solitary gloom of her wardrobe began to haunt her. Her gaze wandered, her tongue stumbled, she kept involuntarily switching from Russian to English, and the tears ran uncontrollably down her cheeks. Once, she tried to find out from Ludmila whether there was a good dry cleaner in Moscow. Ludmila said tartly that Moscow was not an African jungle and of course there were dry cleaners, but nobody in their right minds would take anything worthwhile there because after being dry-cleaned all that would be left was a damp spot. In short, if Lena cared to show the spot she would find the right household remedy. Naturally, Lena tried to change the subject and make sure that the coat was not left unguarded because it was obvious from Ludmila's persistent questioning that she knew more than she let on; it was as if the spot were not upon the coat lining but on her reputation.

She and Sergei contrived to go home after rehearsals as late as possible and arrive separately. Lena would quietly unlock the apartment door with her key and tiptoe into her room like a thief in the night. In any other circumstance anywhere else in the world she would have left long ago and gone to stay in a hotel. But she tried to tell herself it would not only be suffocating to pen herself up in a hotel room but dangerous to be stuck in Moscow without friends at her side; and that was true, as it was also true that she was not keen on spending her hard currency on a hotel: she had become infected with Soviet stinginess. She told herself that she had to think about her financial future in London in case the English version of the show really went ahead and the theatre came to London on tour.

Returning from the theatre long after midnight she would notice light coming from under the door of Ludmila's bedroom, showing she was not asleep but waiting up for Lena's return. Lena would barricade herself in her room and listen to Ludmila's footsteps patrolling the apartment like a sentry, as if trying to inspect the damage done to her family life and household. Was Ludmila trying to find out what the spot on Lena's overcoat was? If they happened to come in together, Sergei would immediately disappear into his wife's room with a guilty smile on his face, from where demonstratively erotic groans would be emitted by Ludmila a little later.

It was humiliating but theatre was theatre, the game was worth the candle, even the loss of her own sense of self-esteem. That heady sensation of her first few days in Moscow returned, an almost Nietzschean shamelessness in the face of petty bourgeois morality. She stopped worrying about the ignominious stain and when she went visiting would throw the overcoat from her shoulders, displaying to general view its suspect spots. Art demanded sacrifices. But the sacrificial victim turned out to be not Lena but Ludmila, who seemed to wither on the bough, envy turning her skin yellow, tears starting to her eyes, though less from weeping than from alcohol and sleeplessness. On the other hand, Lena blossomed before everyone's eyes, glowing with an inner light and enchanting the rest of the cast with the artistry of her abandon, her inspired frivolity, the poignant wholesomeness of her Anglo-Russian dichotomy, and her uniquely universal character. On the eve of the premiere she slept soundly all night long with a triumphant smile on her face.

The same triumphant smile was on her lips when the cast gathered to celebrate the first night of "The Rousseauphobe", chattering about the absurd collisions and comic absurdities in the show, anecdotal misunderstandings and interruptions, and how successfully they'd managed them, the play had come off brilliantly. The din of the celebration resounding in her temples with the counterpoint of voices, echoing the roar of applause at the theatre, the enraptured whispers and head-turning gales of laughter or outbursts of repressed sobbing from emotional spectators; there on the stage, her head had spun from the smell of sweat and dust. How many times at the end they had bowed and curtsied she could not recall, but she felt a pleasant weakness in her knees, she was blinded, hypnotized by the gleam of enraptured eyes, while the crowd rose as one from their seats to clap and cheer her in an uninterrupted chain of bravoes. She was applauded for being Russian but understanding the whole tragedy of the small-minded Rousseauphobe. The public knew she was a foreigner but also that she had drunk deeply of the tragedy of the Russian soul. She was mysterious in her simplicity and simple in the sense of mystery she radiated. She had stood front stage in her fake English costume, which still conveyed her inimitable foreignness. With bated breath all Moscow repeated her killingly English accents and malapropisms. Those hundreds of high cheek-boned Slav faces were fixed on her, awaiting a revelation from her and when it came the revelation was a gift, transmuting a life that is alien to all of us into something close to our hearts, and vice versa. She was both here and there, she was everywhere. It was freedom. She no longer regretted the humiliation of recent days, as art required sacrifices. It was a triumph. It felt as if the footlights along the stage would burst from the emotional incandescence of the theatre.

At that peak of emotion and ovation she spied a strange figure in one of the dress-circle boxes, a suspect figure clad in a heavy black overcoat with an astrakhan collar. But she could not understand why the person had not been made to check the overcoat in the cloakroom. She took fright at the idea that it might be her own overcoat taken from the dressing room by the man in the box. True, the overcoat was not really hers as it belonged to the theatre, but Lena had been given it to wear so long as the rightful heir could not be found. The idea that the heir might have been found, breathed life into the motionless figure in the box, and he rose to his feet, straightening out to full height and turning toward the stage as if listening to the play not with his ears but with his huge white forehead. One hand was thrust forward, hanging like an artificial stump, and he clapped on it with the other as if in time to a rhythmic dance, joining in the general ovation. The auditorium suddenly spun before Lena's eyes, her legs gave way and she fell against one of the wings, cracking it down the seam, in a vain effort to keep her balance.

She was carried to her friends' home all of a-tremble, agitated, wrapped up in her incomparable overcoat – it had been recovered whole and untouched from an armchair in her dressing room; and now she would not take it off. The blurry faces crowding around her offstage with valerian and smelling salts were still solicitous when they gathered round the festive table. Only there was she revived with glasses of vodka and yet another stunning toast. People leaned across the table to kiss and embrace her, with flirtatious familiarity and risque compliments.

While all that was going on, Lena's recent interview for the weekly magazine "Stolitsa" was being passed round the table. In it she had discussed the Iron Curtain as akin to theatre and emigration as a theatrical device, a stage exit, if you like. It all sounded highly original, particularly the bits about the Pirandello elements in our lives, when (in contradistinction to Stanislavsky's "fourth wall") it was not clear where the audience ends and the stage begins, which way the Iron Curtain really faced, who stood behind it and who stood before. Everyone welcomed the idea as it allowed no-one to feel patronized, East or West.

"The press is chasing after me like a foxhound after a rabbit," she announced in her peculiar Russian to those present, not understanding why they burst out laughing. Ludmila's contorted drunken features looked even more distasteful as she staggered to her feet, as if about to collapse and drag the tablecloth to the floor with her, threatening to bring glasses, plates and ashtrays crashing after her:

"D'you think this is some kind of rabbit hutch here then?" she squealed, rocking in the middle of the room. Mouths were still twisted in laughter but all eyes were on Ludmila. "And as for you, you randy old foxhound", she swung round to face Sergei, "what do you see in her? In this little English rabbit, ready for the fucking? Just look at yourself, will you! You've dirtied yourself in her blood, but who washes your underpants? Me, that's who!"

"What blood are you talking about?" muttered Sergei.

"Her blood, you arsehole. Menstrual blood, you stupid git!" And she stumbled along the edge of the table in Lena's direction. Everyone rushed to stand aside, leaving a circle where Lena stood face to face with her. Ludmila dragged the cursed overcoat from Lena and shoved it in Sergei's face. "She thinks I don't know where these bloodstains come from," she simpered at Lena.

Lena tried to wrest the coat from Ludmila, who suddenly threw it down, leaned across the table, drew herself up to full height, working her jaws like a camel, and spat right in Lena's face. Then, stumbling backwards to the door, she suddenly declaimed in faultless English amid the ensuing silence:

> A base foul stone, made precious by the foil
> Of England's Chair, where she is falsely set.

"What's Shakespeare got to do with it?" muttered Lena wiping her face with her sleeve, as most of those present rushed after Ludmila. Ludmila screeched something insulting and hysterical from the landing outside. Lena began mechanically to don the overcoat and follow the others, but slumped back on the chair as her enfeebled legs gave way. At the now empty table a pair of elderly alcoholics from the make-up department were swilling cheap wine, from time to time leaning their foreheads against one another so as not to fall off their chairs. One of them stared through bleary eyes at Lena as she sat in the middle of the room in the overcoat and moaned. The alcoholic muttered:

"So that's the overcoat. His overcoat."

"Whose overcoat?" asked Lena.

"He had it made specially for himself," he hiccupped, "to hide his hump. His hump was why he was so good as Richard."

"Why hide your hunchback when you play Richard? Richard has to have one according to Shakespeare," mumbled Lena.

"According to Shakespeare, sure. On stage he wouldn't have thought of hiding it. On the conn-con-trary. But in life he was a hunchback too. So he used this coat, to conceal his hump, see."

"What the hell is he talking about?" she thought. At the same time she tried to listen to the screams and shouts from the landing.

"Our Honoured Artist was not only a great actor," the drunk said hiccupping again, "but he was good at literature too. Denunciations were his speciality." Etc. etc. The theatre's Party Secretary since the beginning of time. Honoured Artist. Order of Lenin. And all the rest of it. Even after he died no-one else was allowed to use his dressing-room. But when perestroika began, both in society and on the stage, the doors to his totalitarian dressing room were also thrown open.

"Darling, wouldn't you just hate to wear something like that?" said the drunk, grabbing at the tails of the great black overcoat.

"I'm not worried by the underpinnings of things," said Lena in a conscious effort at a pun, and strode out on the balcony, from where she could hear the querulous voices below. The street was lit by street-lamps like a stage set illuminated by footlights. The recent merry company had re-formed out on the icy street in a coatless huddle, trying to restrain Ludmila. Clouds of vapour were issuing from their mouths like the exhalations of a smoke-breathing circus conjurer. Ludmila tried to break free, her swearing could be heard along with hysterical laughter. Protected from the icy cold by the heavy overcoat, Lena watched Ludmila finally wriggle loose and rush across that stage-like street, and away down a side-street over and beyond. But at that moment round the corner lurched a trolleybus, as if on instructions from a director hidden in the wings. It seemed to be a part of the stage set, a mechanized prop from the special effects department. Lit up from inside, the transparent body in the metallic carcass of the trolleybus raced horrifically across the set like a frightened insect. Ludmila ran blindly down the street straight at it, cursing and paying no heed to the screams of warning from the panicking crowd behind her. With a crunch of snow and a hiss of brakes, the trolleybus swallowed her skull under its bumpers, chomping her under its wheels. The sudden grind to a halt made the trolleybus booms fly loose from the wires and sway up and down, showering firework sparks into the air. From her grandstand view, Lena had to keep herself from applauding the magic theatrical staging and its anonymous author.

* * *

She was woken by a familiar tired shuffling sound, as if she had never left that bed of hers in London. It was the way mice had rustled in the wainscot a year earlier, when Moscow had seemed like some mirage from the past, a fairy- tale country from her father's tales, a far-off story of someone dear who had long since passed away. No more than a year had elapsed since Ludmila's death, but it seemed an eternity. Lena rose up on her pillow and looked around her room. Not a shred remained in it of the squalor that she had fled from to Moscow, to go anywhere, to get away, wherever she could be free of the rotting draught through the window, the squeak of wintery branches outside the window, the rustle of rubbish on the pavement and that stirring of mice behind the walls. While she was in Moscow, the rat-catchers had destroyed the mice, their children and elders down to the seventh generation. In addition, during her absence the local Labour-run council had been replaced and the wind was no longer leafing through old newspapers trampled under the heels of passers-by. And the trees outside her windows no longer disturbed her with their funereal creaking; outside the window the May-time garden was rustling as the rhododendrons and golden rod swayed and heaved.

Her own loved one snored lightly beside her, and Lena guessed at the source of the rustle that brought mice to mind. Sergei slept with pursed lips like an infant, and his every breath caused a corner of the light linen sheet to rustle against the wallpaper. This discovery made the rustling seem like a hymn to comfort and domesticity, and was echoed by a rustling from under the sheets when she pressed herself to his naked body in that tender May night.

She had won him by right, that curly Cupid's head of his, his big and mobile body, and his genius as a director. Any fool could see what his stay in England would do to his theatrical career; and if it hadn't been for her he would never have come. His extravagant interpretation of *Richard the Third* had been a sensation among London theatre-goers and discussions were already in progress on a proposal for the Almeida Theatre to stage an English-language version of the "Rousseauphobe". Initially, of course, he had pretended to resist the idea of coming to London. Not a month had gone by since Ludmila's funeral and they had still been surrounded by the grief-stricken faces of stunned relatives and by problems to do with the apartment. But Lena saw him following every movement of her body while her tongue waxed eloquent over the importance of Anglo-Russian theatrical links. How could such a gorgeous lover have wasted his life on a flat-chested, cantankerous and ungifted

The Moth

stage-girl, whose egoism and ambitions had matched only her lisp and slight squint, for some reason admired by her crowd as a charming flaw. The question of scruples obviously arose; yes, she was with Sergei, no, perhaps they hadn't been so noble in their behaviour to Ludmila during rehearsals, hiding things from her and leaving her to suffer alone at home while they spent nights together, as it were offstage. Scruples are all very well but we have only one life to live, and if it hadn't been for those carryings-on in the wings, the show would never have been so successful. That dreadful bloody mess of torn flesh and shattered bones sticking out from beneath the wheels of the trolleybus still preyed on their minds like the shameful spot on her coat-lining after that first night in the theatre. But it was a sacrifice in the name of art and, as we know, art demands sacrifices.

Something was interfering with her elegant train of thought. She tried to concentrate but was distracted by a gentle shimmer of night-light streaming in through the window from behind the curtains. It was as if maybugs were floating into the room from the garden. A restless thought, or rather a hint at one, fluttered vaguely and took on the form of a glimmering spot that zigzagged round the room and jumped up and down in the reflected glow of the night sky from far-off street-lamps. This half-mosquito, demi- butterfly, this dot out of some pointillist painting kept moving from side to side, before appearing close beneath her nose. In a sudden cat-like move, Lena clapped her hands on the importunate creature and annihilated it, but its double immediately appeared to one side, pirouetting in the air in the same way. They were probably midges or other night insects invading the room, together with a heavy aroma of jasmine. She rose carefully from her bed, trying not to disturb Sergei, and closed the window. Then she tiptoed, as if in a scene from some ballet, after the tiny dancer towards the wardrobe in the far corner of the room. The floorboards creaked under the carpet and Sergei, with a sudden snore, turned over when Lena, in the measured leap of a feline, caught the next moth in the palm of her hand. The bust of Lenin acquired in that Moscow school stationery store jumped as if shaken by surprise on the card table alongside. At the same time, the door to the wardrobe creaked open. But then, yet another invader appeared in the room as if from nowhere, and Lena switched on the table lamp to find out where it came from. The secret routes were either coming from or ending up in the wardrobe.

In the gaping door of the wardrobe, the silk lining of the museum overcoat gleamed and the curls on the astrakhan collar shone with the same green reflection as the bronze of Lenin's bust. It stared out at her like something totally alien, obviously from a stranger's shoulder, hostile and out of place in London.

In the first few days after her return the overcoat had been a wild success. In London she dined out on her tales of the fascinating horrors of Moscow life. But after a few months the fashion for Soviet punk and Russia had vanished and the overcoat lost its lustre. Lena came to consider it out of place, clumsy and twice as heavy as an overcoat should be; her back groaned under its weight. Then it was consigned to the depths of her wardrobe. Moscow only returned to her now in the shape of a recurrent dream about that triumphant moment when she stood front-stage, the theatre choking from the echoing bravoes, the spotlights swimming from the applause, and the overcoated stranger up there in the box clapping her with one hand. On one occasion she thought she saw him standing on the corner of her London street; she recognized even the black overcoat with its padded shoulders and the hints of baldness and a widow's peak. But coming closer she realized that it was just a local drunk scraping around in a garbage heap. Soon after, the derelict must have moved on to another part of London or drunk himself into a better world, because he never appeared again on her street. Eventually, the nightmare of his double in the theatre box ebbed away too.

She pulled the overcoat from the wardrobe, laid it on the armchair and under the bright light of the lamp noticed that the fringes of the astrakhan collar and its lapels were covered in tiny holes: as if eaten away by the tiny teeth of mice, or riddled with buckshot. Maybe the mice had come back for her coat instead of cheese. Even its wonderful silk lining had begun to fall apart at the seams. Where the traces of that shameful spot could still be seen, it was now sticking out monstrously, coming adrift from the wadding. But instead of wadding she saw that something odd had been stuffed into it like newspapers, the way Soviet soldiers use old papers as boot linings in freezing weather. When she tried to smoothe the wadding back into place her fingers felt something bulky and a moment later a packet fell out from the seam. It was an ordinary-looking brown-paper envelope, rather official-looking, sealed with the theatre's crest impressed on it in red wax, and bound with coarse string for added security. Lena made herself comfortable at her card table beneath the lamp and the frowning bust of Lenin. She unsealed the envelope and drew from the packet a bundle of sheets from an ordinary school exercise book, which she spread out on the table. The first page was covered in plain handwriting with no flourishes, and was headed:

MARTYROLOG

Now is the winter of our discontent made summer. No, it was not beneath a foreign sky, like some arty-farties but wherever my audience was, fortunately, always up there with my audience, on a cloakroom hanger, I was always there, bearing the load of civil strife in the shape of people's furcoats and other winter wear. In my mind I am always aware of the greatness of my allotted role, but my hands have been shaking so much recently from nervous excitement, that I was totally unable to hook the coat onto the hanger when I was taking a coat today from that out-of-town touring actor, that small-town redneck, that creep. My fingers trembled so much that he must have thought I was afraid of him. Me afraid?! He should have eaten worm-infested meat on the "Potemkin" and not played Richard. But in our liberal times this stock-player gets to eat grouse and pineapple and swills champagne with the girls to a NEP-man's gramophone music in the company of my little brother. My little brother is a slob too. Director of this theatre, what's more. So he had apparently got some order from the Party high-ups to give the part to that little nonentity and brown-noser with a butcher's looks. He hasn't a shred of the evil it takes to play Richard. Out of this miserable theatre company who but me can possibly understand the inner essence of the hunchback? Can he really know what it means always to be facing the world with your best side, to hide your hump? I may be deformed but I'm not defective. Unlike some. I may not have been born to court an amorous looking-glass and am not shaped for sportive tricks or acrobatics with the fair sex. I may have been sent unfinished before my time into this breathing world, but I have consequently had more leisure than my fellows to study the human kind.

* * *

What a rogue of a genius lies in me going to waste! Brother George is the director. My other brother, Ed, is ruining our theatre. Another fine member of the family. We got him the job as artistic director, head of actors' equity and so on, but he leaves me stuck as cloakroom attendant. He doesn't give a damn about anyone, let alone his brother. But I'm not complaining. A cloakroom attendant's work is so fascinating, isn't it? I'm serving the people, aren't I? Anyhow, it's got invaluable advantages for my purposes. I'm the first to know anything, who's doing what and with whom and why and wherefore. Everyone talks too much for their own good, because I make them embarrassed with my hump, my humiliating situation and my supposedly defective appearance; and I shake my hump under their noses, turning it deliberately towards them so they can see the depths of my suffering. Fools that they are, they underestimate my hump and don't understand the historic role of hunchbacks on the nation's stage. They can't see that my hump is my pride and joy, my trump card in my efforts to play the part of Richard in the Soviet theatre. But let that be my secret. I keep on pretending it is unbearable for a weakling like me to carry furcoats for the bosses; a few groans help too; they encourage me with tips and indiscretions.

* * *

Yesterday I gave brother George his raincoat. He is another example of brotherly love. He feeds me on promises. Brother Ed tries buying me off with money, promising to get me a pay rise, and young George is forever hinting he will put in a good word for me with the casting committee. His idea is that I could occasionally play stock characters. I told him I was happy enough to have a bit part as a cloakroom attendant. He's so naive it makes me sick. And worst of all, he has no talent, he's a blockhead. When he plays Clarence and kneels before the two murderers with his panegyric to the effect that only God can sit in judgement on His laws, giggles ripple through the theatre. Soon people will stop coming to see our shows. My two brothers are letting the theatre down with what they put on. And both of them are crap-artists, complaining about their health but always out at restaurants, taking champagne baths with our cinema stars.

Brother George says Ed was very poorly yesterday; he had terrible stomach pains. George has nightmares. They both shouldn't drink so much. George complains about Ed: a gypsy at the Sandunovsky Baths supposedly told brother Ed that he would lose his job to someone whose name began with a G: George. My surname begins with a G too, but I keep quiet about that. We live in parlous times, and sometimes art requires sacrifices, sometimes unnecessary ones.

* * *

Yesterday I helped brother George with his coat. He got drunk again last night. Ed is threatening to have him run out of the theatre. So what, as I'm always saying, art requires sacrifices, but George's disappearance from the stage would not be any particular sacrifice so far as the arts are concerned. He suffers from nightmares. He dreamed he was aboard a ship about to leave on tour for Europe. For Burgundy. From the deck he could see the shores of long-suffering Russia recede into the distance. A storm got up. The deck was rolling. He said I was there too. All of a sudden I stumbled on the heaving deck and pushed him overboard, straight down into the sea. He was drowning and sank to the sea bottom, where he could see heaps of corpses and skulls. And all the while he was shaking my shoulder and saying to me over and over again: "Yuri, what is the country coming to?" An anti-Soviet remark if ever there was one. Unpatriotic shit. So our country is marching on history's floor. I wonder where Burgundy is, anyhow.

Where had he got Burgundy from, anyway? Lena walked over on tiptoe to the book-case and took out her annotated school edition of Shakespeare. Brother George had repeated Clarence's dream more or less word for word; in it, Richard had stumbled and pushed his brother Clarence overboard, the corpses, it was all there in Shakespeare. Word for word. Which came as no surprise. George must have been playing Clarence. She turned the page.

I spoke to Ed as I gave him his fur coat, incidentally telling him of brother George's dream. At first the fool paid no attention to my words, just complained about his liver and kidneys, and latest hangover. He was turning to leave when I stopped him and told him straight: all that stuff about Burgundy that George's been telling us is obviously no dream. It's just our little brother deciding to go on tour to Burgundy and flee from there to Europe. People like that are undesirables on the revolutionary ship of Russia, I said. Ed tried to shrug it off. Don't be crazy, he told me. But I reminded him that George always did have itchy feet and now he realizes he's no better off than he used to be, he's decided to fix himself up with political asylum in Burgundy. Once there, he'll go to work for the arch-enemy of our theatre, Mikhail Chekhov, the renegade emigre and brother to the famous pre-Revolutionary writer. It's quite possible that the plan is all in his head and nothing will come of it, but we cannot allow ourselves to harbour a potential turncoat in this theatre. What about the other actors? What about Ed as director? He'll pay for it with his head if anything happens.

* * *

Last night brother George was taken off in a Black Maria, straight from the dressing room, just before the show was due to begin. There was panic on a grand scale, what with there being no-one to take his place. Nobody else knew the part. Except me, that is. The entire company came to the cloakroom to persuade me to play Clarence. But I turned them down flat, saying how could I act the Duke with my hunch-back. And I turned to one side to show them my hump so they could see for themselves, as any idiot could, the part I was made for. But now that George had disappeared, I recommended someone who really could act Clarence. One of us who had been working in the theatre bar and whom I had specially rehearsed for the part. For the first time after its long apathy the audience applauded.

For my part, I did my social duty and returned to my humble post as cloakroom attendant. Sorry, George, but you always were a milksop. Nothing to be done: I must hew a path of my own to art.

Off-stage of course, rumours are circulating that I informed on my own brother. I have only one reply: art demands sacrifices. There was an obvious change for the better: the working atmosphere improved, the acting became more enthusiastic and the players obviously began to love their parts. But the company has still not totally rooted out that traditional actors' envy at the success of others. Derbin, Hastin and Buckin were whispering with one another in secret. They must have been saying I had informed on George.

* * *

When Ed learned of George's arrest, he completely collapsed. A bad conscience. His heart's been giving him trouble. The doctors told him he'd live a long time. Derbin, Hastin and Buckin all behaved badly to me yesterday when I was handing them their overcoats. Derbin is the Party Secretary, Hastin is the theatre administrator and Buckin the trade-union leader. I wasn't tipped. They refused to shake my hand. But while they were busy putting the wrong arms into the wrong sleeves, I had time to hint that the grassing on George came not from me but from relatives of Ed's wife Elizabeth. Derbin and Hastin had old scores to settle with her. Taking advantage of her husband's illness, Elizabeth and her relatives had formed their own little clique behind his back. On their initiative a general assembly of the Party cell was convened to investigate my case and ethics. I was, for example, accused of exceeding my powers as a cloakroom attendant and of intriguing. But I was about to hint that it was not me who wanted to get rid of George but Derbin and Hastin. However, the affair turned by chance to my benefit without my having to do anything; for into the meeting wandered that ancient harridan, Margarita. She lives in the apartment of her late husband, L.N. Kasterov, which has been turned into a museum honouring the great actor whose immortal name embellishes a gilt commemoration plate in our foyer. Of course it is hard to deny that Kasterov was the father of our theatre, the founder of a whole theatrical movement and acting method but his family's emigre connections should never be forgotten.

Her relatives, incidentally, are in Paris or possibly Burgundy, for all I know. It doesn't matter about your past services, you'll answer for the present. Anyone else but her would long ago have been sent to the furthest corner of Siberia. Kolyma's too good for her. And

Kasterov's theatrical method seems suspect to me: all those hints at the fourth wall and the fifth corner of the stage. That long-toothed old cow Margarita limped up onto the stage where the committee was sitting and banged her fist on the table, screaming that all of us Bolshevik swine had done her husband to death, they had destroyed Kasterov, he had been a genius, and they were not fit to lick his boots. Who'd let her into the meeting? Her tsarist attitudes brought me and Elizabeth unwillingly closer together. All that remains is to insinuate to Elizabeth that Derbin, Hastin and Buckin had a part to play in the slanders on my little brother George. It would also be worth seducing his widow. Too much to do, my back hurts. Time to ask the theatre administration for someone to assist me in the cloakroom.

* * *

I have decided to order a new winter overcoat from the tailor. The coat may be of black cloth with an astrakhan collar. I long ago worked out the cut by myself; it conceals my hump perfectly. I must not show off my back too much but conserve it intact for my historic role on the stage in the not too distant future.

* * *

Ed has passed away. Standard Party funeral, First-Class. Everyone weeping, including me. Great pity of course, but he was a chump. The word is out that he will be replaced by Elizabeth's adoptive son, an upstart boy, wet behind the ears, all because his mother has connections in the Politburo. It'll be a long time before we root out corruption at the local level. The brazen bastard came down to the cloakroom and took his coat with its rat-fur collar, shamelessly reciting Shakespeare at me (he must think I've never read any), comparing himself to an ape unworthy to be borne on my shoulders. Self-abasement, it would seem, wouldn't it? But really this milksop agent-provocateur wanted to let it be known in public that I was the clown, because on who else's shoulder does a monkey sit? But that young ape's head will roll, mark my words. Art needs sacrifices. Ed and Elizabeth had given jobs in the theatre to their entire family, handing out parts right, left and centre to friends. While such giants of the stage as Hastin and Derbin, or even Buckin of the Equity group had been sidelined, more or less. Not to mention the constant free trips to holiday resorts that they'd awarded themselves. And what about State awards? When had Buckin last been given the cheapest of awards or medals?

Buckin? Buckingham? Why hadn't she been able to work out straightway that the names in the diary were in code? Hastin was Hastings, Buckin was Buckingham, and so on. Our Soviet hunchback was moving up the hierarchical ladder in the theatre from cloakroom attendant to offers of bit parts in shows, point for point repeating the strategic moves of Richard the Hunchback. Even Richard's number with the dry hands recalled Stalin's problems with his withered extremities.
Lena leafed through several pages and looked at the end.

Yesterday Buckin came with the company to the cloak room. They tried to persuade me to become the theatre director and run the repertory side of the company. I refused. I'm not interested in administrative work. But I would be ready perhaps to play Richard, I said. If, of course, I'm asked. And that crap-artist who's been usurping the role of Richard all these years, that fat-faced untalented slob, was carried away today in a Black Maria. This time, I swear, there was no need for my literary talents. The actors themselves agreed to put an end to the reactionary past, backwardness and obtuseness in art. The company decided to bring someone on, as it were from out of the depths, from the cloakroom; without hesitation everyone speaks of my talent and genius. The theatre may begin with the cloakroom hanger but for some it ends with the hangman. However, art is higher than the evil we do. And the art of evil is higher than evil itself, even if evil of the kind I had committed was on the level of art. Because by its degree of perfection it bore witness to the Almighty.

Then there must have been some pages missing.

Our work is already bearing fruit. The professional level of acting has noticeably improved. Yesterday there was endless applause again. When I bowed, bending slightly to one side because of my hump, I saw out of the corner of my eye a scarcely visible figure in the dress-circle box. I couldn't believe my eyes. It was Stalin himself standing up there and clapping. Or rather, he was clapping one hand against the other. I could not restrain myself, straightened up and, turning towards the box, began applauding him in turn. All stood. It seemed as if the footlights would burst from the emotional incandescence in the theatre. It was as if both of us were being applauded, two godheads of our great world theatre.

The diary ended rather abruptly, in a few laconic notes obviously written many years later.

It's a tragedy. My overcoat's been stolen from the cloakroom. That scoundrel, the cloakroom attendant, has been making excuses. But he'll pay for it.

* * *

I duly made him pay. I'll have to tell his family that a terrible accident occurred behind the scenes during a rehearsal. Let's say, fracture of the skull from a coat hanger smashing against it. But the overcoat turns out to have been stolen not by the cloakroom attendant but an extra. Not a year out of acting school and already playing a spear carrier in "Richard". The cheeky bastard claimed he had not stolen it, but simply wanted to wear it for a while as a relic from one of the stage's great heroes, to try and put himself under my skin. Well, that's what he said. At his age I was handing out other people's skins on coat hangers in cloak rooms, but he's been here less than a year and already wants to take my part. Richard the Third or Richard the Second? Somehow I've lost count.

* * *

There's something wrong with my beloved winter coat. I saw all these tiny holes in it as if it had been hit by buckshot. Moths! That's all it took: just a week in the lousy wardrobe of that dreadful extra and suddenly you've got moths. It'll eat the whole astrakhan collar.

The Moth

It'll eat everything. There's something wrong with my heart. I've got to get away and have a rest. Where can I go? To Burgundy? My kingdom for a horse!

Lena stuffed the diary back into the dirty official envelope, threw the black overcoat to the floor, and sat down in the armchair. As she raised her eyes she saw a moth zigzagging before her nose. The glimmering morning light, diluted by the light from the night-lamp, was making the moth almost invisible. She tried to concentrate on the spot leaping about in front of her eyes and at last guessed at the thought dawning in her head: all those years before the events happening to her in Moscow she had nurtured a secret of her own, at a corner of a far fence of her soul, concealed among the thistles and weeds, wild raspberries and nettles of her childhood. When you were completely alone you could look into it and find something where you were the chosen person to whom the secret had been entrusted. All those years up until her Moscow trip, a vague image of some forgotten country, some other homeland that continued to dwell in some far corner of her mind, as one's parents are always present in a corner of one's mind. It was like the name of her old childhood doll, engraved on her memory forever, a name known only to herself. Russia had always been like that for her, part of her childhood, a secret she had always carried in her memory.

That Russia had now disappeared for good. The image had vanished, eaten away by some still unabsorbed vision and she had been orphaned by its loss. But it was now time to begin a new life on her own without that homeland, a strange spot on the map like a birthmark in a hidden place under her armpit, in the corner of her memory. What would remain: her gnawing conscience? The scurrying mice? Before her eyes, the jumping reflection of light again flashed into view, the shadow of the moth, and another and another, and without getting up from the armchair she began catching the leaping and fluttering ghosts. Sergei again shuddered, snored again. He raised himself suddenly on the pillows. squinting from sleep, yawning and scratching. He caught sight of Lena, sunk in her armchair while the infamous black overcoat with its burst lining lay on the floor in front of her like a corpse. From one corner, the bronze Lenin stared down at her, throwing a weak shadow in the light of the lamp as dawn

121

approached. Lena had a look of self-abandonment but a tremor flickered under her cheekbones; from time to time she kept going through the same mechanical motion: jumping up and clapping her hands together.

Yawning, Sergei asked:

"Hey, what's the applause for?"

1996

The Moth is an insert novella from Zinik's recently finished novel **Facing the Original**, as yet unpublished.

The protagonist of **Facing the Original**, Eugene, is a Russian-born British author who arrives in post-perestroika Moscow after many years of absence. Although he is lionised there as a celebrity he is aware that his standing in the British literary world is not as high as it seems to his admirers and especially women. He keeps coming across and hearing about another London-based Russian emigre (Alec) who seems to be his double or alter ego. Gradually Eugene realizes that he shares all his Moscow lovers with Alec and he starts following him everywhere like a sleuth. Despite the ideological and spiritual differences between the two men, their different backgrounds and social standings, their bond grows stronger, and Eugene becomes convinced that Alec has an evil influence on him. In fact, all the unpleasant changes in his life are related to his mid-life crisis and simple ageing, but he increasingly feels resentment against Alec and a kind of obsession with him. Alec's and Eugene's sides of the story develop independently and their relationship resembles that which exists between the author and his hero. Their story is reminiscent of **The Picture of Dorian Gray**, where the picture is a live entity. The novel also portrays present-day London and Moscow, where political changes in Russia have an immediate effect on human relationships.

Zinovy Zinik is a novelist, born in Moscow in 1945, but living since 1976 in London. His five previous novels have been translated into several European languages, and the most famous one, **The Mushroom Picker**, was adapted for BBC television in 1993. A recent collection of short stories and essays, **One-way Ticket**, was published by Harbord, London, in 1995.

Zinovy Zinik
ONE-WAY TICKET
Harbord Publishing, 58 Harbord St., London SW6 6PJ, UK

One-way Ticket is Zinik's first collection of stories published in English. Set across the width of Europe and a time span of almost 20 years it follows the destiny of the generation which left Russia — like Zinik himself — in the mid-1970s.

With the same intellectual vigor and the distinctive comic touch of his earlier novel, *The Mushroom Picker*, Zinik catches brilliantly the repeating motifs and inherent duality of emigre life. The final stories of Zinik's collection bring him back to his Moscow roots, when, after the collapse of the Iron Curtain, the once-locked past was again opened to returning emigres.

"Typical Zinik: a scary, hilarious feat of conjuring."
— *The European*
"A subtle, playful collection..." — *TLS*

Robert Greenall
MOSCOW: AN EXPLORER'S GUIDE
With 12 specially drawn maps

IF YOU ARE VISITING MOSCOW THIS YEAR, YOU WON'T FIND A BETTER GUIDE TO THE CITY

A series of 12 conveniently organised walks in central Moscow. Full guides to Moscow's two major museums, the Pushkin and the Tretyakov. Excursions to out-of-centre attractions.

Comprehensive listings cover accommodations, transport, safety, as well as a succinct list of restaurants, cafes and bars and an Insider's Guide to what's worth seeing on the city's cultural scene.

A long-time resident in Moscow, Robert Greenall is the author of the 1994 An Explorer's Guide to Russia, *acclaimed by* The Sunday Times *as "a book which in many ways sets the standards for guides to post-Soviet Russia."*

UK edition: Harbord Publishing, 58 Harbord St., SW6 6PJ, UK
US edition: Zephyr Press, 13 Robinson St., Somerville, MA 02145, USA

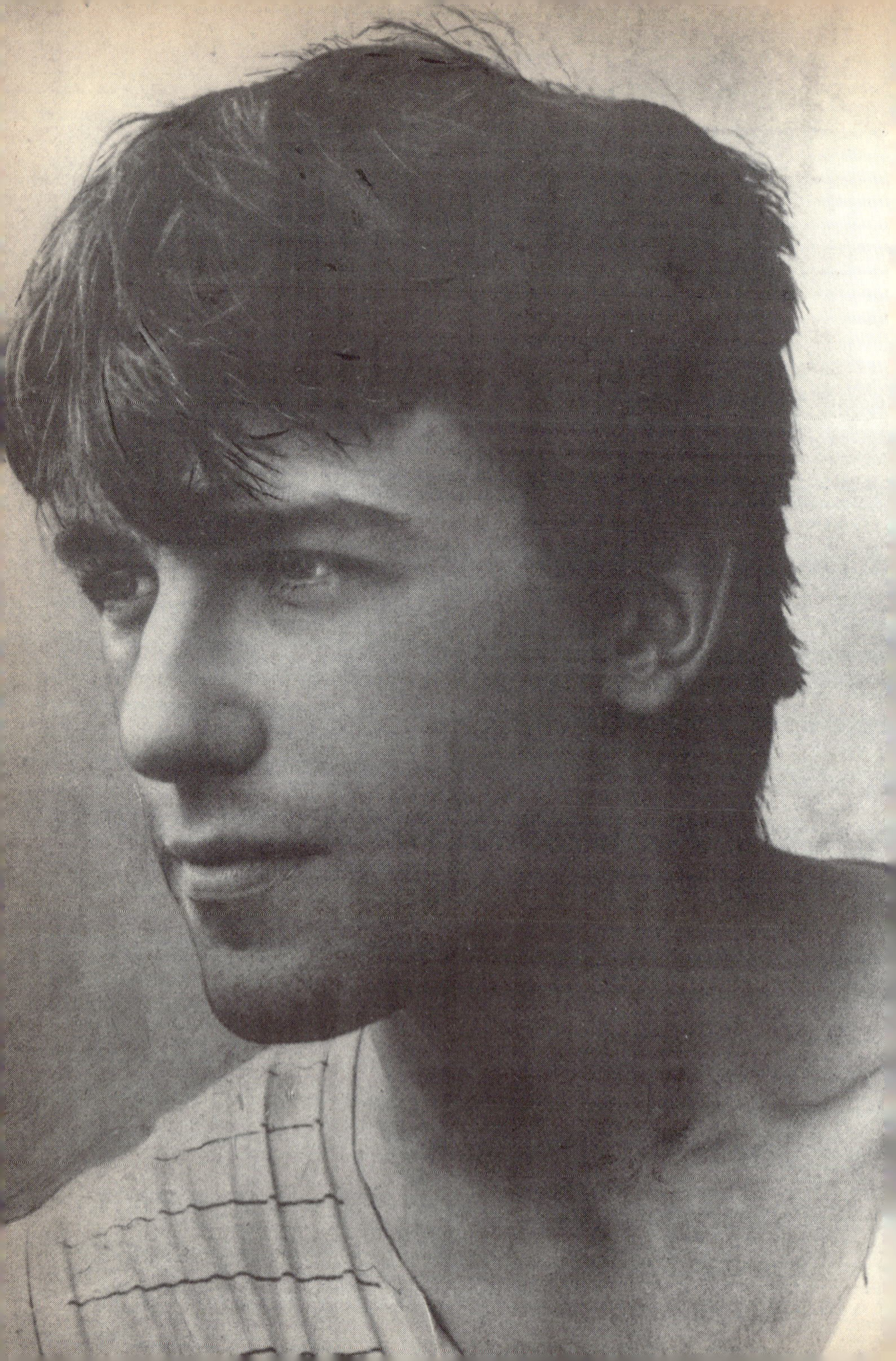

Alexander
TEREKHOV
The Rat-killer
Translated by Andrew Bromfield

Happiness
Translated by Martin Koffer

Alexander Terekhov

The Rat-killer

[The town of Svetloyar is bidding to be included in the list of historical towns making up Russia's famous "Golden Ring" around Moscow, which is a major tourist route. The town is due to be visited by the President of Russia and the Secretary-General of the United Nations. Apart from the relatively minor difficulty that the town has no historical past, having been entirely constructed during the Stalinist period (there are, after all, ways of adjusting history), it has one serious problem: rats. They have infested the place, and they have to be removed, if only temporarily, if Svetloyar is to avoid disgrace and acquire the coveted and profitable "Golden Ring" status.

Two exterminators, or "rat-killers", are summoned from Moscow to deal with the most sensitive site, the town's central hotel, where the rats simply drop from the ceiling in the banqueting hall.

Svetloyar's historical (and geographical) credentials are created by burying exhibits from museums in the region, together with ill-assorted bones, to create a fake archaeological site (when the army workers accidentally uncover the genuine site of an ancient graveyard, it is rapidly reburied to avoid unnecessary complications):

"What's this you've dug up for me, you bastard? Where did you get this garbage from?..."

"Right, lads, bury the fucking tombs again. Cover them with clay and smooth it all over... Smash the bones to pieces and scatter them in the fields..."

"For history?" Sviridov twisted his face into a grimace. "You shut up about history. I know what kind of history we need around here."

Pipes have been laid from the Don to establish a "source" for the great river on the territory of the town, and a connection has been invented with the hero of old Russian folk-lore, Ilya Muromets (he must have passed through here at some point on his travels!).

In order to greet the President and the UN Secretary-General in fitting style, the real inhabitants of the town are evacuated and a motley collection of soldiers, actors, blind women and female prison-camp internees is put into training by the local army command as a "welcoming crowd" stage-managed with immaculate, if ludicrous, care.

Meanwhile a power struggle develops, involving factions in the army and the security forces. The outcome, inevitably, is the emergence of a provincial military dictator. Pretence becomes reality as different military factions become embroiled in bloody combat. Eventually Svetloyar (now populated entirely by the military) is threatened by a new wave of rats, turned against the town by the rat-killers who were brought in to help exterminate the rodents.

The Rat-killer

The narrative is told in the person of the younger of the two rat-killers (he refers to his boss simply as "the Old Man"). A biologist by education, he is supporting himself as a rat-killer while he struggles to complete his dissertation on flies.

When he and the Old Man have successfully rid the hotel of rats, they are about to leave, but instead are arrested because they protest against the army's plans to set captured rats on fire in order to destroy their burrows. The young rat-killer becomes ill, and as his condition worsens the narrative assumes more of the characteristics of delirium or nightmare.

The links between human and rodent behaviour are drawn tighter when his own constant attentions to women (including the bride of the military dictator Gubin) are strangely mirrored in his pursuit of a particularly cunning female rat that takes refuge in the local branch of the savings bank. It is only at the end of the book that we realise the rat-killer is in fact mortally afraid of rats. And in metaphorical terms, of all that they stand for. Throughout the book he has been engaged in far more than a simple struggle with destructive rodents].

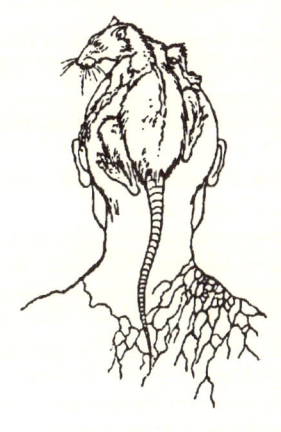

"Still dribbling into your pillow?" I asked the Old Man when I phoned and woke him up. "You can get the money tomorrow and pay for the basement, before they turf me out of it." Then I dropped and slept, right there in the basement. We'd rented a basement for our office because we were struggling to make ends meet on small orders.

For millions of years the common and black rats known as sinanthropes after their home country of China remained dammed into the rice-swamps, locked into that foul place by the Himalayas, the desert, the jungles and the ice. When people moved in there looking for gold, they melted the glaciers and cleared the passes, and in a flash rat hordes broke out. Skirting round the Himalayas, up to the North! — to Korea and Manchuria. To the fleshpots of India — South! The East submitted without even raising its head to protest. The first to congratulate Buddha on the New Era was a rat, the symbol of joy and prosperity.

127

From the twelfth century Europe complained and would not accept its fate — for it was believed there were no rats in Golden Hellas! — not knowing that black rats in ships and attics pressed ancient Egypt so hard that even the accidental killing of a cat was punished by death. Greece and Rome had only one refuge: they kept mum, or they mumbled "mice". And we used to be proud of their cleanliness, what fools we were! Excavations have made it quite clear just what kind of creatures it was that Aristotle described: born of the filth in the ships, conceived by licking salt. Who did Diogenes reproach with lust? Who was it Cicero reproached for his gnawed sandals? The god of "mice" is Apollo. Their history began when the Gods overthrew the Titans and the earth shook and split open. And the mice came pouring and tumbling out of the black cracks.

And they put the people under siege.

There were no windows in the basement. The night was coming to an end when the Old Man switched on the light. He stuck the key into the lock and picked up the piece of paper that had unstuck from the door: "RAT Cooperative".

I went to bed late. The Old Man was a real swine, he could have shown up later just as well.

Streaming after their black brothers came the common rats, the victors! With the Arabs they crossed the Persian Gulf and the Red Sea, the Crusaders carried them further on from Palestine, Venetian mariners delivered the plague-carrying rats to Europe together with pearls and spices. In the fifteenth century the church cursed them. It was too late. The bones of a common rat were dug up in the palace of Shirvan-shah in Baku.

The common rats made their way across medieval Rus. Convicts in the stocks at the Solovki Monastery paid with their noses and ears for the commercial liberty enjoyed by the towns of Pskov and Novgorod. The rats moved into St. Petersburg with Peter the Great. In 1727 the earthquake in the Kuma Desert drove a huge army of common rats to Astrakhan. The pincers were closed.

In 1732 a vessel from the East Indies delivered retribution to England. Thirty years later Paris fell, and twenty years after that the beggars ate rats during the siege of the French capital.

In 1775 America capitulated.

In 1780 it was Germany's turn.

When the Russians reached the Aleutian Islands, they were swarming with rats, and so that was what they called them, the Rat Islands. In 1809 Switzerland fell to the horde.

The Old Man walks about, sneezing, the pig, stands a carton of milk right under my nose, puts a bread-bun beside it, rummages in his bag. He's the boss, he gets the table, and I get the camp-bed. I have to sleep with my legs bent up.

They carried on. At the end of the nineteenth century they celebrated the capture of Tyumen, Tobolsk, the Crimea. The Russo-Japanese War bequeathed rats to Omsk and Tomsk, and by 1912 the common rats had occupied the Siberian Railway.

The First World War gave the black and the common rats more fodder than they could eat, and not a single place was left in Europe without them. During the Siege of Leningrad the rats warmed themselves in the children's beds and occupied the front lines of defence (where the corpses had more meat on them). The evacuation carried them off in all directions.

"Get up out of that bed," said the Old Man. "Enough sleeping. I've paid for the basement."

I ripped open the carton of milk and took a bite from the bun. A thickset, grey-haired man came in, scratching his neck. He produced an advertising supplement out of his pocket:

"Here," he said.

The advertisement I had put in read as follows: "An opportunity not to be missed. Rats and mice exterminated anywhere in the world. Prices well below international rates. We saved the Vandome Islands from rats. We saved Thuringia and the public toilets in Geneva (three hundred seats). The 'RAT' Cooperative, winner of a special award from the Swedish Academy! Reach us via metro station "Medvedkovo" and bus No. 661 to the stop for the State Polytechnical College. Walk along the concrete wall on the opposite side of the street to the break, then through the car park. Ask for the All-Union Society of the Blind. We are in the basement at the first entrance, sixth door on the left. Telephone such-and-such, from 22.00 to 24.00, Vladimir and Larissa."

"Yes, that's us," said the Old Man. "Have a seat."
"I'm glad I found you," said the man. "I have a way for you to earn some good money."

***

...We had the meeting in the school gym.

On the floor lay a huge sketch map of the town. An army colonel, dressed in field uniform, was pushing a string of toy trucks across it, as if it were the president's cavalcade.

"Mokrousov Street, transit time sixteen seconds. Welcoming crowd," the ginger-haired Baranov read from a piece of paper, "one hundred and seventy-six. Twenty-four on balconies. Sixteen at windows. Nine posters, forty-six flags. Dress from the civil defence reserves."

"Okay," agreed the Governor, and climbed down from the volley-ball umpire's tower.

Take a gutful in the evening and next day you'll suffer for it. I sat by the mineral water, close up beside a bald old man in glasses. He didn't even turn his shrivelled skull of a head, he was too busy watching the governor.

Shestakov towered up in front of the flags of Russia and the United Nations, leaning with his fists on the oak table that was crowded with telephones and winking army walkie-talkies, waiting for me to finish opening a bottle of mineral water with my teeth.

"Time. We're losing time," Shestakov hissed, as soon as I'd drunk my fill and wiped my mouth. "The job is a big one, but we don't have enough people. We're expecting three companies of police from the district centre. The reserve has been called up. Just in case there's any nonsense the district command has provided another three battalions. They're training in Kriukovo Forest. For a day like this there should be a division, with tanks. Our garrison is keen for action, isn't it, Comrade Gontar?"

"Very keen," agreed the army colonel.

"On the fourth we start operation 'Clear Field'." Shestakov glanced down at the telephones, and his cheeks quivered. "Expulsion from Svetloyar of all outsiders. On the sixth, operation 'Clear Sky', removal to village schools of residents from the town centre and the visitors' entry and exit routes. Responsible officer, Baranov of the police. I am in overall control. We'll have no nonsense. No attempts to contact the President. Or any questions. Please don't make any notes."

Everyone glanced around cautiously. Especially at the Old Man. And at the door, which was guarded by two men in civilian dress with automatics sticking out from under their jackets.

"From our side Colonel Klinsky's people will be the closest to the visitors." The governor pointed to a puny bureaucrat with slick, wet-looking black hair. He was the only one without a tie and he had ear-phones glued to his head.

"The town is almost in ruins. That's what the mayor's office has done for it. The evacuated residents will have to be paid for two days off work and given hot meals. We'll have to guard them. To be on the safe side. Do not explain anything to them! If you do, it will all be turned against us. There are two areas causing me concern. First, we have to have people who look right to play the part of the residents along the route of the procession and at the festivities by the monument to the 'Source of the Don'. The organisers figure we need about ten thousand. Men are no problem. We can dress up soldiers and cadets. The theatre will help out with hair styles. There aren't many children, but we do have some. Two nursery schools have been assigned. Our people in the front rows."

Shestakov breathed out loudly. "The women are a problem. Where can we get so many women? The blind workers' cooperative will give us fifty units, they can be paired off with soldiers as guides and kept at a distance. Maybe the ballet dancers will have time to get changed after their concert. But we've had to request most of the women from the corrective labour camp. Special train here and then back again. Five hundred women with shattered lives. How do we explain the march from the station and back again under guard? Maybe we could say it's a cross-country march of soldiers' mothers? We'll have to arrange them on the square with officers, three to one. It's hard to keep an eye on people in a crowd. We were thinking perhaps we should take their shoes off. Or perhaps handcuff them together at the elbow. We'll come up with something. We'll put together a task force from actors and police veterans, about a hundred men. They'll be following the visitors in two vans, just in case..." Shestakov put his palms against his cheeks and continued in a hollow voice, "in case the visitors want to speak with the people. An extreme situation, as you appreciate. Personally, I don't believe it will happen. But everyone has to be able to smile and say hello. The reception and the dinner will last one hour forty minutes, but the escort will arrive earlier, so the festivities will drag out for about six hours. I understand, believe me, it's all really far too much for us. But as they say, we have to go for bust. The life of our town depends on it, from now on forever, comrades. If we do a good job, then the government will include Svetloyar in the "Golden Ring" of Russian towns and the list of national historical monuments. And that means hard currency, comrades."

His audience came to life and began applauding.

"The second thing worrying me," Shestakov cast a significant glance towards our corner, "is the rats, comrades. Repulsive creatures. They gnaw everything, that's why they're called rodents, it means they gnaw. They've been building up here for decades, and in the last few years the mayor's office has fallen down badly on the job. They bite the dogs. People are afraid for their children. On my initiative we've set up a rat control corporation, 'King Rat'. They'll use a traditional folk method to rid the area of the festivities of rodents. In a single night, just before the visitors arrive. Free of charge."

Now even the guards were applauding. Skull-face beside me was lashing away so hard, his spectacles slipped down his nose. The Old Man stared gloomily at the map.

"But the banqueting hall in the hotel 'Don'... You know yourselves what it's like. Some of you... had first-hand experience. We had to go to the capital for help. The governor employed them, but we'll have to pay, and it's a lot of money." I was watching the governor as he spoke. He had turned pale. "It can't be allowed to happen, it just can't be, not even for a moment. Not even for a fraction of a moment. Imagine. During the celebrations... One drops on to the table. Or the floor. Or on someone's head. Even just droppings. It's absolutely out of the question! So let me warn our highly paid businessmen here and now, in front of you all. Just so they have things clear."

The gathering turned to face us. I smiled. The Old Man fidgetted.

"Colonel Gontar will announce the orders of the day."

"Right. Let me inform you that from six o'clock the H.Q. will be under barracks regime. Sleeping quarters have been laid out in the staff room and the head teacher's office. The mess is in the library. The latrines remain where they were. Military rank must be respected. On the ground floor two classes will begin the normal school year. The external guard will be in the queue for kvas and in the school lunch van. Passes to be shown to the sentry with the pram. Duty officers will inform you of the colour of the pram. Dismissed!"

Everyone got up, kicking aside the basketballs skittering about the floor. I winked at my neighbour. Well?

"So you're the ones who are robbing us blind."

"And who are you?"

"Here? Captain Larionov."

"Well, captain, all this reminds me of a mad house."

The old captain grimaced:

"I'm no doctor. I'm the town's architect."

He said goodbye and left. The Old Man sat on his chair. It was a long time since I'd sat in a schoolroom until blue twilight filled the windows. Just like being at a dance, not a single girl in sight. I said:

"Tell me, Old Man, what did we come here for?"

* * *

On the square a cordon in full-dress uniform was dying of boredom as they taught alsatians to lie and stand, lie and stand.

In the centre, an officer in a peaked cap stood on a wooden crate, blowing down a megaphone to test it, with a herd of bodies pressing around him. Plodding piously over to join them came a portly priest with a big round medallion hanging on a chain round his neck. Mincing behind him at a respectable distance came several rosy-cheeked lay-brothers in gold surplices, carrying an icon, a censer, a cross and a gonfalon.

"Stage one!" roared the megaphone. "Put out that cigarette! Who's that there spitting on the ground? Sviridov, the visitors, who are the visitors?"

"Comrade lieutenant, com...". A rotund warrant officer with sweaty eyebrows who had the look of a light-weight wrestler came shooting across to me. "Comrade lieutenant, seven seconds. This way please." He dragged me over, clutching my wrist in his moist palm. "Here's your visitor, comrade colonel. He's the right size."

Garrison commander Gontar looked me over from up on top of his crate: "He'll do."

A captain clambered up on the crate and held the megaphone to the colonel's mouth with both hands.

"Stage zero. Comrades, general rehearsal. Remember, total security, responsibility. The goal: determine who follows who. Finalise the general picture. Right then, to your starting positions. One run-through, and we're done. Sviridov, who's visitor number two?"

The crowd stirred and formed up into ranks.

"This way, please." The warrant officer prodded me toward the crate. "You're still in the car. Now who else... Comrade colonel, I can be guest number two myself!" He sniffed and wiped the drops of sweats from his eyebrows.

"Ten-shun! Listen. 'September twelfth. Twelve hundred hours. The sun has gilded...' Right, I'm not reading all of that. Right then, the President and the Secretary-General of the United Nations... they're out of the car, they've arrived!"

The warrant officer led me forward two steps and stopped. We were on the spot.

"Ours is on the left, the other's on the right. Who's that not looking? Remember who's where. Just to help you, theirs is an Arab. That's a kind of a Gypsy. Orchestra!" Colonel Gontar waved his cap and over on the boulevard someone thumped a drum. "The blessing, the blessing, what are we waiting for?"

The warrant-officer moved aside and twisted his face into a pious grimace. The priest advanced, wrapped in something that looked like a water-proof army cape: cloth of gold embroidered with pearls, stuck all over with blue and scarlet flowers with six petals. Sharp reflections from the jewelry glittered on the faces of the meek-and-mild servitors; the priest waved incense over the crowd, crossing himself with broad, sweeping gestures. I stood up straighter and lowered my head with the rest. The warrant officer put his hands on his hips in a haughty gesture.

"Now comes the blessing. Kiss his hand," Gontar hissed.

The priest handed his censer to a lay-brother, then took my hand and kissed it respectfully.

"Kravchuk! What the..." the colonel swore in his exasperation. "Get that goat's beard of yours out of there! Who's the bishop?

You're the bishop! You do the blessing, and he does the kissing! He holds his palms out, and you stick your mitt on top! He kisses it, and you make the sign of the cross over the back of his head! Stop tugging at your beard! Too hot? Sviridov, we can do without the beard today."

"What if he won't kiss it?" inquired the "bishop".

"He will. It's a clean perfumed hand... He'll be told what to do too. If he hesitates, then cross his fat face and move on. What d'you mean, where to? What about guest number two? You've got to bless the Gypsy! Girl, bring up the bread and salt!"

Suddenly there was music from horns and a psaltery, and a fine buxom girl with a face as red as a traffic cop's came bouncing over happily, holding an empty chased-metal tray.

"Girl: 'Pray taste of our bread and salt.' Hold it out, and don't straighten up, let him get a good look down the front of your dress! Don't look down. 'Smiles.' Give him a wink. Once. With your right eye. He takes a bite and chews it. Passes the bread to the nigger. 'Without straightening up the girl takes a present out of her bosom. Speaks:

"Beloved, I have sat up through the night waiting for you and embroidering the shorts'". Sho-orts? Is that right? Sviridov!"

"That's right, comrade colonel. That's what it says in the book."

"In the book! Sviridov, you'll end up in the guardhouse! He reads books now! Anybody here from the museum?"

"Yes, comrade colonel," someone shouted from the crowd. "It should be 'the shirt'."

"Alright then. Come on, girl."

"My beloved, I have sat up through the night waiting for you and embroidering this shirt." The girl ran her tongue over her moist lips and thrust a hand into her crowded bosom.

The colonel rapped out his approval:

"Good girl, good girl... God grant everybody will do as well. 'The girl runs off, the hem of her skirt rises so her underwear can be seen...' It doesn't say what colour, but it should. Sviridov, check that! Cossacks, let's have the Cossacks!"

Two policemen on light-brown horses rode over from the boulevard and around the crowd, whooping as they went.

"'Out runs a girl.' Where's the girl?"

"Here!" A female gymnast in white sports shoes stepped forward. She was about twelve years old, with sharp pointed elbows and totally flat-chested.

Gontar thrust the megaphone away from his lips and hissed.

"Sviridov. Haven't we got any healthier looking specimens?"

"She's the district champion." The warrant officer shrugged and spread his hands, stung by the comment.

"Alright, alright, what does it say here? 'Out runs a girl feeding pigeons!' Alright then, she feeds them, turns a somersault, does a cartwheel. Then a thousand pigeons, the age of the city, go flying up in the air. 'The cover falls from the monument "The Source of the Don" and a stream of water raises up Ilya Muromets over the square, with the flags of Russia and the United Nations. Orchestra. Exultant citizens press the guards against visitor number one' (don't get him confused with the black!) 'and a woman with a blind child break through.' Right, quick march!"

The crowd pushed forward, and a woman with a face wasted from exhaustion lifted a boy in a blue T-shirt up above the swaying shoulders of the bodyguards, keening mournfully:

"Lay your hands on him, saviour."

The child stared upwards in torment, as though an invisible palm were pressed across the bridge of his nose, and he kicked his legs so hard his sandals flew off.

"That way they'll crush the woman," Sviridov hissed.

I tapped my hand stupidly against the child's scarlet forehead. His head trembled on his neck and he bawled out:

"I can see. Mama, I can see! The sun and the grass and our beloved city. Who is this good man?"

"He is your saviour," said the mother with a sob, pressing the child to her and caressing it. "I can hardly believe it myself but we shall pray for him..."

"'She is pushed aside'," Gontar read slowly. "Hold him good and close so he doesn't get photographed. 'The city's chief medical officer certifies it as a case of healing. An ambulance takes him away.' On the corner of Sadovaya Street and City Father Mokrousov Street the midget gets out and the child gets in, and you go to the flat. 'An old woman tumbles out of the crowd.' Alright, Larissa Yurievna, let's see you tumble, please."

The Rat-killer

A woman with her face caked in powder, wearing a velvet jacket and silvery silk trousers, crept under the cordon of bodyguards. She spread out a newspaper at my feet and then knelt down heavily on it, supporting herself on the servilely extended elbow of the stooping Sviridov. She thrust a fat hand covered in rings and bracelets into my face.

"'The visitor attempts to raise her to her feet'."

"Oh, let me be, I am older than you are, and you must hear what I have to say." The woman gave a feeble smile and adjusted an imaginary head-scarf. "I never thought to see the face of an angel, but now I have I can die in peace. When I tell them in the village they won't believe me, they'll say I'm making it up. Hear now the one thing I must say. You are our hope, make our land beautiful, pay no heed to our transgressions, curb the power of despotism, dry the tears from the people's eyes. Do not forget you are Russian. Remember where you come from. If you ignore the earth it will not forgive. Do not give way to vain pride, do not be ashamed to repent, do not seek harm to others. We have waited for you so long." The woman sniffed and her tall bouffon hair-do swayed to and fro in its net. She held out an ordinary post-office envelope containing a sprinkling of sand. "A gift to guard you, earth I gathered from the burial mounds of our own Kriukovo Forest, it will save you in the dark hour of night."

"The old woman is carried away," Gontar prompted. "The visitor breathes in the smell of the earth. Song: 'O Russian land, beyond the hills afar...' Is that right? Isn't it 'so fair', not 'afar'?"

"A fart, maybe?" suggested the captain holding the megaphone.

"Five days' close arrest in the guardhouse! Sniff that earth! What kind of way is that to sniff? They're not offering you shit on a shovel! Watch this, I'll show you how to sniff your own native earth!" The colonel jumped down off the crate, took the envelope from me and stuck his nose into it. He took a deep breath, screwing up his eyes in ecstasy, then he suddenly grunted and barked out: "Sviridov, where did you get this?"

"I did as you ordered... I got sand," Sviridov said in a startled voice. "I got it from the sandbox, in the yard... Let me have a sniff."

"At the double. Take down all the dog owners' names, sieve all that sand, find out which animal shat in it and take it to the veterinary station. Put the mangy cur down! And do it now! Now for everybody: in three days' time full dress-rehearsal. Know your lines. First company, right turn! Second company, left turn! At the double. On the command 'at the double' elbows bent at ninety degrees, trunk inclined forward with the weight balanced on the right foot. Quick march!"

Warrant officer Sviridov slouched off about his business at top speed, holding the envelope up to his nose and then holding it away from himself at arm's length. I finally recovered my wits. Everything had been so well-ordered I didn't have any time to laugh or even think...

Published in Russian in 1995 in the literary journal, *Znamya*, and in book form by Sovershenno Sekretno Publishers.

Drawings by V. Losev

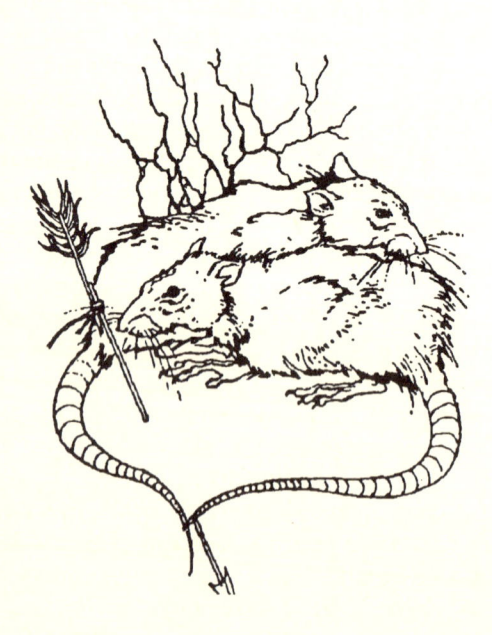

Happiness

I always find it difficult to answer the question whether I have ever been truly happy. I try to recall something meaningful and important, but all sorts of silly nonsense which it would be embarrassing to write about always comes to mind. Not embarrassing because it's obscene or anything like that. It's just that when I'm asked this question, this is all that comes to mind.

It's just like you leaf through a photograph album, at random, but you always end up in the same places. While we're on the subject of photographs, incidentally, there is one in my album in which a tiny moment of my happiness is preserved.

I was learning to walk at my grandmother's. My mother and I moved away from the grey, famine-stricken Tula region when I was all of two weeks old to her birthplace, a green, cheerful little town on the border with the Ukraine where cherry trees grow right in the streets, where vicious dogs are kept chained up and where, when maize is being cooked (an endeavour that lasts from very early, about six o'clock in the morning, right until dinner time without a break) the whole house and courtyard are suffused with a heavy, exciting smell which makes you drool in anticipation of the moment when your teeth will sink into the firm golden flesh of the corn cob, and the bittersweet salt you have painstakingly rubbed between the grains will crunch in a way that drives you wild. There I lived with my mother, and grew plump and healthy. My grandmother, choosing a time when the local priest was in our area, had me christened along with three other infants, all of whom behaved themselves admirably, while I raised Cain like a goose facing execution, obliging the priest to curtail the ceremony in view of my manifestly atheist future.

In any case, I was plump, my grandmother found me too heavy to carry, my mother was very frail, and father had stayed behind in the Tula region. He was a locomotive driver and missed us terribly, but it was healthier here, there was more food, and we had an enormous number of relatives ready to help out. There was sun and fruit dumplings, and pumpkin seeds to chew and front gardens full of golden globes in bloom. There were important-looking turkeys with bizarre striped feathers and nights of inky darkness with the barely audible sighing of wind on the shutters, and our neat white house. And this was where I lived.

And so I took my first step, and gave everyone cause for celebration. My auntie ran to uncle Stepan who lived next door but one. (I don't actually remember him, only his funeral, a little. My grandmother led me by the hand half way down the street behind a truck on which Natasha, Uncle Stepan's granddaughter, sat looking completely bored. It was terribly hot and I was looking at the earth under my feet, which was covered in long cracks from the heat. Everyone kept giving me sweets which I didn't want to eat.) Anyway, Uncle Stepan came running – no, probably he just walked – with a camera, and preserved my happiness for posterity. It was in the orchard. In our yard there was a little pond, and behind it an orchard with cherry trees, plum trees, apple trees, pear trees, gooseberry bushes and beds of strawberries. I was standing in front of a currant bush. To my left my sweet mother was crouching down, looking very young and cheerful, her hair very black and curly. She was smiling and clapping her hands and I was standing. I was quite tow-haired at that time, with a long forelock combed to one side of my big round head and wearing a white shirt, the sleeves of which barely came down to my plump, sugar-white elbows. I was wearing a pair of brown shorts, which had obviously been pulled up over my firm little stomach a moment before the photo was taken. Little folds of skin were visible on my chubby knees and my right hand was raised behind my ear as if I were dancing, and I was smiling such a broad happy smile that you couldn't even tell what sort of eyes I had then.

It must have been a bright day. The grass was tall and lush, there was a smell of currants, and the gentle hum of dragonflies' wings in the air. My mother said, "My darling son!", and from over on the other side of the pond my grandmother was looking out from the porch at her fair-haired grandson in his clean white shirt and crying, remembering how her little daughter had nothing to eat but oily black cake made from the pulp left over from the processing of sunflower seeds. And who could have known then that she would survive the war, that she would have a grandson, that he would be named after his grandmother, and that, God willing, his future would be as bright as this day. Back on the other side of the lake my mother was clapping and laughing out loud as Uncle Stepan, who was soon to die, limped on his bad leg leaning over his camera. And starlings flew out of the currant bushes when a locomotive hooted from the station...

I seem to have this bad habit of smiling in photos, and always somehow managing to look sarcastic or sly. Only ever once have I looked honest and endearing. Then.

One evening years later my mother was crying in the kitchen. Our white house had been sold off for timber, and I just laughed impassively and reasonably explained to her that the house was old: grandpa had built it before the war which took him in its embrace and no more was ever heard of him. During a raid a bomb had exploded in the garden and the ridge was no longer straight, and grandma no longer had the strength to work herself silly every spring, and we didn't visit her that often. What was so terrible if she had the chance of a flat with a telephone where she wouldn't have to go out for water and she'd be closer to the hospital? What was wrong with that? But mother just cried, not looking at the letter from auntie which lay on the table in front of her.

The new owners were well-heeled. They replaced our house with one built of brick, and then eight lorries arrived laden with topsoil. They filled in the pond and tipped soil over where the orchard, now cut down, had been. Well, it was old, neglected and overgrown.

Actually, it's a bit odd. I sometimes think in those days I could hardly have been walking around in that white shirt all the time. I expect they dressed me up in it specially for the photo.

If there's one other thing that comes to mind on the subject of happiness, happiness actually experienced rather than simply remembered from being told about it and photographs, happiness that set my heart pounding, then what I usually remember is a girl from school. I haven't even got a photograph of her. You give someone your picture when you part from them. To be honest, my memory of her is really rather vague now. I remember her flowing chestnut hair, soft and downy, her thin, childish lips, and her eyes, with an anxious, darting gleam in their depths. And that's it. No, there was a blue jumper with white deer on it. I don't think she even wore it very often, but for some reason I remember that jumper more clearly than anything else. To this day I sometimes see people wearing a similar pattern in faraway towns where nobody knows me, and my heart skips a beat, as if a bird from those distant times had hurtled past above me, on to a time when people won't wear jumpers like that one anymore, because you can't expect our manufacturing industry to go on producing them forever. Then the only memory left with me will be of April and that courtyard, blue in the falling dusk, where every step you took was agonizingly sweet, where the air was full of the smell of budding poplars, and there was still a glistening crust of ice on the puddles. Table lamps flickered mysteriously yellow and green behind warm, cosy curtains and blinds, and the birch trees stretched the quivering tips of their black branches out towards the crisply shining stars.

I was sixteen years old in that far-off April. I walked round school, morose and swollen with self-importance, as befitted the editor of a justly infamous school magazine. Anyway, I took a liking to this girl in the year below me. It seemed to me then that she was beautiful beyond measure. I only had to look at her for my heart to beat wildly, and when I walked past her I probably, no, I definitely, blushed; and all because I had been told this girl supposedly read my much-discussed magazine, and had once expressed an interest in me. This was enough to give me trouble getting to sleep at night.

So one day I was walking down the school corridor looking particularly irascible and weighed down by the burden of being the resident prophet, and she came straight out of room 23, right in front of me. Our eyes locked.

She was evidently happily talking away to someone else and turned to look at me with a smile still fading on her lips; or maybe she just gave me a smile of complicity. Who can tell at this distance in time? Her eyes, as I later discovered, were actually green, but it was a sunny day and the eyes I saw were huge and lilac coloured, as if hundreds of droplets were quivering around the enticingly dolorous wells of her pupils.

I skirted round her and went on my way with that same fierce look in my eyes, but I was completely, completely changed. Something warm and disturbing had lodged in my heart, and does so again even now. I would call it a confident expectation of happiness. Something was, without a doubt, about to happen. It was as if I felt the excruciating snares of fate about my shoulders and knew that I had found my path in life.

Happiness

I walked off quite unafraid of losing her. I felt confident something was about to happen.

When I walk along the school corridor now, out of place and not needed here, I am puzzled myself as to what it is I am looking for. I stop by a ginger clearing of light spilling in through some windows and, just as before, I see that fleeting smile on her thin lips, and her eyes so perfectly clear you can see lilac-coloured droplets in them, and time licks its tongue over my heart, nostalgically and rapidly. I am as much a stranger to this school as it is to me. Everything has changed beyond recall. Nothing remains, except for this corridor running through my life, those yellow squares of light framed by shadow, those eyes. I sense the unfocussed, animal, gnawing of time regained, a time of blank sheets of paper and my first pages of writing.

But back to happiness. That girl introduced herself to me at a disco. I was horribly shy. I shuffled from one foot to the other and tried really hard to say something intelligent, but somehow everything came out wrong and I blushed crimson, and the instant a lock of her ethereal hair touched my cheek I started shaking like a lightning conductor discharging a storm in the muggy night of an Indian summer. I breathed in her understated perfume and wondered how I could possibly deserve someone as beautiful as this. Well, all right, perhaps this wasn't really happiness.

But the next day I was back in school on some business long since forgotten, and stopped by the noticeboard where there was a programme of events for the spring holidays. I read one line and shuddered. What was it? I could smell her perfume!

I began feverishly sniffing the air like a dog, scared to death of being mistaken or, even worse, of losing that wondrous smell, a token of breath-taking changes and new directions. And so I stood, breathing in my happiness and smiling a blissful smile, confident and calm. I was sixteen years old then. It was a slushy April and she wore a blue jumper with white deer on it, although of course she wore other things as well. I can remember them even now. There was a grey checked coat, short boots, a red scarf with black stripes and fluffy round bobbles. Why was it that jumper made such an impression on me?

I don't have a photograph of her. We split up without that touch. Seven days later.

We were sitting one evening on a bench under a lilac tree. I was scared of her. She had sprung this unexpected question on me: "Do you know how to kiss?" I was scared of her serious expression, her imperturbability, and how sensible she was. I did not know then that this was called being grown-up. And when she touched me by chance, I started so noticeably that she couldn't hide her feelings and smiled irritably.

She told me she had recently been going out with this boy, but he had dumped her. Tremulous tears even shone in her eyes and made me gulp. Anyway, she had wanted, or rather hoped, that I could replace him since, after all I cut quite a figure at school. She talked on, explaining it all, her eyes fixed on a sandpit, and my mouth felt drier than it had since I was at nursery school, when I had been filling my little bucket with sand and suddenly decided it was water and tried to drink it down.

She went in the entrance to her flat, and I knew she wouldn't turn around. It wasn't her style. I could carry on staring at her back for all she cared. I stood there alone in April, mulling over everything, the blood hammering like a tram in my brain, the intoxicating gusts of wind, the stained-glass fragments of sky set in a tracery of tree branches, snatches of conversation, shuffling footsteps, the frenzied swooping of sparrows. Dust particles danced in the sword thrusts of the sunbeams, and my whole youthful body felt like a huge power in an unknown, boundless universe, hurtling through the unknown and the boundless, delirious with itself. Me. Which me? Nothing?

That's when I made my first big mistake. I packed it all in and went back to that tiny town on the border with the Ukraine, to grandma, and auntie, and all my numerous Ukrainian relatives. I went back to learn how to walk.

At first I thought I would return home in a blaze of glory. I slept six hours a night and studied five hours a day after work. I didn't go out to the cinema, or parties. I read other people's words of wisdom, wearing myself out with textbooks and long cross-country runs in the mornings. Grandmother just sighed and said, "If only some young flibbertygibbet would turn up and set you in a spin. What are you doing sitting around like an old man the whole time?" Auntie kept inviting various shy young girls round, laughing affectedly. It all went completely past me. But after a year I wearied of my heavy head and my own stupidity, and the limitlessness of everything. I started observing how the people here lived, and tried to live the same simple, cheerful way, singing cheery songs at the festive table, going round singing carols on feast days, pouring water over people on Midsummer Night, drinking, digging the soil, going fishing, eating kebabs by the campfire, having an arranged marriage, sitting on a bench with a girl, or playing dominoes with friends, or later on with the other old men, and then dying peacefully and without fuss in their sleep and being buried in the ground under a mulberry tree whose berries made people's mouths black. The rain would wash the dye out of the wreath, and it would wash the pint jar with the shrivelled daisies till it shone like crystal, and dissolve the toffees in their yellow wrappers. And everything started to go right for me.

As soon as I stopped trying for university entrance I was accepted. I gave up studying, and became an "achiever". I stopped being interested in girls, and they started being interested in me. I stopped worrying about work, and it started to go well. It seems that in order to have, you need perhaps to be able to relinquish.

Since then I've been living at ease, having understood that you don't need a lot, and that actually you're better off with a little. You need enough to eat, you need to be able to sleep in peace, and to be free to go wherever you want. I didn't think about her much. It was all the same to me whether she was alive or dead, or what sort of husband she had. When I returned to my home town I realised that much had gone forever. I didn't recognize people who nodded to me in the streets and smiled back at them in confusion. The town didn't love me, and I had forgotten it.

She called out to me one day in the street. I was walking along unshaven, avoiding the spring-time puddles, and munching a curd cheese bun. That was the spectacle I presented, and still she recognised me. I saw a pleasant looking lady in a thick fur coat, wearing uncompromising lilac lipstick and smiling ingratiatingly. We talked haltingly about school, about the passing of time, and about how rapidly we were turning from black sheep into pillars of society. We talked about college and shared some gossip. I rubbed the stubble on my chin, holding the bun in my hand. It was very strange. It was as if she were talking to someone standing behind my back and I was talking to someone behind hers. These invisible partners of ours were talking from the other side of a wall of time, out of their burial mounds, communicating through interpreters.

When you're a child you assume that absolutely all change must be for the better. That's why the drumming of train wheels is always so joyful. That's how it seemed to me when I came to visit my grandma, and the first thing I did was go to the orchard and hide under a currant bush, and the rushes in the pond swayed and creaked so sadly.

"Come round and see me this evening," she said. "What luck bumping into you like this! About six o'clock then, okay? Remember where I live?"

Sometimes my memory amazes me. I remembered not only where she lived, but every day we had been together and every word we had said.

"You haven't changed a bit," she told me, and it was the truth. In this case, though, the truth was like a rotten nut. Outwardly, for sure, I looked just the same, but inwardly... it didn't bear contemplating.

At five o'clock I dressed, went down to the market, bought some red carnations, and wandered around the town, which was full of April restiveness. I saw the people, the shops and the cars and eventually ended up at a birch grove. I didn't actually go into it, because the birches were knee deep in cold, lifeless water which still looked back to winter, while spring looked at itself in alarm in this torpid mirror world. I stood confronting the trees with my lacy blood-red bouquet, and listened for the music inside me. There was none. I was empty.

My mother loved the carnations.

I was so sad about the girl in the blue jumper with white deer, so sad about having to kill her. What was I going to have left?

I wondered too, where does it all go?

What sort of deeds or days teach us not to cry any more? What sort of people open our eyes to this not very godly world, blotting out something unfathomable, yet good and holy? Why have I suddenly ceased being able to listen to my own heart, hearing it nowadays only at the doctor's when he puts his stethoscope on my chest and says, "Hold your breath"? Why has it suddenly become so impossible to breathe and listen to my heart? What fire has burnt out my home, leaving me still tramping round trying to find the window from which I used to see that lush orchard. And why can I now narrate things which before I only thought, and was the happier for it, and found it easier to carry on.

It seems to me that when I die, and when the world has died, and what once was me has become a pink droplet in the aura of a giant star, a handful of dust in the tail of a comet, a speck of nothing, it seems to me that this speck will sometimes feel very strange; it will suddenly feel as though space has perceptibly lurched and time become tangible; it will not know that this is called sorrow, and like a faint twinkling, like the twitching of skin around a healing wound, strange, incomprehensible, unnecessary visions which it cannot hold in memory will begin to impinge upon it with inexplicable insistence: the sultry world of a deciduous forest after rain, the sparkling of grass in a waterfall of sunlight when there is stillness and only the breeze, when a loud sound breaks in, the insistently aching iron thundering of the blood pulse of an enormous train, and again the breeze, and blurred birds, and a girl in a blue jumper will walk through woods, pushing aside the branches from her face, only once turning round with a painfully bitter look, and then she will carry on, leaving a trail trampled in the grass, crushed blood red strawberries, breaking a glass jar with daisies, and the ground will be hard and damp and the world will rock beneath the chubby white feet of a little boy in a white shirt, a round-headed boy with a happy, trusting smile open to everything in this crazy world; and like the lash of a whip, a forgotten voice will reach the speck: "My darling son!" And that droplet of light in the aura of that enormous star, and that handful of dust in the ragged tail of the comet, that speck of nothing will feel somehow strange and at odds in their endless movement, and the thing which once was called anguish of soul will be upon them, and there will be so much of it that everything, all around will be anguish of soul, endless, ever-present.

So there we are, whenever I am asked whether I have been happy I try to recall something terribly meaningful and substantial, but only a lot of silly nonsense comes to mind.

From *Forgiveness*, a collection of stories by Alexander Terekhov,
Glas Publishing, 1993.

Alexander Terekhov (b.1966) graduated from Moscow University's Department of Journalism and originally won acclaim as a writer of short stories, of which two collections have been published to date: **Forgiveness**, Glas, 1993; and **Memoirs of Life in the Army**, Vagrius, 1994. His novel **A Winter Day Starting a New Life** has been published in France. English translations of his work can so far only be found in Glas 2 (**Buddy and Charon**) and in Glas 4 (**Communal Living and Black Void**).

Terekhov's early literary themes were largely drawn from his formative experiences during service in the Soviet Army (the Army High Command described his works as "slander"). He spent his childhood in a small industrial town in Central Russia, which still preserved "the spirit of the early builders of communism". This background and his own subsequent disillusionment underlie the complex structure of his **Rat-killer**, in which the main action is set in a similar town named Svetloyar.

The town was conceived by an idealistic architect, Mokrousov, who was never able to build anything as he wished: "...He never actually finished building anything... he came here to build the city of communism from the ground up, and what have we got here? Certainly no Palazzo Montepulciano. A meat-processing plant. A sugar factory... He drew and he drew and he had good ideas! But they twisted it all out of shape... Ideas are always twisted out of shape here. If we're short of something to finish a project, then we're not capable of just saying: 'Stop!'. We go on and do it with whatever we have. And you can't make everything just out of what you happen to have!"

Overwhelmed by the dark embodiment of the narrator's nightmare the novel draws a clear parallel between the rats and human beings. As the political intrigue of phantasmagorical post-communist reality develops into nightmare the greed, cunning and malice of the humans more and more resembles the behaviour of the large communities of destructive rodents, while the rats acquire more and more human features.

Terekhov introduces descriptions and explanations of the complex social organisation of rat society, with its dominant and subordinate males, and of the means used to fight rats, up to and including other rats specially trained to kill and disrupt communities.

Terekhov's language is packed with forceful imagery and the slang of modern Russian. If we wish to identify precedents for his work we might look to Saltykov-Schedrin from the 19th century for his satire of provincial life, and Platonov in the early Soviet period for his range of imagery and individuality of language.

Terekhov, however, is a young and vital writer drawing very much on his own resources and experience, with a distinctive and individual intonation. In **The Rat-Killer** he has produced a racy read which is at the same time an extended metaphor and a satirical novel very much in the Russian tradition.

May We Recommend

Sovershenno Sekretno
(Top Secret)

Founded in 1993, this publishing house is an offspring of the popular daily of the same name. It started with detective and love series for teenagers, "school thrillers" and adventure novels and immediately won acclaim among readers of all ages.
The first 60 titles were translations from European languages but this year the publishers have included a number of Russian thrillers for children. This new series is inaugurated with
THE MYSTERY OF THE CHOCOLATE MARSHMALLOW,
by Valery Ronshin, an exciting adventure novel
which is at the same time an amusing parody of the genre.

Sovershenno Sekretno also caters to adult readers. Apart from a very successful series of world bestsellers in the detective genre they have a non-fiction series which includes
memoires of the ex-Foreign Minister
Boris Pankin, 100 DISRUPTED DAYS;
collection of pen portraits by RTR Russian TV
independent-minded ex-president Oleg Poptsov,
CHRONICLES OF THE TIMES OF TSAR BORIS;
reminiscences of the ex-Foreign Trade Minister V. Sushkov,
A CONVICT NICKNAMED MINISTER.

In press:
THE KGB GUIDE TO WORLD CAPITALS. Contributors include Soviet secret agents working in Paris, London, Rome, Berlin, Washington, New York, Cairo, Bangkok and Tokyo.
A BAD BOY, by Andrei Karaulov, a famous journalist and TV presenter who knows the political "corridors of power" inside out.

Alexander Terekhov's novel THE RAT-KILLER stands apart in the publishing output of Sovershenno Sekretno. The editors fell in love with the book because it shows better than any documentary what is happening in Russia today and where she is heading.

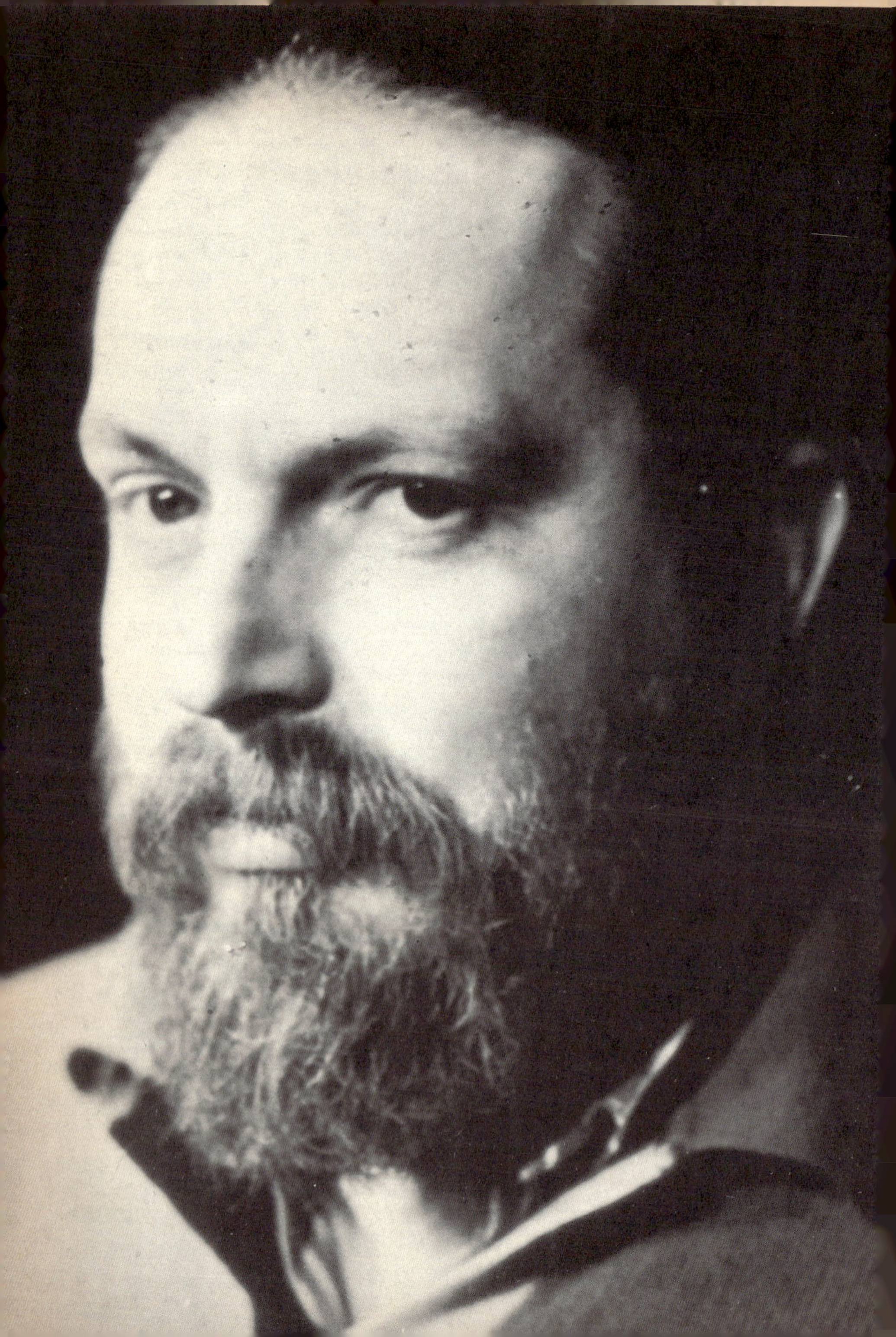

Mark
SHATUNOVSKY
The Discrete Continuity of Love

Translated by Patrick Henry

...in the morning the train came bowling out into the expanse of the heedless Motherland. A popular version of her native landscape as she knew it from trips to the countryside – Tolstoyan, passively resistant to evil – rolled past the window, an endless, doleful film reel. The railway, built much later than the unsuspecting villages, ran right through them without taking any notice. Piercing them wherever it pleased, the railway exposed their seamy side, pitilessly displaying the unsightly panorama of provincial life. As if she were being taken by train on an excursion to meet the common people, who existed only as exhibitions. An abstract love for the people had been instilled in her from childhood, and she loved them abstractly with all her might, doomed to this inevitable abstraction counterbalanced in turn by the monumental indifference of the people toward her feelings, including her innate feeling of guilt. The fleeting variegation of countless trees strewn between the small towns and villages facing the railroad tracks across kitchen-gardens left hapless by the arrival of autumn oppressed her with the spectacle of the incomprehensible abundance of all the unknown, nameless lives that had ended up along this line. The sight left her tormented by her innate feeling of guilt because the statistically overwhelming number of people living in her native country automatically trivialised the value of each individual life, precisely because it exceeded her powers of comprehension. She could not grasp the justification for birth and death, or most importantly for the approximate, simplified existence in the gap between them led by the absolute majority of people, dissolved without a trace on the boundless land. And if everyone is equal before God, does this mean that she, too, could have been born to live out her days in some backwater, perhaps in that peasant cottage painted a wild, toxic green rolling past along with the lonely landscape? Should her resistant soul have submitted to a purely logical, direct dependence if proof based on numerical superiority and high mathematical probability alone had proven insufficiently coercive? And what was to be done with her own independent identity, however insignificant, which did not consent to merely mathematical equality although intellectually she was prepared to admit that it was silly to cling to a social hierarchy that was becoming all the more illusory the farther they travelled from the old capital. She came into contact with the levelling of rights at once, in the doorway of the train's common toilet. The exercise of natural needs in these tight, rocking premises, which instilled no faith in their sanitariness, became an obstacle for her that required additional spiritual effort each time to overcome. She had no doubt that few of the people whose lives she passed as the train moved ever farther in a southwesterly direction, and with whom she came into contact on remote station platforms during long stops when the hospital train, not part of the plan, made way for trains running according to schedule, and no one traveling with her on this train, experienced a similar difficulty, and visited the toilet without attaching particular significance to the act. And if simple mathematical equality does not take its own course, and if all on your own you do not imperceptibly begin to go to the toilet with genuine spiritual simplicity like the overwhelming majority of people, then there is no point in acting as though you are in no way exceptional or in thinking that since you alone are so fastidious you are worse than everyone else.

She was diverted from her extensive reflections at the window by Vera, who had been the most forthcoming in talking with her that first day. They confided in one another, encouraged by the unhurried idleness of the road. This was her style, to accept someone's favor while at first experiencing something akin to indifference or even vexation at this attempt on her peaceful, self-sufficient solitude. Then she would get carried away, tripping over her tongue with well-intentioned, sincere emotionality but without getting into revelations about the other person's life or going into details and almost immediately forgetting their exact circumstances. Such that after Vera finished telling the story of her life, she recalled only that Vera was traveling as a nurse together with her husband, an army doctor, but that she had undertaken the journey on account of another man entirely. They sat on the lower bunk half-turned toward one another. Shadows played across Vera's laconic face, a face executed with limited means. The anemic autumn sun darted in and out of view behind the moving trees, chasing the train that sped along parallel to it. Vera's functional, clasped hands, coupled in a mutual handshake, lay on her practical, tidy skirt, and Vera as a whole gave off the impression of an expedient, energetic being not overburdened with useless details, free from doubts and insurmountable internal prejudices. But when she let Vera pass in the doorway of the compartment she got a whiff of the stuffy, stable, characteristic fustiness, ensconced in the severe pleats of her heavy clothing, that permeates fabric after prolonged wearing as it absorbs the microscopic bodily excretions that accompany the vital activities of the human organism. This smell accompanied Vera's further presence as a subtext, and as a result she began to think that in camp conditions Vera limited herself to regularly washing her face and hands. She forced herself to bring hot water from the kitchen before breakfast, locked herself in the shower-room and bathed, pouring the water over herself with the copper ladle newly given her by the quarter-master. The showers did not yet work, and the train looked largely uninhabited. The crew and the medical staff dispersed and went to their compartments through its narrow, attenuated, rocking and tenantless space. Somewhere up ahead in the immediate vicinity of the unimaginable and fearsome front line this space would be filled with those for whom it was intended. She had gone through the high school nursing course with the usual lack of concern, but now she faced something serious that instilled in her an instinctive, sucking fear. The experience and protective composure that emanated from Vera comforted her, however, and therefore she felt herself obliged not to focus overmuch on Vera's faults. The lunch bell sounded. And if at breakfast she had still maintained a relative sovereignty that saved her from the wearisome obligation of formal intercourse with the others, at lunch they categorically included her in their circle. Vera introduced her to everyone and because of the burdensome cordiality, with its implied reciprocity, of this now unavoidable company made up of doctors, soldiers and nurses, she, as always, immediately forgot all their names. This absurdly awkward absentmindedness compelled her on several occasions to narrow her eyes unctuously and flash a disarming smile which stood in for a name and signified a personal liking for whomever she happened to be speaking with. But at times, intently applying herself to the rather inedible army rations, she caught herself in the creeping self-recognition that she was trying to compensate with heightened politeness for the vague, unfounded indifference toward new acquaintances that she had experienced in the first minutes with Vera. They were so uninteresting to her that she was too lazy to render them concrete, linking together the freely varying collection of random external features – hairdos or bald spots, beards or shaven chins, the shape of noses and ears, the color of eyes, the style of dress, etc. – found in any arbitrarily selected community of people. Only one handsome fellow stood out. He resembled a grenadier who never lost sight of his beauty, and who easily broke into a sweat from intensive attention to his appearance. The rest all looked alike to her, especially the women, and their existence passed her by. None of the variations on generally accepted manifestations that they exhibited touched her: their laboured good nature, imperturbable readiness to collide with the approaching war, or the many forms of personal or national patriotism in which she discerned an unconscious desire to convince others, but themselves above all, that they were right at home here and knew what they were doing. She perceived everything that happened against the background of the constant sensation that she was not at home anywhere, and the definitive meaning of events was utterly unclear to her. Their shared, simple optimism wearied her more than anything as it implied an elated, business-like consciousness of entering the theatre of military operations that in itself invested the war with meaning and even justified it as a cause in which it was reasonable voluntarily to take part. This consciousness contradicted her seditious, apocryphal desire to steal a single, dear person from this beastly war which otherwise held not the slightest interest for her. She did not intend to prove anything to anyone, and amidst the general certainty in the correctness of the common endeavour and the authenticity of commonplaces she preferred to keep silent. She could conceal from all but herself that in the depths of her soul she was persistently indifferent to those around her. This unaggressive coldness, which nevertheless caused her pangs of conscience, was taken by everyone else – to her constant amazement – for a capacity to please and to produce a pleasant impression. No one guessed at the process of self-reflection that took place within her in the presence of others, nor did they see any disparity in her behaviour. But she knew of all sorts of disparities within herself. They finished lunch, having arranged to get together after supper for a party. She avoided Vera now. At some point she would come to terms with her lack of common ground with the people with whom she had to spend the upcoming interval of her life, but at the moment she was exhausted by the feverish stream of heightened consciousness that had tormented her since the day before, when with impetuous haste she had planned and executed her departure, fleeing the possibility of changing her mind or talking herself out of going. She disconnected herself from her overloaded self-reflections, burst fully dressed on her assigned, unwelcoming bunk and fell asleep. Vera woke her up shortly, and along with everyone else they tidied up the dispensary and the examining room. She sorted through boxes of medicines and bandages and stacked piles of linen on the shelves, and amongst the other nurses she suddenly and easily lost sight of herself. The room smelt soothingly of sanded wood from the fresh shelf boards, and the work-therapy definitively dispersed her "I". Then the train screeched, jerked, scraped and stuck at the next godforsaken railway halt, and as one they dropped the unsorted boxes and the remaining packages of linen and poured out on to the platform. They ate their fill of hot pies in the station restaurant. As she bought some big nostalgic winter apples, that seemed to have been specially grown for a still-life, from an amorphous country woman who was phlegmatically hawking her wares on the empty platform, her head was filled with frivolous, consoling sayings: everything is in God's hands, somehow it will turn out all right, there's always a chance.

...the party broke up on its own, but not before she had been persuaded to take a shot of pure spirits to commemorate her joining the medical profession. They filled her glass with a heart-rending liquid and set a tall glass of water beside it. This new situation of being face to face with herself, outside the customary order of things left ever farther behind in Moscow, unexpectedly provoked a relapse of open-heartedness which had seemed completely subdued by refined scepticism. She wanted to be like the rest, and she tossed off the apocalyptic jigger and drained the glass of water. They applauded her, and the handsome grenadier struck up a stumbling march on the guitar. With childish satisfaction she verified that she had been needlessly afraid and nothing terrible had befallen her, only her scorched larynx burnt a little. Now she prepared to take herself seriously in hand and keep track lest she get drunk. But nothing out of the ordinary happened, and they convinced her to have another drink. She was persuaded by the Don Juan lieutenant who sat down beside her, a shortish, significantly unattractive tow-headed man. His deep, fleecy voice seemed to emanate from a wooden box within his chest lined with green velvet or the felt from a billiard table. He looked straight into her eyes with a hypnotic, merry impudence. The simplified interactions of the road pleased her all the more. She liked the way everyone, even the women, drank this dodgy thieves' brew. Vera's unabashed flirtation with the handsome grenadier, and the way her husband was boozing with a gloomy disinterest, methodically nodding assent to the sceptical observations of the hale, grey-haired surgeon. It was obvious that not only was her husband not annoyed by their flirting, but on the contrary it amused him, and he watched them with a cunning approval, almost encouraging and even loving them. This was what lulled her most of all: everyone here loved one another. They were well disposed to one another. They willingly laughed at old, well-worn anecdotes and oft repeated jokes. They were together, and no one was unhappy or lonely. She wanted to grow dull, and she did so. Their unanimous acceptance heartened her, how they all liked her straight off. The lieutenant was blathering in a velvet whisper, hovering above her right shoulder. She liked his attractive, intelligent hands, one of which peremptorily clasped her waist while the other insinuatingly covered her hand as it rested on the edge of the table. Not idle hands in the slightest, their ennobled active outline bore the stamp of the physician's reasonable profession, and with a vague, surprising sluggishness she suppressed her deeply felt, minute impulse to kiss them. A moist, tickling warmth swelled in her lower abdomen, now heavy with the same pleasant and shameful warmth she had felt in her rosy-cheeked, allergy-plagued childhood when she wet her knickers. As if some tightly sealed, concealed anguish about the arbitrary life that had flowed through her fingers, a life for which she could find no justification, had come uncorked. She was overcome with repentance for her useless, wasted life. Without leaving her place she wanted to confess every painstaking trifle to this first soldier to come along who now embraced her. But she was distracted by the weak enthusiasm aroused by her illusion that perhaps now, among these people – made more simply, soundly and genuinely than herself – her life might change. And as a train changing directions at a switch leaves one set of rails, which flies off to the side, soon disappearing entirely from view, her former life flew away from her, leaving not even pangs of conscience behind but only the sarcastic observation that she had only to set out on a railway journey for her associations to acquire a railway hue. With a fresh outburst of her growing simple-mindedness she was carried away by the obvious truth she had discovered for herself: all these doctors and nurses, and the grey-haired surgeon painting a vivid picture for his fellow revellers of his campaign with Skobelev to Bulgaria to fight the Turks, and the whole zemstvo doctors' corps voluntarily dispersed throughout the country in out-of-the-way places, among the very towns and villages whose spectacle had so impressed her that morning — healing, curing, soothing, patching and tending to the needy, hearing confessions, none of this compensated by salary or any other mercantile notion — they constituted the real meaning of the abstract concept "salt of the earth." And now that they had all been drawn into this war they did not judge whether they ought to take part. They were en route to take part in it without experiencing a false and onerous innate feeling of guilt. And although the lieutenant was too impudent, and too boldly squeezed her knee such that beneath her skirt her legs felt as though they had been pinched at the scene of a crime, he listened to her attentively and understood everything appropriately. And he was clear and reliable. When Vera's husband crashed to the floor, stood up, reeled and collapsed on the grey-haired surgeon, raised himself once more and pushed away everyone who tried to help him, destroying the smooth flow of talk round the table, the lieutenant abducted her by the hand and having pressed her shoulder blades against the hard, chill wall of the carriage platform began without warning to suck on her lips, wetly kissing her eyebrows, cheeks and eyes. He rumpled her skirt, which rode up in unsightly fashion, bunched to one side and sticking out as on some circus monkey in one of Durov's costumed attractions. She did not like Durov's attractions or monkeys or even Charles Darwin. Monkeys were disgracefully caricatured specimens of his theory of evolution. And she herself was a disgraceful specimen. A shameful specimen, so shameful that the lieutenant laying siege to her could not have understood. Unless perhaps she just up and wet herself right here, in his presence, as she had in her serene childhood. Unsticking his importunate hands she said that she wanted to pee. He did not understand, but let her go out of surprise. She set off down the long corridor and ran into Vera on the way, but Vera walked right past. To the lieutenant. They exchanged a couple of loud, scarcely audible comments drowned out by the regular clacking of the train wheels. But from the opposite end of the corridor she could not make out what they were saying, and she couldn't be bothered to go find out.

...the young woman had a strange dream as she slept on the decrepit six-legged bed with a bulging spring in the middle. She dreamt she wore a respectable grey satin dress with an ample skirt, which she raised along with her petticoat and held up as she contorted in a humiliating pose over the soul-wrenching stool in the shaky toilet, her satin elbow propped against the thin wall in hopes of greater stability. She stood on the frail vibrating floor over a small round hole torn in it for some unknown reason through which she could see how the dark earth covered with sleepers rushed along below. Having completed the task that had brought her there and pulled up her underwear, so old-fashioned that it astonished her to the depths of her soul, she washed her hands in the sink whose handles she was painfully obliged to touch and went out into the corridor where she experienced deliverance from this custom, so unacceptable it made her skin crawl. She walked back to her compartment through the swaying, unsteady corridor against the direction of the train which rushed through the night past green signal-posts, and she had hardly entered when the shortish, rather toy-like lieutenant who had been following her appeared from the platform. (She wondered in the dream how she recognised his insignia, and had no answer). Lithe as a hungry cat he came after her, the two crosses on his chest knocking against one another and jingling slightly. In the closeness of her cramped compartment she pulled off her crackling dress, her elbows brushing against every possible protuberance, and hung the dress by the first buttonhole she found on the metal dress hook screwed into the paper-thin wall. The hook astounded her unaccountably, but at present she didn't have the strength to go into exactly why. At this point the door opened and there was no time to pluck up the courage to admit whether she had forgotten to close it or had intentionally left it open. She was waiting for something all the time, some kind of continuation, or a very specific continuation. And this continuation followed. The lieutenant came through the half-open door and closed it behind him without wavering. Once more his sure, capable hands devoted themselves to her, reducing her to a state of ecstatic weakness. They unlaced her bodice, from which her heavy breasts immediately tumbled out, and penetrated beneath her petticoat o her bare skin. The lieutenant remained dressed, but he stealthily, childishly unfastened the zipper on the riding-breeches that he wore tucked into his boots. This made her laugh. She had no desire to see the lieutenant in all his final and exposing nakedness. He threw her down on someone else's cramped bunk and pressed down on her, but nothing came of it. The bunk was impossibly narrow. The lieutenant's leg and then the lieutenant himself slid off the edge. Then he unceremoniously lifted her up, turned her back to him and, with one arm wrapped around her stomach he bent her forward. There was nothing she could do but lift her backside toward the lieutenant like an animal, her arms leaning on the folding table. She found herself face to face with her own reflection in the night-black window that appeared before her and began to scrutinise her humiliating pose with real voluptuous delight, her blazing, dishevelled and harrowed face, her breasts hanging down side by side and flapping to and fro in time with the synchronous swaying of the train car and the forward movements of the lieutenant, who resembled a jockey towering behind her from the waist up. She also saw in the window how the fiery points of villages flew by, intersecting her smoothly swaying breasts, villages filled with the same people for whom she had since childhood felt a useless, oppressive, innate feeling of love identical to a feeling of guilt. But now, on account of her obvious bestial humiliation – in full view of the villages flowing past beneath her nipples – this was balanced with a feeling of guilt toward herself, and these two guilts cancelled each other out, delivering love from the aggravating makeweight and allowing her to feel ripe and freely flowing. An irrational, uncontrollable readiness to submit herself to commonplace shame made her even with all the rest of humanity, supplanting useless conceptions thrust upon her by her upbringing of an innate, one-sided obligation, of some sort of debt before whomever it might be. Her feelings became just what they should have been, simply feelings, summoning her to nothing and obligating her to no one. Freed by this desperate downfall she allowed herself to be glimpsed in the lower part of the window, in the space between the two short shades lowered on a thin horizontal metal bar, along with the distant nocturnal villages drifting by, along with nearby railway crossings, like models, ripped by the train's light from the black cotton wool of the night, along with the dark silhouettes of trees, the untidy blots of bushes and single disorderly poles. At this moment in a speculative stupor she discerned that a worm-like blue monogram ran at intervals in slanting lines across the white curtains, coiling into the simple bureaucratic abbreviation "MOC", for Ministry of Communications, the very one that had stuck in her mind from last year when she took the train to Leningrad on a business trip for her publishing house. And that the table she was leaning against was covered in light-blue plastic and bordered with aluminium trim. Suddenly the elusive source of her astonishment about the hook screwed into the compartment wall on which she had hung her satin dress became clear. Its design was from another time entirely. From the time in which she slept, in which there was no place for the ceremonious satin dress or the affected trousers or this lieutenant out of a musical comedy. And just then in her dream she found the explanation for this. She had simply never ridden in pre-revolutionary trains and hadn't the slightest idea what sort of tables, curtains and hooks they had. And the presentiment of some important discovery gripped her in her dream. Something to do with history. That there is no history. That the costumes and decorations change, but all historical events are a vain masquerade performed by their participants. That the most grandiose turning-points in history change nothing except fashion. And the pettiest individual life, utterly inconspicuous everyday events such as going to the toilet or the process of spreading butter on bread are the only truly vital events worthy of our attention. All the rest requires no personal participation. We are all interchangeable in mass spectacles, and the less you take part in them the more you remain yourself. And although in this she completely contradicted her ardently beloved poet Tyutchev, through her dream she experienced exultant liberation even from Tyutchev. The state of freedom that seized her in her dream was so strong that she had an unbearable urge to pee. Or she had wanted to for some time but could not wake up. It was true, she recalled, that she had already dreamt of going to the toilet and had even felt how naturally and authentically she had urinated. From the inarticulate, childish fear of wetting the bed in her sleep she awoke, but having examined herself she calmed down. The bed was absolutely dry. Then with a degree of psychological relief she threw on her robe, passed close by a mournful male shadow prudently blended in with the wall and made invisible, and set off through the corridor, peaceful now amidst the all-embracing night, to the real toilet, already mentioned many times and in great detail.

Published in Russian in *Postscriptum*, No.2, 1995.

The Discrete Continuity of Love is a novel about love. A thirty-year-old woman sleeps and in a persistently repetitive dream she sees the events of another's life and another's love story which took place long before her birth, before the Revolution. At one point she returns home from work. She unlocks the door with her key and in the locked apartment she discovers the protagonist of her dreams seated at a table.

The Discrete Continuity of Love is a neo-novel, returning the Russian novelistic tradition to postmodernism with all the consequences that issue from this:

- a text combining refined metaphor with classically simple, sincere writing;
- an historical space made up of mutually penetrating and correlating pre- and post-Revolutionary periods;
- personal reality and life reproduced down to the sense of touch;
- a world seen from within by characters located within themselves;
- a scrupulous psychologism inherited from Tolstoy-Dostoevsky immersed in the most excruciating and obscene details of the human soul and physiology;
- the discovery by one of the heroines that the reduction of life to a minimum, to a practically continuous dream, provides a no less vital presence in life than the most feverish activity;
- the discovery by one of the characters that the Revolution in Russia came about not because of the Lenins and Trotskys, but because he parted with the woman he loved.

It is a novel about what each of us experiences when we are alone.

POEMS

UNTITLED

a child in a room,
                now he's a boy, now a curtain,
the floor absorbs his sandals
his gaze becomes substance – an inquisitive chisel,
fidgeting in the drawer, overturning the table.

from his kidneys, an impudent ash-tree grows,
and in his right lung salt begins to blossom.
he's a complete fragmentation, visible, though muddied,
the hearing sprouts within him, shackled to a bean.

he's no longer split in two by chromosomes,
he's more simple and transparent than fish fry,
and all five of his senses are familiar to my touch,
and his whole soul is wrapped in a paper cone.

(I know that the soul is a flexible hose,
inside, the blood completes its death work
– that our internal space is an uncomplicated aqualung,
but in the boy the soul grows, breathing nitrogen.)

the grass will take root inside him, and he'll let fall
some chance object from his hand to the grass
so that I might find either stars or comets there,
and collect them in an empty, crushed milk can.

Translated by John High and Patrick Henry

BANAL OBJECTS

these years, myopic — hovering behind the
mirrored, peeling wardrobe,
>a guilt-ridden smile, a baggy raincoat,
they don't resemble my father:
the frail figure
>too bloated
melts away in a slow high.
or when you'll go into the garden through
>the paralytic back door —
back to the garden where the passage is almost harmless,
even if the weather's fine
>in the end, you'll only get your feet wet,
in evaporating puddles, a childhood once lived on alimony.
who brought on this terror
>that shook you from the photo albums,
pre-war boys, connoisseurs of old sayings
and wrestling tricks — sent to the corner and absenced by life,
>your facial expression coincides
with something forgotten.
>your outstretched shadows
on the lunar surface of fear —
shadows of monuments, which once stood on the bare earth.
you feel feverish at the slightest agitation in your groin,
the documents in your shirt pocket
>bring you chills.
the deaf compartments where life has ceased —
>parallels the apartments you live in,
someone looks out from this place
as the General Secretaries stare out from their portraits
>and our capital is bustling in its patterns of morning
>>exercise

or then in the neglected stairwell —
>you'll meet yourself
but not knowing what to say
>no conversation occurs —
you only watch, in anticipation

at this other wearing a second-hand cap.
– he says, let's stay a while,
        no reason to hurry off.
like snails the things that go unnoticed in their living.
here, the lips tenderly mouthing the tube of bright lipstick,
two keys and a ticket –
        are they evidence,
chance objects asking, disgracefully, for mercy.
this petty life extorts simplification from itself,
a handful of sweet tears
        washing from the deceptions of childhood,
after a rain, having received absolution,
crawling from handbags, pockets,
why should they be spared
        would that reflect the characteristics of a true killer –
and where can we go from here, and then if we return
for what, what can we find
        or want to be convinced of –
that children grow up
        and the earth continues to revolve.

Translated by John High and Patrick Henry

Reprinted from the Five Fingers Review # 11

Mark Shatunovsky about himself

There is not enough external evidence of Shatunovsky's existence, which cannot be taken for granted.
He was born on March 6, 1954, but this event stamped itself weakly on his memory. He studied at school and then in the philological department at Moscow University, but this had no particular affect on him. Only his stint in the army temporarily concretised him in the form of a reserve lance-corporal.
At some point after that he recited poetry somewhere with the poets of the "new wave", with Zhdanov, Yeremenko, and Parshchikov or with Bunimovich, Arabov and Iskrenko, but no one recalls exactly with whom or when, and this is almost a legend by now.
He has a wife and daughter. But when his daughter fills in questionnaires at school she never knows how to answer the

question about her father's occupation. And his wife, seeking any sort of evidence of her husband's literary success, finds mention of him in the category "and others".

He even became a member of the Writers' Union, an accomplishment largely due to the considerable efforts of Kirill Kovaldzhi, whose once famous poetry seminar in Moscow he attended quite regularly. But since this seminar has receded into the realm of legend and tradition, and only the restaurant remains of the Writers' Union, now frequented by characters little resembling writers, even this fact does not permit us to consider the existence of Mark Shatunovsky as proven.

His play "The Trajectory of a Snail, or An Anecdote About Stalin's Death" played an entire season at the Moscow University Theatre, but subsequent stormy nationwide events dispelled the authenticity of this rather minor event.

There is one further piece of material evidence: a book of poetry called **The Sensation of Life**. But the very fact of its release from the AMGA publishing house in Paris arouses doubt. What was the point of publishing it in Russian in Paris? And then, can poetry really constitute an even a slightly serious piece of evidence? For the same reason, his other book of poetry, **Thoughts of Grass**, published in Moscow this time, cannot, likewise, be taken seriously.

It's true that his poetry and prose have been translated into English and French and published in American and French journals, and he received an official invitation from the United States Information Agency to take part in the prestigious International Writers' Program at Iowa University. But then the latest factual evidence, the (neo)novel **The Discrete Continuity of Love**, written by him over six years and published in the St. Petersburg-based literary journal **Postscriptum**, betrays the fictitious nature of Mark Shatunovsky's existence. Think about it — could any real, living person write a novel for six whole years in the current conditions of Russia so unfavourable for literary endeavours?

W. Booker Winners

*"My life would be the poorer
deprived of Glas,
and Russia,
for all her paradoxes,
is definitely and permanently
in my bloodstream."*
Francis Greene

Winner of the Booker   Russian Novel Prize

GEORGY VLADIMOV
A General and His Army
(excerpt)

Translated by Arch Tait

What picture did the words "General Headquarters" conjure up in the mind of a driver sitting numbly in his seat, peering dully at the road ahead, blinking his red eyelids and trying periodically with the doggedness of a man who has not slept for a long time to drag the cigarette butt glued to his lip back to life? Probably in the very words he heard and imagined something high and enduring, soaring above the Moscow rooftops like a fairy-tale turret, while at its foot would sprawl the long-anticipated car park, a courtyard surrounded by a wall and covered with vehicles like the court of a coaching inn which he had once read something about. Somebody would constantly be arriving or taking their leave, and the endless chit-chat between the drivers would be well up to the level of that which their bosses the generals would be exchanging in quiet, dimly lit chambers behind heavy blinds on the eighth floor. To venture in imagination beyond the eighth was beyond the reach of Driver Sirotin, his own life having been lived hitherto at the ground (and only) floor level, but neither would he have the brass located any lower. They must surely be allowed a view of a good half of Moscow from their windows.

How cruelly disappointed Sirotin would have been to learn that General Headquarters was buried away deep underground at Kirovskaya metro station, that mere plywood partitions divided off its cramped offices, while its buffets and cloakrooms were tucked away in railway carriages. It would have seemed reprehensible, meaning as it did that it was deeper underground than Hitler's bunker. It would have been quite wrong for our Soviet Headquarters to be thus tucked away because the German HQ was justly derided precisely for being in a bunker. In any case, how could a bunker inspire the same trepidation with which our generals would proceed into the entrance hall, their knees half giving way beneath them.

It was there, at the foot of the turret where he would have positioned himself and his jeep, that Sirotin anticipated discovering what fate now held in store for him, perhaps again melding his destiny with that of his General, or just as possibly decreeing it a separate course. If he kept his ears open he might well pick up some useful intelligence from the other drivers, just as he had picked up on this journey ahead of time from a colleague in Headquarters' motor transport division. Settling down for a lengthy smoking session while they waited for a conference to end, they had first talked of abstract matters. Sirotin recalled expressing the view that if you were to mount the engine from an eight-seater Dodge in a jeep you would get a great little buggy you couldn't wish to better. His colleague had not denied this but observed that the engine of a Dodge was on the large side and might well not fit under the hood of a jeep. You would have to make a special panel to cover it, and they then jointly concluded that things were best left as they were. From here the conversation moved on to changes in general and whether they were all that good a thing. Here, too, his colleague pronounced himself a believer in tradition, in which connection he hinted that they in the Army could expect some changes too, literally in the next few days, and the only question was whether they would be for the better or for the worse. What precisely these changes might be his colleague did not let slip, saying only that a final decision had yet to be taken, but from the way he lowered his voice you could gather that the decision when it came would issue not even from Front Headquarters but from a higher level, perhaps indeed from such a height as the two of them were never destined to see. "Although," his colleague suddenly said, "you just might. If you get to Moscow, tell the old girl hello from me." To register astonishment at the idea that he could possibly find himself in Moscow in the middle of the present push would not have been commensurate with Sirotin's status as the Commander-in-Chief's driver. He just nodded, while secretly resolving that his colleague couldn't have any hard information, had heard some distant echo, and might indeed have been the origin of it himself. But it had proved to be no echo, and he was ordered to Moscow for good and real! Being a prudent sort, Sirotin had already started making preparations on the off chance: he fitted new tyres, "Mother's own", American tyres which he had been keeping until they would drive into Europe, and welded on a bracket for an extra fuel canister, handy on a long journey. He even pulled on the tarpaulin they usually left behind whatever the weather because the General disliked it: "It's as muggy as a dog kennel under that thing," he said, "and it hinders dispersal," that is, jumping out over the sides at the double if you came under fire or were being bombed. So, all in all, it was not that great a surprise when the General suddenly ordered, "Harness her up, Sirotin. Let's have a bite to eat and then we're off to Moscow!"

Sirotin had never once seen Moscow, and was both delighted at having his long held, indeed pre-war ambition realized, and at the same time apprehensive for his General abruptly recalled to GHQ, to say nothing of himself. Who else might he end up driving, and might he not do better to ask to transfer to driving a one-and-half-ton truck, where you got less hassle, and there was also a slightly better chance of staying alive in an enclosed cabin which would keep out at least some of the shrapnel. He also had a strange sense of relief and even of a kind of deliverance which he did not care to admit even to himself.

He was not the General's first. Two earlier drivers had come to a bad end if you counted from Voronezh, and that after all was where the Army's history began. Before that, in Sirotin's opinion, there had been no Army and no history, just sheer wretched chaos. So then, since Voronezh the General himself had not suffered a scratch but two jeeps had, as they said in the Army, been shot from under him, on both occasions along with their drivers, and one time also with his aide. A persistent legend had grown up that the General had a charmed life, and confirmation of this was seen in the deaths of those who had been right next to him, literally a couple of paces away. Admittedly a more detailed account revealed a slightly different picture: the jeeps had not exactly been shot from under him. The first time his vehicle had suffered a direct hit from a long-distance high explosive shell. The General was not actually in the jeep when it happened, having been held up for a minute at the divisional command post. He emerged to find everything a shambles. And the second time, when the vehicle was wrecked by an anti-tank mine, he had just got out to walk along the road and check how satisfactorily the self-propelled artillery was camouflaged before an attack. He ordered the driver to move away out of the open, and the idiot went and drove off into a grove of trees. The road had been cleared of mines but the sappers had left the grove as no traffic was projected to pass through it... What difference did it make, Sirotin wondered, whether the General was too early or too late to get himself blown up: that was all part of the charm. The trouble was, it did not extend to those accompanying him, only took their common sense away. When you thought about it, his invulnerability had been the cause of their death. The experts had already worked out that almost ten tons of metal went into killing a single soldier in this war. Sirotin did not need them or their calculations to know how difficult it is to kill a man at the front. You had only to last out three months or so to know not to listen to the shrapnel or bullets, but to listen to yourself, to that inexplicable chill which warned you, and the more inexplicable it was the more you could rely on it, to get the hell out of somewhere. It might root you out of the world's safest dug-out with seven layers of logs in its roofing, and send you instead to some totally useless ditch to shelter behind an insignificant clump of grass, and the dug-out would promptly be reduced to a log pile, while the tuft of grass protected you from harm. He knew that this crucial survival mechanism lost its edge if not constantly used, if you were away from the front line for as little as a week, but while this General of his was not obsessive about being at the front, he certainly had no aversion to it. Sirotin's predecessors could not have got that unused to it. So it must have been their own silly faults. They had not listened to themselves.

As far as the mine incident was concerned, you didn't know whether to laugh or cry. It was against regulations and against common sense. Could he imagine himself driving off the road into a grove of birch trees for cover? He could not, even if every shrub had a notice stuck in front of it proclaiming: "Checked for Mines: Clear". There might well be none for the guy who had checked the area out, he would be well out of harm's way by now; but you could bet your bottom dollar that in his haste he had left just one little anti- tank mine specially for you. But supposing he had swept the grove from end to end with his belly button, everyone knew that once a year even an unloaded rifle goes off. The shell took more explaining. Choosing to argue with a mine was something you did yourself, but a shell chose you. Some unknown hand traced its trajectory beneath the heavens, corrected a slight error with a rippling of the breeze, deflecting it two or three thousandths to the right or to the left, and all in just a few seconds. How were you to sense that your one and only, the one chosen for you by destiny herself, had already left the barrel and was rushing towards you, whistling, droning, except that you heard nothing while other men needlessly ducked their heads. But why would you have stayed in the open when something held the General up at that command post? It was that same inexplicable sixth sense that would have made you stay, that was what had to be recognized.

In these musings Sirotin was invariably conscious of his superiority over his two predecessors, but who was to say that this was any more than the eternal dubious sense of superiority of the man who is still alive over the man who is dead. That did occur to him too. The trouble was that it was something you were not allowed to feel. It could disorientate you even worse, driving away that saving chill. The science of survival demanded that you be always humble and never weary of begging to be spared and then, maybe, you might be all right. The main thing, however, that the chill whispered constantly to him was that he would not see out the war with this General. Why not? If you could have put a name to the reasons there would, of course, be nothing inexplicable about it... Somewhere, some time it would happen, there were no two ways about that. It was always at the back of his mind, and was why he was so often morose and depressed. Only a very experienced eye would have seen behind his bravado, behind the extravagantly dashing, gallant appearance, to that concealed presentiment. Somewhere the rope must have an end, he told himself. It had been winding round and round for a long time now; he had been too lucky, and how he longed to be let off with just a wounding, and after his hospitalization to start afresh with a different general who did not have such a powerful charm protecting him.

These were basically the misgivings, there was nothing else, that Driver Sirotin imparted to Major Svetlookov from the army counter-intelligence unit, Smersh, when the latter called him in for a talk or, as he preferred to put it, "for a bit of a gossip about one or two things." "Only, you know what," he said to Sirotin, "you can't have a proper talk with anyone in the unit. Somebody's bound to come charging in with some crap. Let's see if we can't find a better spot. But in the meantime, not a word to anyone, because you never can tell, eh?" Their meeting took place in a small wood not far from headquarters. They met there at the edge of the trees. Major Svetlookov sat himself down on a fallen pine tree and took his peaked cap off, turned his stern, bulging forehead with the red line left by the capband towards the autumn sun, and seemed thereby to neutralize his superior rank, disposing one to honest and open conversation. For all that, he motioned to Sirotin to sit down on a lower level than himself, on the grass.

"Come on then," he said. "Tell me all about what's on your mind, and why our soldier boy is sad at heart? I can see something's bugging you, not much gets past me..."

It was not wise for Sirotin to be talking about things which the science of survival bade you keep silent about, but Major Svetlookov immediately saw his problem and was sympathetic.

"Never mind, never mind," he said without a trace of irony, vigorously tossing his flaxen locks as far back as he could. "We quite understand all this mysticism. We are all superstitious, not just you, the Commander-in-Chief is too. And I can tell you a secret, his life is not all that charmed. He does not care to remember it and does not wear the badges he was awarded for being wounded, but he was, as the result of his own stupidity, in 'forty-one, near Solnechnogorsk. He earned himself eight bullets in the stomach. You didn't know? His orderly didn't tell you? He was there when it happened. And there was I thinking you had no secrets from each other. Ah well, I expect Fotii Ivanovich ordered him to keep it quiet. So we'll keep quiet about it too, eh? Here, listen," he suddenly glanced down at Sirotin with a merry but piercing gaze. "I don't suppose you are, you know, holding out on me? Keeping back the one thing that really matters about Fotii Ivanovich?"

"What would I have to keep back?"

"You haven't noticed him behaving strangely lately? I should mention that one or two people have. But you haven't, nothing at all?"

Sirotin shrugged, which could equally well have meant that he had not noticed anything, or that he did not see it was a matter for the likes of him. He had, however, detected a danger, as yet unclear, which threatened the General, and his first impulse was to distance himself if only for a moment in order to understand what threat there might be to himself. Major Svetlookov was peering straight at him, and it was not easy to meet the gaze of those piercing blue eyes. He had evidently figured what was behind Sirotin's confusion, and this gaze was to put him back in his place as a member of the entourage of the Commander-in-Chief, which was the place of a devoted servant who trusted his chief implicitly.

"Don't tell me about sundry doubts or suspicions or miscellaneous other nonsense," the Major said firmly. "I only want facts. If there are facts, it is your duty to alert me to them. The Commander is an important man. He has done a lot of good things, he is valuable, and that puts us under an even greater obligation to do our utmost to support him if he has stumbled in some respect. Perhaps he is tired. Perhaps right now he needs special care and attention. He is not going to ask us for it himself, is he, and we might not notice, we might miss an opportunity, and then we would kick ourselves afterwards. It is, after all, our job to look after every man in the Army, and as for the Commander, well, it's obvious, isn't it?"

Who precisely this "we" was who had to look after every man in the Army, he and the Major or the whole of the Army's Smersh in whose eyes the General had evidently somehow "stumbled", Sirotin did not know and, for some reason, did not feel he could ask. Their talk was ever more obviously drawing him in a particular direction, towards something mightily unpleasant, and the thought vaguely occurred to him that he had already taken a small step towards treachery in having agreed to come here to "gossip".

From the depths of the forest there came the damp freshness of the breeze which preceded evening, and into it a cloying sickly stench insinuated itself. That wretched burial detail, Sirotin thought, they had collected our own dead but not bothered to pick up the Germans. It would have to be reported to the General, he would teach them not to fall down on the job. They hadn't felt like picking up the corpses while they were fresh, and now everyone else had to hold their noses.

"Tell me one thing, though," Major Svetlookov said, "what do you think his attitude is towards death?"

Sirotin looked up at him in astonishment.

"Same as the rest of us, I suppose."

"You do not know," the Major said severely. "The reason I ask is that just now the protection of our command personnel is very high on the agenda. There has been a special, classified directive from GHQ, and the Supreme Commander has stressed on more than one occasion that commanding officers are not to put themselves at risk. Thank God, this is not 1941, we have worked out how to force a river crossing, and that there is no reason for the commanding officer to be there in person. What was the point of Fotii Ivanovich making the crossing along with everybody else under fire? Perhaps he was deliberately placing himself at risk? From desperation of some kind, from fear of failing to cope with the operation? Or maybe, you know, he might have gone a bit odd. Who's to say. To some extent it would be understandable, this is after all a very complex operation..."

It might not have seemed to Sirotin that the operation was actually that much more complicated than any other, and it seemed to be going perfectly smoothly, however those up there at the great height from which Major Svetlookov had condescended to him might well have considerations of their own.

"A one-off incident perhaps," the Major was meanwhile wondering aloud. "No, there is a pattern behind it all. When the Commander-in-Chief of the Army moves his command post ahead of the divisional posts, what option does the divisional commander have? He moves even closer to the Germans; and the regimental commander has to move in right under their noses. Are we trying to show off to each other how brave we are? Or take another example: you often drive up to the front line without an escort, not using an armoured car, without even taking a radio operator with you. You're asking to be ambushed, or you might be trying to cross over into German lines. How are we to establish afterwards that there was no treachery going on, and that it was all just a mistake. We have to foresee these possibilities, and head them off. And that means you and I first and foremost."

"What can I do about it all?" Sirotin asked with some relief. The subject of their talk had finally become clear to him and was close to his own anxieties. "It's not up to a driver what route he chooses."

"It certainly isn't for you to give instructions to the Commander-in-Chief! But it is within your competence to know in advance where you're making for, isn't it? Fotii Ivanovich does say to you, doesn't he, 'Harness her up, Sirotin, we are heading over to the hundred and eighth?' Doesn't he?"

Sirotin was properly impressed by such knowledgeability, but objected,

"Not always. Sometimes he gets in first and then tells me where we are going."

"Quite true, but you don't just have one destination in the course of a day, you inspect three or four positions: half an hour in one then, maybe, a good two hours somewhere else. There's nothing to stop you asking him whether you are going to be there long and where you are going next, as if you want to be sure you are going to have enough gas. And there's your opportunity to ring through."

"Ring through where?"

"To me, of course. We'll exercise general oversight, and contact the position that you are heading for at any particular time so they can send someone out to meet you. Of course, I realize there are times when the Commander-in-Chief wants just to turn up unannounced, to catch everyone with their pants down. One thing does not need to get in the way of the other. We have our own job to do. The divisional commander will not know when Fotii Ivanovich is going to show up, but we will."

"I thought," Sirotin said smiling uneasily, "that your job was catching spies."

"Our job takes in everything," the Major said. "The main thing is that we should always know what is happening and that the Commander should never be left without our protection. Will you promise me that?"

Sirotin furrowed his brow, stalling for time. There seemed nothing wrong if every time, no matter where he and the General were heading, Major Svetlookov should be in the know, but he didn't at all like the idea that he would be having to report behind the General's back. Sirotin asked straight out:

"What, do you mean, keep it secret from Fotii Ivanovich?"

"Uh-huh," the Major mocked him. "You don't like the idea, but the whole point is to keep it secret. Why trouble the Commander with it?"

"I don't know," Sirotin said. "It doesn't seem right, somehow."

Major Svetlookov heaved a long sad sigh.

"And I don't know either, but I do know that's how it has to be. So there we are. There used to be political commissars in the army and it was all so simple. What I have been trying to get out of you for an hour already the commissar would have promised me without a second thought. Nobody would have found it strange in the least. The commissar and counter-intelligence worked hand and glove. Now military commanders are trusted more, and it has become infinitely more difficult to do our job. You can't just drop in on a member of the Military Soviet. He is a general too, and values that more than being a commissar. You're not going to get him to waste his time with this sort of nonsense. But we lesser mortals have to get on with it and work away on the quiet. Yes, our Supreme Commander has made life difficult for us, but he has not let us off doing our duty."

The sadness and concern in the Major's voice and his openness and also the burdensomeness of the task designated by none other than the Supreme Commander all came together to leave Sirotin feeling he did not have a leg to stand on.

"Yes but, phoning through, you know... The signaller's line is nearly always busy, and when it is free he's not just going to let you use it. And you have to tell him where you are phoning to, and before you know it, it will get back to Fotii Ivanovich. No, it's..."

"What do you mean, 'No'?" Major Svetlookov thrust his face towards him, instantly amused at such naivety on Sirotin's part. "What a funny fellow you are! Are you really going to go and say, 'Please put me through to Major Svetlookov in Smersh?' That really would land us in the soup. The simplest way is to play the lovesick soldier phoning his lady. That line works every time. Do you know Kalmykova in the military police? The senior typist?"

Sirotin had a vague recollection of a bosomy, flabby and, in his twenty-six-year-old eyes, ancient old bag with an unrelentingly bossy expression and thin, pursed lips yelling authoritatively at the two girls junior to her.

"What, not your type?" The Major smiled, a blush rapidly suffusing his cheeks. "She has her admirers, you know. They even say she's dynamite in the sack. Let's face it, love is blind. In any case we are not running a convent. When we do move into Europe, this year or next, they have monasteries there specially for women. More precisely, for virgins, being as how these lady monks, 'Carmelites' they are called, give a vow to stay virgins till the day they die. Think of the sacrifice! So their purity is guaranteed. Choose whichever one you fancy, you can't go wrong."

The austere Carmelites somehow got associated in Sirotin's mind with caramels, and seemed very enticing and sexy indeed. For all that he just couldn't see himself making a pass at Flabby Breasts, or even chatting her up over the telephone.

"*Sehr gut*," the Major conceded. "Let's think of an alternative. How do you fancy Zoechka? Not that one that works for the MPs, the one who's a telephone operator at headquarters. With the curls."

Now those ash-blond curls spiralling down from her forage cap on to the curve of her little porcelain forehead, the surprised look in her little eyes which yet sparkled so brightly, the neatly taken in tunic with a single button undone (never two, which might have got her into trouble), the little custom-made chamois boots, and the slender manicured fingers, that was all much closer to his heart.

"Zoechka," Sirotin repeated dubiously. "I thought she was going with that bloke from the operations section, practically married to him."

"That 'practically' has just one secret obstacle, a lawful wedded wife in Barnaul who is already bombarding the political section with letters. And two dearly beloved offspring. We shall have to do something about that. So... You wouldn't turn up your nose at Zoechka? I suggest you get stuck in straight away. Roll along to see her, start building bridges – and then phone from wherever you can. You think the signaller isn't going to connect you, the driver of the Commander-in-Chief? All right. You just don't need to be a shrinking violet, remember your status in the army. Just give Zoechka the old 'How I miss you, long to kiss you' routine, and then drop in in passing something along the lines of, 'I've got to go now, sweetheart. Ring you again within the hour from Ivanovo.' There's a lot of loose talk goes through signals, one more slip won't make any difference. But we can even get round that, we'll work out a code later, a password for each position. Anything you don't understand?"

"No, but somehow..."

"What do you mean, 'No but somehow...' Eh?" The Major was suddenly irate. Somehow it did not seem in the least surprising to Sirotin that the Major already had the right to get angry with him for being slow and tear him off a strip. "Do you think I'm doing all this for my own benefit? I'm doing it to safeguard the life of the Commander-in-Chief of the Soviet Army! And yours, incidentally, also. Or are you seeking death too?"

He heatedly slashed at his boot with a stick which whistled as he brought it down. God knows where that had come from. The sound it made was nothing, but for some reason Sirotin cringed inwardly and got a sinking feeling in his belly, the same dismal, anguished feeling produced by the whistling of a shell after it has left the barrel of an artillery piece and splashes down into marshy ground. The sounds are all the more significant and terrifying precisely because the roar of splintering steel and the splash as a fountain of brackish water rises in the air and the rending of branches severed by shrapnel are by now no longer any threat to you. You have been missed again. This meticulous, limpet-like Major Svetlookov who could see everything, had recognized what was bugging Sirotin and making his life a misery, but he had also intuited something more important, and that was that there really was something up with the General too, something dangerous and leading ineluctably to his destruction and the destruction of those around him. When he had stood up full height during the river crossing in his conspicuous leather coat so picturesquely exposing himself to the bullets coming from the right bank and from the swooping Fokker aircraft, it was not bravado or 'setting a personal example of bravery,' but that same mysterious thing which Sirotin was sure he had seen from time to time afflicting certain other men: he was seeking death. Sirotin wanted only in every way possible to help this concerned, omnipotent Major, to give him as much detail as he could about the oddities of the General's behaviour in order that he should be able to build them in to whatever calculations these were that he was working on.

Published in Russian in *Znamya*, Nos. 4 and 5, 1994.

A General and His Army

Georgy Vladimov is already well known in the West for his novel **Faithful Ruslan**, published by Harvill in 1979. His **Three Minutes of Silence** (1969) was published in **Novy Mir** and greeted with a barrage of official criticism. In 1977 Vladimov resigned from the Writers' Union and assumed the leadership of the Moscow chapter of Amnesty International. He was forced to emigrate to the West in 1983, and edited the emigre journal Grani from 1984-6. He lives in **Germany**.

Vladimov began writing **A General and His Army** after ghost writing the memoirs of leading Soviet generals about the conduct of the Second World War. The KGB soon took an interest, and his manuscripts were confiscated. Persistent rumours were spread that he was writing a novel which would attempt to rehabilitate General Vlasov, commander of the Russian Liberation Army which fought on the German side against Stalin. In fact, he describes the main concern of his novel as being the phenomenon of large numbers of Russians, variously estimated at between 400,000 and two million, taking up arms against their own country.

Vladimov is a skilled writer in the style of classical Russian realism, and Tolstoy influences the characters directly and indirectly, from Major Donskoy, General Kobrisov's adjutant, who tries unsuccessfully to model himself on Prince Andrey Bolkonsky, to the German tank commander Heinz Guderian, his headquarters based at Tolstoy's estate of Yasnaya Polyana, who reads and re-reads **War and Peace,** trying to fathom the mentality of his Russian foe.

A major theme of the novel is the relationship between the mentality of rebellious Russians and the despotism of Stalin and his secret police in the context of war. Khrushchev is present as a prominent Party representative on the Ukrainian front, and Brezhnev figures as a character so insignificant that no one can remember his name.

The novel is densely written, with constant allusion to events past and future, and a completely original perspective on the Russian conduct of the Second World War as an ambiguous history of criminal brutality, incompetence, and heroism. At the same time, Vladimov concedes great shrewdness to Stalin in his understanding of the people over whom he ruled.

The novel is framed by the fictitious General Kobrisov's never accomplished return to GHQ in Moscow after his recall from the Ukrainian front. Travelling with him in his jeep are his driver Sirotin, his batman Shesterikov, and his aide Donskoy. All the three of them have been questioned by Major Svetlookov of Smersh (the Army's secret police) and made to inform on their boss. The naive driver Sirotin is a reluctant but ultimately an easy prey. The batman Shesterikov, who once saved Kobrisov's life, gives nothing away but fails to warn his boss of the fact of his having been approached. The ineffectual Major Donskoy finds Tolstoyan morality no defence against the plebeian brutality of Smersh.

181

There is a flashback to the day when Kobrisov accidentally blunders into a village occupied by the Germans, gets himself shot in the stomach, and is dragged to safety by Shesterikov. Shesterikov then has to find a way of getting the wounded general to hospital in Moscow, along a road flooded with demoralised Russian deserters who are heading into town ahead of the (in fact no less demoralised) Germans. His contact with Vlasov comes when the latter hijacks fresh Siberian troops intended to reinforce his own army, and drives the Germans back with them, breaking the encirclement of Moscow. Vlasov's disciplined troops enable the wounded general to be put on a sleigh back to the capital.

This same day Heinz Guderian, commander of the tank army moving on Moscow from the south, finds himself humiliatingly stranded when his tank falls into a shallow ravine. Hitler's decision to divert the Blitzkrieg towards Kiev (captured) and Leningrad (unsuccessfully besieged), delays the advance on Moscow until the cold of winter wreaks havoc on the ill-equipped and supplied German troops. Finally returning to his headquarters at Tolstoy's estate, Guderian writes out the order for his troops to retreat from Moscow for the winter.

The next flashback is to the autumn of 1943 when Kobrisov, who has now formed the 38th Army, has established a bridgehead on the right bank of the River Dnieper in the Ukraine. He finds himself outmanoeuvred at a war council chaired by Marshal Zhukov, where it is decided that a Ukrainian general should liberate the first major Ukrainian city to be recaptured, Predslavl. Unlike Zhukov or his fellow generals he has an acute awareness of the value of human lives and cannot reconcile himself to the "four-layer theory" of Russian warfare, whereby three armies pave the way for a fourth to advance over their corpses. (Zhukov was to sacrifice 300,000 Russian lives in the attempt to get to Berlin by May Day 1945 and without the aid of Eisenhower.)

In order to delay Kobrisov's advance on Predslavl he is instructed to encircle and capture Myriatin, a town he has been leaving alone because he knows most of its defenders to be Russians fighting against Stalin. He fails to present a plan of campaign to his superior and is sent back to Moscow to "recuperate". Just as he reaches the capital the radio broadcasts news of the fall of Myriatin to the 38th Army and of the decoration of Kobrisov and his promotion to Lieutenant-General. He gets very drunk as he looks down on Moscow, recalls how, just before the outbreak of war he was arrested by the GPU on a charge of attempting to assassinate Stalin (two of his tanks had broken down in front of Lenin's Tomb during the Revolution parade), but was saved by the outbreak of war. He imagines the mass executions which Smersh will now be instigating in Myriatin. The mistake in decorating him as commander of the 38th Army (or has Stalin deliberately disregarded the decision to send him away?) allows him now to turn away from Moscow and return to the front to fight on.

OLEG PAVLOV
An Official Tale

Translated by Alla Zbinovsky

"Potatoes"
(excerpted from Chapter Two)

...On the first day the potatoes were trucked into Karabas, Captain Khabarov kept his men back. He prattled on and on at the hungry unfortunates about the necessity of sorting through the potatoes to discard the rotten ones and see how much can be allotted for each ration. While sorting, the soldiers furtively devoured the raw potatoes – they had arrived from headquarters slightly frozen, which made them crumbly and sweet. The captain watched it all, but he didn't kick up a fuss. He decided that they would nibble on them a bit, and reckoning on tomorrow's rations, they wouldn't even bother hiding them in their shirts.

Khabarov was afraid to fall asleep that night and didn't undress at all, lying on top of the blanket on his bunk which was as narrow as a bench, as if waiting for a summons. Hungry mice roamed about the office trying to nibble at its primitive equipment. The hours ebbed by, and the captain felt weak in the predawn cold. For the remainder of the night he deliberated: the soldiery would refuse to dig the garden, and if the allotted rations were not handed out, then they might even burn down the barracks. The captain got up in the half-darkness and sat at the window. Under his gaze, the sky grew light and unveiled itself, and the boundless hills of the steppe began to appear in the dark mist.

His voice, filled with anguish and intoxication, rang out in the sleeping barracks. The captain raised a battle alarm, armed his men with sapper shovels and drove them out of the dead light of the barracks courtyard into the steppe. Gasping for breath, the soldiers whispered to one another: "Where's he driving us to? That drunkard, what's gotten into him?" And the captain began gesticulating, as if he were commanding a battlefield. Looking around with confusion as if to ask "what're we diggin'?" the soldiery attacked the empty earth stretched out before them, entrenching themselves, following Khabarov's orders.

The captain weaved along the swarming lines as if he were drunk, brandishing his pistol if the digging ceased without his permission, rousing them to action: "The more you lean on those shovels, boys, the sooner you'll get your cigarette break!"

There was more and more dug-up land. He measured it with unbending strides, and when he had no strength left, he ordered everyone to line up on the edge of the field.

Sacks were dragged out before the motionless ranks, and then came the cries: "Hey guys, look, they're going to bury our food rations!" "So he's not drunk, he's stone cold sober, the fool, he's playing with us, he's trying to trick us!"

Khabarov nearly smothered their howls with a scream burning with desperation: "Silence! We're not burying our rations, we're planting our future in the earth. In half a year we'll be gulping down mashed potatoes by the bucketful, from one potato we'll get one bucket, or even more."

"Boys, we refuse! After all, these rations belong to us!"

Khabarov made another attempt to persuade them: "They'll grow by themselves, no more work is involved... I'm doing this for you! I want to secure our future..."

However, they had already surrounded him with their roar: "We refuse! Give us our grub, company commander!"

Then the captain poured out all the potatoes and began placing the spuds in the ground by himself. The soldiery didn't dare attack him, remembering he had a pistol. However, this formidable weapon didn't save the captain from an outpour of obscenities and lumps of dirt – which they threw at him, fearlessly. But he was glad! The ground was plowed, he wouldn't have been able to manage all this on his own. Cognizant of the fact that he had deceived them, he didn't bother shielding himself from the flying lumps. He quickly hid the potatoes in the rows and covered them with soil.

The mob dispersed... After spending the whole day working in the field by himself, Khabarov completed his task and thought wearily about his return to the barracks. However, all was quiet in the company, they were all in their positions. They avoided him or gloomily gave him a wide berth. Still, one of them laughed under his breath: "You could use a good sleep, old man, I dare say you look wiped out."

The captain woke up late in the morning with the thought that his soldiers had completely forgiven him, since they had called reveille on their own. After washing up, he strode over to the canteen, and he even found soldiers inside. His belly was lashed by a strong fried smell emanating from the kitchen. "What's cookin'?" he wondered. A merry cook stuck himself out of a peeling little service window. His frying pans still sizzling, he grinned and yawned: "Potatoes, potatoes! Chow down, all you can!"

Beside himself, Khabarov ran to the field. His potatoes lay scattered like stones all around the courtyard. He dug into the dried out earth with his hands and found one potato, left there to rot, and then another one. That was why they hadn't started any disturbances! They took everything they thought belonged to them, while the commander lay collapsed in his bed. And now the captain crawled on the ground, saving what had been thrown away, what they hadn't carried off.

When he returned to the barracks, the first soldier he came across was lazily smoking a fat cigarette on the stoop. He almost choked on his own smoke, recognizing Captain Khabarov in this twisted, dirty person, dragging what looked like a sack stuffed full of stones along the ground.

Having eaten up the fried grub to their heart's content, the soldiers felt overwhelmed and slept sluggishly with a quiet midday sleep. They forgot all about him, and now he exclaimed in a tired, strange voice: "Get up! Where, where are the rest of the potatoes? You couldn't have stuffed them all down... Do you hear, I'm not going to let you sleep, you bastards, I won't allow this!"

The soldiers in the barracks began to wake up. "Get off your high horse, who the hell do you think you are." "Now really, guys, why's he on our case?" "Y'hear, Khabarov, we're in the right on this one, we're going to write to the procurator!" "Come on now, cap, frisk us – whatever you find is yours. Or get lost, don't ruin our party." "Now-now... And if you're going to wave your barrel, we'll do you in ourselves. Just try and touch us, everyone will sign, and you'll be sent away to the zone!"

"So, you want to see me dead?" sighed Khabarov. "Now you listen here: the potatoes must be returned, you must put them back in yourselves, with your own hands, every last one. If you refuse, then to hell with you, at the evening roll call I'll shoot myself in front of you all."

He fell silent and again sighed with disappointment, looking around at the now quiet men. He had spoken out irresponsibly, in a fit of temper. Realizing now with cold reason that he had condemned himself, Captain Khabarov softened, he felt as if all his bones were melting, and he dragged himself off to his little room in the office.

* * *

...Dying will be painful, thought Khabarov. It also occurred to him that he would have come to nothing; people had lived before him, storing up their lifeblood to pass it on to him and now he would sink it back into the black mire. He was such a mess, it really would be better if he just kicked the bucket.

Khabarov lay down on his bunk in a half-conscious state; in that same half-consciousness he imagined shooting himself thousands of times, but came to when he thought he heard a shot go off in the office. From the sound it could have been a blank. He was now wide awake, which made it even more painful to think about that promise, which had burst out of him in a fit of temper. Forcing himself to lie in the bunk, pretending to be asleep, it needed a power of self-deception to keep him in the office and not go out to face them.

It was getting dark in the yard and voices were becoming more muffled, as if melting into the quiet of the evening. Nature called the captain so intensely that he couldn't bear it. A small bucket stood in the office, a slop pail. He squeezed his eyes shut from shame and relieved himself in the pitch blackness. He shook all over, thinking they would hear him.

When they knocked on his door he gave no sign of life. They leaned heavily on the door posts, making them crack. "Comrade captain, comrade captain!" "Come on, it's a shame to break it, it's a good, solid door." "Who heard the shot?" "Kiryukha did. That wasn't smart: you can hang yourself without making any sound at all." "What have we done, what have we done? Who'll be held

An Official Tale

responsible?" "Comrade captain, speak to us, are you alive?!" And Khabarov uttered: "I am here." Joyous sounds from the other side of the door. "We've given you the potatoes back!" "What's that?" asked Khabarov in agitation. "Just like you said, right back into the earth. We, um... decided to make it up to you, meaning, we did wrong, and there's an end to it."

Pausing for breath, he opened the door to the envoys. They were taken aback and stared at his bare, bluish feet. "You see, I'm alive," he said. The soldiers held back, waiting. "We thought it would be best if, well, we kept some of the potatoes back, or should we plant those too?" The captain muttered: "It's up to you."

To prevent any more looting, the captain chained two large sheepdogs at the edges of the field, trusting to their ferocity and lusty barking. But in the morning, the sheepdogs were found with their skulls split open. The guilty soldiers were exposed by their dog bites, and Khabarov drove them out into the steppe, bidding them not to return. Staggering around, they froze to the bone and almost starved to death, but did all the same return, complaining about their injuries and demanding rations. They had nowhere else to go.

Closing ranks, the company promised Khabarov the looters would loot no more, but they self-seekingly negotiated to keep the potatoes procured in the night, as well as the defunct sheepdogs. Having secretly skinned them, they secretly roasted them. They could after all be regarded as army property no longer serviceable.

Many really did keep their word, they gave in and from then on even helped the captain look after the field. They surrounded it with barbed wire, which uselessly rusted everywhere in enormous rolls. And some others opposed to the good souls came to hate the field, inciting the rest to create disturbances. However, the potatoes quickly sprouted in the ground, that was why the number of doubters grew in the company; it was too bad about the rations, but it was a pity to destroy the sprouts, perhaps they should be left alone, come what may. And then the most rancorous, those who couldn't live on groats anymore, denounced the captain on paper.

They reported that the captain was a drunkard who railed against Soviet power. That he deliberately planted the reserve of vegetable rations with the intent of profiting from every potato with a whole bucket and letting the soldiers starve. And even though they, the soldiers, tried to stop the captain's rule and refused to participate in his schemes of personal aggrandizement, Khabarov began to threaten them with his own death and forced them to bury the potatoes, and surrounded the field with barbed wire that he had stolen from the state.

They sealed up the letter and addressed it to: "Central Asian Military District. Our Chief Procurator. To be delivered to him personally. Soldiers of the Sixth Division of the Karaganda Regiment."

Everyone in the company knew about the denunciation, but they soon forgot all about it. The letter was in the possession of the quartermaster, who kept forgetting to send it off. And then the letter was finally dispatched, in a very casual fashion, with a stranger, the first civvy to come along, leaving it a secret for the captain alone.

"Comrade Skripitsyn"
(excerpted from Chapter Three)

(They had an unusually good potato harvest, but then the army's secret police came to investigate. The investigator's name was Skripitsyn.)

...It was quiet behind the door of the company office, quieter than the sound of Skripitsyn's breathing. Having established that Captain Khabarov was indeed asleep, Skripitsyn woke him up with his loud and continuous knocking.

There was nothing strange about the fact that he was waking up a sleeping person with his banging, but it looked like Skripitsyn was trying to break into the office. Khabarov woke up quite frightened, which was why he opened the door in a great hurry and stood there half-naked in the cold, while Skripitsyn, standing at the threshold in his overcoat, didn't immediately enter.

Hesitating, as if taking aim, Skripitsyn leapt across the threshold and addressed the captain in the middle of the room: "It's cold in here, you should get a heater," he said. "You do live here, after all."

Attaching himself to the table, as if he had found a place that had been prepared for him alone, Skripitsyn began taking things out with great haste, as if they didn't belong to him; he set up his briefcase and was already unbuttoning his overcoat, even though he had been the one who pointed out how cold it was in the room. Not turning around, busy with his coat, he muttered: "I've come here concerning a certain matter, you should have been informed, properly notified, so I've arrived to deal with this matter, I'll be investigating..."

Through his half-awake state, Khabarov perceived the warrant officer to be squeaky clean, as befitting such an official, and the captain simply stood there, captivated by the weak, whining voice. But then he suddenly cried out, as if it just dawned on him: "So you've been sent by comrade general!" He closed the door, pulled on his boots and threw on his trousers and jacket, resembling a flat dried fish. "What a man, he kept his word, how wonderful!" The captain felt giddy, and shook all the pieces of his uniform with joyous excitement. When he glanced out of the window, he was blinded by the sight of something and took a step back: "What's this? They've sent a truck?! He promised me, he promised, he said: I'll send you everything you need, get ready for work!"

Completely overwhelmed by what he had just heard, Skripitsyn moved – he sat down in a chair and said, "So what about him, this general?"

"What a man, what a man! He inquired, and understood everything. He's far away, but he knows everything, it's as if he's here! Wonderful... Another might eat me alive, but this one believes, he even praises..." Khabarov kept crying out and running around the office, space became very tight.

Skripitsyn grew into his chair and stiffened. "You mean, he praised you?" he finally blurted out. The captain quieted down, he fiddled with the jacket in his uniform. "You think potatoes are stones that shouldn't be praised, if they happen to grow?"

"I'm hearing this all for the first time, this babble of yours," said Skripitsyn despairingly. "I myself serve as senior warrant officer and have never come across any generals wandering around detachments. The name is Skripitsyn, I'm from the special division, although you know all this already, comrade Khabarov."

The captain's spirits fell. He sat down on his bunk directly across from Skripitsyn, who glared at him, his face wrinkled with a sour expression.

"If you're from the special division... But didn't the general send you?"

"That's enough, Khabarov, your choice of tactics, it's all very telling. It means that you've got a guilty conscience."

"I don't really understand what you're all about, what kind of tricks you're up to in the special division. What is your purpose in coming here?" asked Khabarov.

"I thought I would notify you, so that you could collect your thoughts, that is to say, comprehend what's happening. I thought we could settle everything quickly. But now I see you've decided to turn all this to your advantage. So, let's begin from scratch. It's all right here, if that's the way you want it, citizen."

Skripitsyn reached for his briefcase, peered into it, and, shoving in his arm down to the elbow, dug around in the bottomless pit and picked out a cardboard folder from those files, whose "cases" were active. However, this folder turned out to be a thin one, almost empty from inactivity. Four pieces of paper were resting in the cardboard folder, they had the look of grimy underwear. Unclasping the pages and sternly handing them over to the captain, Skripitsyn left the folder totally bare.

"What's this about?"

"Read it, then you'll find out."

"Better say it to me, I know it all anyway..."

"What's this – you've forgotten how to read?" the other one smirked.

"You keep on laughing," muttered the captain and grievously took all the papers at once.

Khabarov wasn't accustomed to reading to himself, it was difficult for him to understand what was written about him, it felt like he was searching for something in the darkness. That was why he began to read the papers out loud, in front of Skripitsyn, without ceremony, which took Skripitsyn totally off guard, and by the end he was torn up inside, upon suddenly realizing what denunciations sound like.

Skripitsyn was drained, it seemed to him that the reading conducted by the captain was intended for the sole purpose of humiliating him. However, the captain read just for himself, gloomily, forgetting about the presence of the interrogator. He tripped up in places and read them all over again, and then he would exclaim with incredulity: "What bastards!"

Skripitsyn sat waiting, as if he were just a messenger in this affair, and turned pale when he heard the swearing. He was forced to listen aquiescently to the captain's effusive speech, such a clear, loud, speech, and to observe with a degree of confusion that this captain was not the least bit afraid of the written word, he even interjected his own opinion as he read the papers slowly and deliberately.

When he finished reading, Khabarov silently spread the papers out on the table, and, seeing that the interrogator didn't understand a thing, he explained: "Sinebryukhov, the prison camp commander, wrote this one. This one was written by somebody who serve in my company. I don't know who wrote this one... Many soldiers ran away from me to Dolinka. Some ran away in summer, and others, maybe in the spring, from hunger."

(The entire potato harvest is then confiscated. Khabarov is arrested after failing to convince Skripitsyn that his initiative was inspired by his desire to feed the ever hungry soldiers. Skripitsyn drives away with the potatoes, but instead of taking them to headquarters, he suddenly comes up with another plan.)

...The truck lurched and spun its wheels. "What, are you really stuck in there?" asked Skripitsyn.

"We'll manage, we'll get out of here..." said the truck driver.

"We're not going anywhere, get out of the truck," Skripitsyn said tersely, obviously knowing what he was doing. "You'll throw the potatoes out of the back of the truck, drown them in this puddle."

"What for? What about the order, you yourself said there was an order the potatoes be brought to headquarters."

"I am now my own boss. What do you really know about me, you idiot?... It's me, I'm in charge of everything here."

"I'm afraid of you, comrade warrant officer. First you say, take the potatoes, that was an order, and for that we almost got killed. Then you say, when we've just driven off, there is no order, you say throw them away, and we almost crash. Perhaps I am also a human being. Why are you doing this? Maybe you've had a concussion, maybe you should go to the infirmary..."

And then Skripitsyn blurted out, his patience wearing thin: "You are alive now, only because I once saved you. Or have you forgotten? I saved your life, I didn't balk, now don't you balk at my words. What I say, you must do, just as I say, I am your commander." And then the driver, Sanka, wordlessly crawled into the back of the truck, remembering anew who had saved him.

Skripitsyn crawled out after him and stood to the side, rooted to the ground on a piece of empty steppe. He stood with his head uncovered, his hair moving with the wind, hiding his hand in the breast pocket of his overcoat. As if shell-shocked, he looked with detachment at the dirt on which the potatoes were being poured. It seemed as if the potatoes were alive. It sounded like they were wheezing inside the sacks before the hardy Sanka emptied them off the side of the truck. They rumbled like hail as they fell, grumbling from out of the dirt. And then they grew into a hill. "That's it, they'll all rot now," Skripitsyn mumbled to himself. Sanka continued to empty the sacks and was silent to the very end.

When it was all over, the truck started and drove away, but instead of dashing forward angrily, it lumbered backwards heavily onto the potato heap, leveling it, and then crushed it with its wheels, until the potatoes were ground into a pulp that resembled raw porridge. It was only then that the truck tore off in a fit of fury...

Published in Russian in *Novy Mir* No.7, 1994

Oleg Pavlov (born 1970) started writing at the age of seven, so there is no wonder that already at the age of 25 he became a strong contender for the Booker Russian Novel Prize in the short list of three. His densely written and very poetic novel draws on his own nightmarish experiences as a guard at a prison camp in Kazakhstan where he did his army service.

Pavlov had his fill of torture and humiliation in the army which he portrays as a contemporary variant of gulag. He refused to cooperate with the authorities and report on his comrades but was compromised anyway. After a particularly cruel beating he faked a suicide to get away from the barracks. He was locked up in a psychiatric hospital for a while where he was so doped up with drugs that he temporarily lost the power of speech. Back in Moscow he could not find a job and had to make a living, like many Russian writers, working first as a night watchman and then as security guard while writing intensely in his free time.

He names Platonov and Solzhenitsyn as his sources of inspiration showing that little has changed in the labour camps since **The Gulag Archipelago**.

Pavlov portrays the very thick of the people's life and uses "the common parlance with a uniformity that envelops the reader in a highly charged atmosphere." (**The Moscow Times**)

EVGENY FYODOROV
The Odyssey
(excerpt)

Translated by Arch Tait

...Nervy Zhenya religiously stripped the bark from the railroad ties. The quota was thirty, but try as he might his poor strength was barely stretching to six. By the end of the third week he was just about managing unlucky thirteen, indifferently finished, although it had seemed that he would never make even ten. After that for some reason his daily output slumped, the graph plunged ignominiously. It was no laughing matter. The skies fell in on him, he developed a vacant look, bludgeoned into listlessness by nightmare reality. Perhaps he might have made it up, might have managed the quota, perhaps he could have focussed his efforts, got into the swing of it if it had not been for the dogs making life a misery: the baying, biting dogs, worrying him, not letting him pass unmolested, dogs the meek youth had to work next to every day. It would begin as they were assembling for the march to work, the hounds leaping all around him, as they had, as they would, furious, violent, irrepressible, giving him no chance of coming to his senses. A wild skirmishing mass of muzzles and snouts, a legion of yapping frenzied hellhounds.

"He'll have to forget college till he's done his time here."

"To Moscow, to Moscow, to college!" A leer.

"It's six feet under for him, not Moscow!"

"Forget seeing momsy again!"

"Pick up a tag on your toe with your number." The voice triumphant, exulting.

"One more week and he's a goner."

"He's all tinkly and crinkly: you can see right through him!"

"Like crystal!" Laughter. Hearty, healthy pleasure. (No doubting their health.)

"He won't hang around, he'll kick the bucket."

"Fucking pansy."

"You watch, he'll pull a fast one and leave his sentence for the boss to finish."

"Oy, you! Pea-brained dummy! Wake up, you're asleep on your feet."

"Chemist, don't give us that shit!"

"Sly-ass."

"You're putting it on, dogturd."

"Wake up, Egypt's night!"

"What a faker."

"He's studying life in a cool climate."

"Oy, you, tight-ass. I'm talking to you."

"Here, know-all, what's a PDC?" They check out his knowledge of the labour camp catechism.

Timid Zhenya answers uncertainly,

"Preliminary detention cell."

Viciously, flakily, vilely, but as if defending a higher moral justice and truth, and pursuant to the demands of the rhyme:

"... Answer me back and I'll give you hell."

A quick slap, slap, slap in the face, before they go to work on him with a will: a living, unresponsive punchbag. The rhyme and metre call for action to complete the poem:

"Piss on him. He's off the wall."

These dogs leaping around him are young, little older than our absurd protagonist: twenty-three, maybe twenty-five. They are strong as oxen, and derided, rejected Zhenya wilts, crushed, more dead than alive, not one of the gang, a snotty student, an intellectual, a blue-blooded college boy, the white crow. He isn't meeting the quota but he's not being punished, he's living off them, sucking their blood, he's a lousy parasite.

"He's dreaming dreams of Moscow."

"Got a mother, have you?"

"Bet she's missing you."

"Momsy's too, too far away."

"Get her to send you your lunchbox, kiddy: some nice bacon fat to keep out the cold."

"The old girl's on a loser waiting for you to come home."

"You'll get used to it, you're young."

"The first ten years are the worst: you get used to it after that."

A burst of shared healthy laughter, young stallions whinnying, braying at him. Gusts of laughter, hostile laughter.

"Hey, Chemist, are you signing your horns in, then?"

He hasn't a clue what they mean. What a moron. More hoots of laughter. Inventively and with gypsy-like stealth they have crowned him unnoticed with a pair of horns instantly fashioned out of wire, and the pathetic, bungling, dismal little weed is so dumb and switched off, so conditioned by life outside the camps to cloddishness and non-survival that he doesn't pick up on this one either, isn't even aware of his crown of horns. Why are they all pissing themselves, why are they all roaring with laughter at him?

He suffered, he sickened, his spirit grew dim. His sunny, angelic soul, open to the world, hungry for love and understanding, had the props kicked from under it by the unrelenting malevolence surrounding him. He became ever more persuaded that he was nothing, useless chaff, something warped and twisted and rotten, a disgrace to the human race because he was not adapted to the vigorous, healthy struggle for existence and survival, because he was destined for elimination through natural selection. He had had an infinitely easier time of it in the investigator's office than here among his fellow-convicts, these unknown warriors of valiant, victorious armies which had cast down Hitler. He had been a student, a sluggard not working for victory but reading books: they had every reason to hate and despise him, to deride him imaginatively and with such sadistic ingenuity. It was Nietzsche's "bilious envy". What a relief to know that someone else is having a worse time of it than you, to see them going down for the last time. "Push the man who is falling": such is after all the philosophy of all living beings. It is in the blood, writ large in the damnable laws of evolution, in the whole idiot Darwinian nightmare, in the aeon-long struggle for survival, in the sickeningly infinite proliferation of living cells. The camps' first commandment is truly, "You die today: I'll leave it till tomorrow." Don't be the last in line, the one who gets it in the neck. The last but one maybe, just not the last. Only at the very beginning had Zhenya shuddered at the clear realization that he was not up to surviving the camp, and that as far as he was concerned Kargopollag was a death camp where he was being crushed and destroyed by the malice of his neighbour; a neighbour who was just as unfortunate as himself but who had the edge over him by not being a student and a Muscovite. His strength failed quickly. The less able he became to resist the environment, the faster his last pathetic powers dissipated. His inner caution disappeared, until he was psychologically ready for the end. He lived for the present like a bird of the air, feeling apathy and indifference to everything, like a stone, like a Buddha. Just last out until break time before you sigh. He stripped his rail tie. Time did not move. On the way back to the camp he just concentrated on not falling, not losing his balance. In the canteen the food was monotonous and meagre. After that his legs carried him back to the dormitory hut. He clambered up on to the top bunk: exhausted, he collapsed into a sobbing slumber of half-being. Until the detail or the brigade commander would tug his leg, communicating the message that it was time to work those muscles again, to put his back into it. He slept on his jacket, not having got round to filling the mattress with wood shavings. He hadn't the strength, and anyway, what did it matter? What did anything matter? His own belongings, what had survived from before his arrest and not been stolen on the journey by cattle-truck or at the quarantine station, he had sold off for peanuts, buying this and that in the camp store. There was little in the way of food. Some time in the past for no reason anyone could understand a huge quantity of absurdly fancy tinned crab from the Pacific seaboard had been brought in. Apart from that the shelves were empty. The crab was no use to anyone, barely nutritious, unsatisfying, it was a waste of time as far as the prisoners were concerned. Zhenya bought crab. His few roubles were soon at an end. What he did still have was his wretched raglan overcoat, which he had practically died defending at the quarantine station. He was hoarding it, reluctant to part with it, trying to kid himself that he was keeping it for a rainy day when no day could be rainier than the present. The only way things could get worse was if Lady Death came to get him (and she was soon to appear, dressed in white). Zhenya's rags were seeing out their second sentence: the old camp overalls and padded jacket looked as though they were on their third sentence and fit only for throwing out, and his shoes were little better. He was kitted out the same as the rest of them, no different, inconspicuous, yet still his mimicry didn't save him. With a sensitivity worthy of a proletarian blood-hound they unerringly sniffed out the class provenance of this uncommunicative starveling: a useless, lousy intellectual, he was, a doomed scumbag, a viper, a fancy boy. There was nothing wrong with their class consciousness.

Morning. It is still black as night, the searchlights dazzling. Time for the roll call. They assemble lazily, sleepily, everyone mixed up together, nobody knowing Zhenya, everyone a stranger. From time to time he notices the heavy, dim, brooding looks coming his way. He is being sized up. They have sniffed him out, recognized a marked man, caught him out. They seem to slip the leash in their thirst to drink human blood and win out in the struggle for survival, to be part of evolutionary progress. They light up, they exult. In order not to be recognized on the hoof, to merge again with the background, he does not this time raise his eyes, looking fixedly at his feet. It doesn't work. "Bonjour. One's humble respects." The whole satanic crew pile into him right there by the gate out of the camp. There is no escape. They zealously pull him this way and that, unwearying. The same unrestrained and unrestrainable hail of articulate malice and viciousness rains down on him: into his ears, into his throat, up his nose. He is in big trouble.

"Hello there, Betty!"

"Oy, you, Lord Muck!"

"Wake up, dummy."

"Time to get your finger out."

"And stop riding someone else's prick to paradise."

"Horny little bugger, horny, horny..."

He finally dislodges the wretched horns with an absurd, pathetic gesture. A shriek of laughter, an idiotic, exultant, life-affirming squeal that might have come from a piglet. Dozens of sturdy, zinklined throats guffaw in unison. Zhenya looks at them with haunted, dry, shining eyes full of anguish. He listlessly throws the horns aside, an impertinence for which the penalty is severe. He reaps the whirlwind. Somebody takes a swing and belts him unhindered, very hard, very unexpectedly, very energetically. Zhenya crumples. He quickly gets to his feet, leaning to one side. He knows to get up quickly before they beat you to death just for the hell of it. They don't let the grass grow under their feet: once you are down they will vigorously delight in finishing you off like a poisonous reptile. Putting the boot in is best. There is no arguing with a good, painful kick, much more memorable than a punch from a massive fist, especially if it comes from a goal-scorer who gets a clear run up. Russians have a talent for football. He gets up again, limping, his knee smashed, his hand crushed. How is he going to strip ties with a split rake like that?

"Black his eyes, make him a clown!"

"Go on, give him it!"

He has deserved more, and they punch him professionally. He sees fireworks cascading out of his eyes. And again. He falls, somebody contributes another kick. There you have it: an encounter with the real Holy Russia and the mystical, eternal, immanent spontaneity of her people. Oh, Rus, the beloved to whom I am wedded for all time! The chief guard hurries up, drags Zhenya free from the frenzied horde, preventing them from restoring the world to harmony by expunging this freakish reject of nature. They come to their senses, and those who a moment ago were beating him with a will melt into the crowd of prisoners, running away like cowards.

It is not so far from the camp perimeter to the timber plant, but straggling along in procession, herded along with frequent halts ("Stand up straight!") to ensure that those at the end do not fall too far behind, they take the best part of an hour. Trimming the rail ties is a labour beyond his strength, despair deepens the weariness, he slogs away making a supreme effort with bruised, sick hands which feel as if they belong to someone else, trimming the damnable, massively heavy ties. Even so, he feels less bad while working than he did when they were lining up to leave, or than he does in the smoking break when the cook comes to dish out the watery soup. In the afternoon it's boiled barley, invariably. His fellow brigade-members crowd together so tightly there is no room to spit: vicious, ugly, degenerate faces, the rail tie brigade, unstable and simmering. As they march salutations fly his way, and again there forms that moral, militant, victorious united front: "Betty!" It begins all over again. The endless, ingenious torture, the same imaginative artistry. The weirdo, the outsider, a pariah for them to attack. He is not of this world. He feels a metaphysical, an ontological otherness; and solitude. How much can he take? One time perhaps, two maybe, but this daily via dolorosa, this daily bearing of his cross. A tortured, tormented God? Why? What is the point? Why should the truth be found in this?

The Odyssey

Over the ten-hour working day his back becomes strained, the hook-like hands become broken and numb and ache from the unaccustomed work to the point where the knuckles no longer bend. Barely able to drag his feet along, he stumbles to the canteen past the faded, forgettable, dull slogans which seem to complain at being walked past. "The Plan Is Law!" "Work Well, Rest Well!" "Fulfil the Five-year Plan in Four!" "Work Is a Matter of Honour, Glory, Valour and Heroism! Stalin" It is feeding time. The aluminium plates clatter, the noise is deafening. And so to his dormitory, number 23, not the one where the brigade of rail tie cutters sleep. He climbs up on to the hard planks and stretches himself out. His body becomes intelligent and serious; and in the morning his bread ration will be in front of his nose, invariable, sacred, awaiting him, urging him: "Eat me." He will hold on to the make-weight crust with a finger, and then eat listlessly.

Before a month had passed, our hopeless, luckless novice was in a pitiful state. He had become even thinner, succumbing to the human venom, he had lost his footing, the sun was veiled, and he heard a rushing in his ears. His pitiful soul had become dark and gloomy, had curdled like sour milk, lost its bearings, had faded, sickened and given up the will to live. He had not even the strength to report sick until his brigade leader chased him, the shadow of a man, off to the medical section, telling him firmly:

"Go for it. They should let you off."

Here was a real crowd, an endless line of human misery, crammed together, propping up the wall, practically dropping from exhaustion. Zhenya joined the misery for three hours or so before his turn came and he heard the summons, "Next!" The voice was that of Iskra, a medical orderly whom the prisoners considered knowledgeable, fair and compassionate, and who was generally respected. She asked Zhenya something, he got the answer wrong, telling her with a staggering lack of nous that he was collapsing from exhaustion, worn out, and simply had no strength left to work. His voice was colourless and pleading, and he gazed with anguish and expectation into eyes as blue as those of a two-week-old kitten. Iskra's eyes grew increasingly cold, increasingly cat-like, more and more irate and when in a black ecstasy of despair (they had pissed in his face) he fell to his knees and cried out with unbelievable folly that he, like she, was in under

199

article 58, sections 10 and 11 and that she should help a brother in misfortune, the compassionate orderly's eyes became merciless and she roared in an outraged womanly alto,

"You pig! Get out of here this instant!"

He was so light that when she grabbed him by the collar she easily lifted him like a cat, turned him round (he did not resist, made no protest), gave him a good kick, and our scapegrace flew from her presence like a sparrow. She valued her warm place working inside, and this ghostly maniac, this malingerer, dared to mention that they were bound with the same fascist rope, Article 58 of the Soviet Constitution, conspiracy. She threw him out fast without letting him near the doctor. So near, and yet so far.

A new day. Formidable snowdrifts reared up, the like of which he had seen only in early childhood. A blinding snowstorm. Winter had begun in earnest. They started calling the roll for the rail tie brigade. When Zhenya's turn came he responded as required with the thin, breaking voice that sounded as if belonged to a young cockerel: the Article under which he was sentenced, the sentence, when the sentence would end: "1957". Would he last that long? The camp was more than he could take.

The camp administration at this time was under the management of Lieutenant Koshelev, a man with the reputation of having a heart of stone who gave no quarter, a brutal, straight down the line fulfiller of the Plan. He was well regarded by his superiors as someone who got things done. Every morning come hell or high water Koshelev personally accomplished the important ritual of vigilantly inspecting each individual prisoner as they left the gates of the camp compound to head for their place of work. He checked to see they were properly clothed, and that his working men had not been robbed by their brigade leader or the guard in charge of their detail. It was obvious that if people were properly fed, shod and clothed, they would work efficiently and fulfil the Plan, ensuring the Soviet Union's advancement onwards and upwards. You could then demand high output levels from the mass of toilers, with their eternal tendency to backslide and and take things easy. Koshelev immediately spotted and pounced on the puny, pining figure of ground down Zhenya. What was this? A worker barely able to stand upright, a skeleton with legs like matchsticks. He was unusable, a clear loss-maker incapable of contributing adequately. With an irritated, masterfully confident wave of his hand he sent Zhenya back into the camp, and had him removed from the statistics of those charged with delivering the plan. He gave authoritative instructions to the medical mammoth, the outraged orderly of yesterday, and Iskra stretched out her neck in fright and inclined her head as if laying it on the block, firmly put in her place. In the end it was not the compassionate medic but the hard-driving efficient workhorse who came to Zhenya's aid, took him off work, sent him for a fitness examination, and from there straight to the clinic. The head of the medical section palpated our hero's pathetic buttocks, wasted by hunger and hopelessness, with a brisk, professional hand, encountered his sad, repulsive coccyx, and pulled back in disgust. The black coccyx could be seen through his skin. It was to such as Zhenya that Nietzsche bequeathed the maxim: "The weak and the failures are doomed. They should be helped to their doom."

It seemed odd that he should have been reduced to this spectral state after a single month in the camp. The first thought to occur to Koshelev was that he might be simulating. The big boss took an interest in our sickly martyr and called him in. It does no harm to check. You can't trust prisoners an inch. It's a fact of life.

"You aren't drinking vinegar, are you?"

He is only asking for the sake of form. Vinegar eats into the liver. He's doing his job. His experienced eye tells him straight away that there's no suggestion of malingering here. He has before him an overtired physical wreck incapable of work, with a black eye; a half-dead prisoner who would blow away in a stiff breeze. Not promising material for his labour camp.

"Sit down," he says coldly, drily. It is part of the ritual.

Zhenya sits down and places his scrawny hands on his bony, skeletal knees as he had been taught by the unforgettable pugnacious Kononov. The darkness thickens. He is going to be invited to collaborate with the security organs. It would give him a chance. He will pretend not to understand, then sluggishly, listlessly, refuse, and that will be the end of him. Let this cup pass from me.

"Are your morals troubling you?"

"I do not know," he replies with a weak, sluggish voice which seems to be coming out of his boots, every inch the dying swan.

"What article are you here under?"

As if he doesn't know! Keep your wits about you when being stalked by a lion. Zhenya tenses, puts out his prickles, hardens himself, blinking rapidly and listening even more intently. He stammers out the name of the article and falls silent. Silence is the best policy: give nothing away. He knows from bitter experience only to answer direct questions, not volunteer general opinions.

"How did you get landed with that?" the Commandant reproaches him in mock distress (with a fatherly intonation, as if to say, "We've seen it all before"). "Section 11 is bad news. We can't release you from constant supervision by the guards."

The Commandant patiently, dully, as if trying hard not to fall asleep (is he faking?) asks whether his mother or father are still alive. Are they helping him? On learning that our retarded shadow has not yet established contact with his home base (Do the letters get lost? They seem not to arrive. At least there is no response and he doesn't know what to think), the Commandant orders Zhenya to rattle off right here and now, in his office, a letter to his mother, and says he will send it himself through his own "channels". Zhenya is shitting himself, figuratively of course. Is it a trick, to let them get at his parents? He just scribbles a few spidery words to say he is alive and well and – adds their address. Love from. Is it a trick? Is it all bullshit? In spite of himself he harbours a faint hope that the Commandant will send the letter and that it will arrive. And so it turns out. Soon the greenhorn receives an answering letter from his mother, followed by a parcel, so the Commandant has done his bit. And he hasn't invited Zhenya to collaborate. It has all blown over, he has got off scot free.

A break. A breathing space, recuperating in the hospital.

A sleepy, lethargic fly, travelling the whole road in a state of uneasy drowsiness. Sleeping, sleeping, but sleeping not the light sleep of Zarathustra which revives body and spirit with cheerfulness and fresh new powers. He seems constantly to be on the verge of waking up and at that same instant to be diving down into an evil, turbid, snow-flecked coma which spreads through all his flickering consciousness. Sleep, they say, never killed anybody, sleep cures all ills, sleep is the healer. They can't be talking about this kind of fitful sleep. His legs are cold, and that is bad, very bad. He opens his eyes

The Odyssey

and sees a figure, indistinct, blurred, milky, ephemeral, illusory, improbable, lacking immanent, solid inner being, structure and substance. Substance. Spinoza's favourite term. And a good term it is too, very useful when you want to deliberate on the material oneness of the world. At times the figure disappears, as if dissolving in its surroundings, blurring. Zhenya knows perfectly well that there is nobody and nothing really down there at his feet, and that this is merely an absurd, empty trick played by his eyesight, a distortion of his faculty for perceiving the surrounding objective world produced by hunger, dystrophy, weariness and the camp. Zhenya inventively, quickwittedly, without warning jumps, turning his head and eyes sharply, violently to one side. The insubstantial, incorporeal figure with its barely discernible eye sockets and something resembling a greedy, gaping jaw, this denizen of a questionable unseen world, no less speedily whisks itself over in the direction of his eyes, losing its outline in the process, violating the optical illusion, and thereby confirming that it is totally without substantial being, identity or reality, that his night-time visitor is solely and exclusively a perceptual illusion, a functional error of the visual apparatus dependent on the direction in which he turns his gaze. And yet, while whisking off to wherever Zhenya turns his gaze, his visitor, unspeaking, embodying profound stillness and perfect calm, is not fully banished: it retains some measure of its milkiness, approximateness, and delusiveness. The weirdest and most unpleasant aspect is that, consisting of no more than subjective, illusory pseudo-being, having been trounced by intellect, it is not in the slightest effaced: it obstinately, ineluctably, capriciously, in defiance of the postulates of reason (this is a visual defect we are talking about, something generated by the eye), as if responding to natural necessity and conformability, perceptibly, wholly within the order of things and not at the caprice of the perceiver, slowly, lazily, just a little slyly and yet at the same time straightforwardly and guilelessly, demonstratively (he notes) condenses, approaches, and returns to its former position by his cold feet which become even more chilled, compromising, shaming reason which is ready to desert him, crushed by a torpid, inarticulate feeling and its own self-evident rule excluding the unnecessary hypothesis (ultimately it either does exist and is real and corporeal; or it does not, in which case it is mere appearance, illusion, a rushing in the ears, a false, empty fiction, a figment of the imagination). Look again, and his visitor has completely and in full measure regained its earlier, lost perceptibility, its specificity, its compromised reality, regaining thereby the strong and important predicate of being and other imperious, incontrovertible rights enjoyed by objects existing indisputably in the three-dimensional material world. Zhenya repeats his already well tried technique and with a physical movement of his eyes and head unceremoniously drives his voracious unbidden guest in white away from her favoured position where she has again been chilling his feet. Hopla! In *Materialism and Empiriocriticism* Lenin defines material as "objective reality present in perception". There was a time when our hero had boldly raised his banner against so primitive and unconstructive a definition. Investigator Kononov tried to nail him with having criticized Lenin. Zhenya denied it. The case against them had largely been plucked out of the air, and Zhenya decided on a policy of outright denial. He even denied having run in the same relay race team as Kuzma. It had never happened! In fact, however, the information delivered to the MGB by their informer Marat was as accurate as a facsimile copy. "Objective reality"? "Present in perception"? Then if you gave a rock a good, swinging kick, the pain in your foot would prove the existence of the rock. What's wrong with that? At first sight it might seem convincing enough, but if you think again, alas and alack! Not only does the pain in your foot not in the slightest prove the existence of the rock, in philosophical terms it does not even prove the existence of your foot. An amputated leg can feel pain, and how! Darkness and confusion! The foot can hurt all right, while all the time the thing which is aching simply is not there, it has been amputated, there is nothing there for you to stroke or scratch. Again the insinuating foe of reason returns to her station at his feet, radiating coldness, moving now quite purposefully so that all attempts to shake her off are foredoomed to failure. The prudent youth firmly tucks his feet under himself just to be on the safe side and in order at least to be saved the irksome, aching, oppressive, murderous cold. It is always best to take countermeasures if you don't want to find yourself forced into checkmate. Atheists christen children just on the off chance. God takes care of those that take care, said the nun, slipping a condom over her candle. Zhenya listens intently to the weak, even beating of his heart. It runs like a well-tuned motor, like a clock. Diastole-systole, then again diastole. But what if it stops? Suddenly, forever?

"Why do hearts stop?" he asked the old man with the ascetic face on the next bed (like a child always wanting to know the reason why).

"Nobody even knows why they beat," came the unexpected reply.

"What about doctors?"

"Doctors don't know anything."

"The ones in here?" Zhenya got drawn into the conversation.

"No, not just them."

After a moment's silence Zhenya blurted out in a frenzy, "I am not afraid of death."

"The soul fears death," his neighbour cautiously contradicted him. "In *Phaedo* Plato tells us that philosophy is none other than preparation for death. Our homeland is there from whence we came, and there too is our Father."

"I am not afraid!" Zhenya exclaimed with naked exaltation, lit up by the closeness of Death and her apparition. "There she is. By my feet."

His neighbour recoiled inwardly from the dying boy, glancing in alarm at the spot the crazed, dry, sparkling eyes of the waxen, angelic youth with his pointed nose eloquently indicated. He was chilled by the obscure, mediumistic message. He felt his flesh creep, but saw nothing, an absence of any presence. Perhaps the soul of this unhappy boy on the verge of passing over into the other world had received the gift of seeing what was by its very nature unseeable.

Published in Russian in *Novy Mir* literary journal No 5, 1994

Evgeny Fyodorov, in his early seventies, an art critic by training, was arrested in 1949 and spent six years in Stalinist prison camps for anti-Soviet agitation and subversive group activities, which in actual fact was simply a study group of young intellectuals meeting every Saturday to discuss art, philosophy and upolitics. One of the members turned out to be an informer and when the group was arrested he also went to prison with the rest to continue informing on his friends.

Young Fyodorov started writing early and had been taking notes for his future novel. Those notes contained a wealth of compromising information on himself and his friends and were virtually a self-denunciation. But luckily the investigator did not bother to read either the notes or his literary works and simply burnt the lot.

Fyodorov has several stories, plays, and novels to his credit written in the manner described as "modern baroque". Despite his dense, sophisticated style the writer insists that content is more important to him than expressive means. He admits the influence of Proust, Rabelais and Sterne, and claims that his main theme is not the gulag but the life of ideas which he was able to investigate in all their stark reality in the camps.

Sergei Potapov

STANISLAV RASSADIN
Chairman of the 1995 Booker Russian Novel Prize Jury

A Subjective Substantiation of a Subjective Choice

"The audience gasped..." wrote the newspaper **Evening Moscow**, describing the reaction of those present when the decision of the Russian Booker jury was announced: the short list consisted of only three novels instead of six. The audience were evidently not aware that six was, in fact, a maximum but not the only number possible, while the minimum was three. The audience did indeed gasp, before starting to conjecture as to why the jury had acted as it had. One critic, known as an intelligent person, wrote that the Booker Prize was now old hat, so the jury had decided to stir things up a bit by taking this extravagant decision. He was forgetting that the jury changes each year, that they are not part of the Booker Committee, and are therefore less worried about the future of the Booker Prize in Russia than about their own professional reputations.

Certainly this jury had no wish to detract from the prestige of the Booker Prize, but our main concern was for literary fairness.

It was quite simple. We certainly did have the ambition of establishing a higher standard for the Booker competition, but that was a secondary consideration; our primary reason for making the short list quite so short was not a lack of novels to choose from but, on the contrary, an overabundance. Let me explain.

If the founders of the Russian Booker Prize are so far from a sense of reality (which is arguably the same thing as a sense of humour) as to wish to play the role of a demiurge in the Russian literary process, they may be under the impression that they actually have fired up novel writing in Russia. The current tendency is to call any piece of writing a novel, be it an essay or memoirs or even poetry; and who knows but that the sole reason for this is a desire to be included in the long list of Booker nominations. This is what you suspect when reading in an interview an apparently casual mention that such and such a work has been nominated for the prestigious Booker Prize. In our day and age when culture has been humiliated and insulted it is only natural that authors should crave any form of recognition, and nominators too are only human. But ask yourselves whether more than forty novels worthy of the Prize, or even of critical attention, can really appear in just one year.

I am happy to hide behind somebody else's criticism of the imperfections of the long list (imperfections which are only to be expected): "Frankly it should be obvious to any reader that Petrushevskaya's vers libre exercises (however musical and talented some people may think them) simply are not prose narrative, and that Nina Sadur's **The Garden** and **Diamond Valley** belong in the same amorphous lyrical department; while Igor Klekh's travel notes and the masochistic memoirs of Mikhail Veller belong to genres all their own. It surely hardly needs to be explained that chapters from a novel do not constitute a fully fledged novel, even if **The Day of the Beast** does belong to the pen of Victor Sosnora (who, incidentally, wrote it quite some time ago). And so on..." (Andrei Nemzer, **Segodnya** Daily)

I hesitate to add to the above list works that should never have been nominated in the first place because of their hopelessly low literary quality. My sympathies are not with those who are proud to have been nominated but with those who are disappointed, who exclaim after the event: how could such and such have been omitted, why were Astafyev or Slapovsky not shortlisted? And, of course, why is Sorokin not there? The present author would be the last person to dispute anyone's right to be disappointed and to disagree with the short list. For three years running I nominated authors who failed to win the Prize, among them Friedrich Gorenstein, Semyon Lipkin, and Yuri Davydov. To this day I remain unrepentantly convinced that theirs were the novels most worthy of the Prize.

Since these notes are purely subjective I can't help expressing my doubts about the value of literary prizes as such.

Indeed... It is not so much the prize itself as the expectation of it ("It could be me!") that is so humiliating for the artist, since art by its very nature resists competitive rating. I admit to not being very logical here, and yet I persist in my lack of logic (on the other hand, is it lack of logic on my part or the paradoxical nature of the whole business of the Prize?). I must confess, however, that when I read in Bunin's reminiscences how he was on tenterhooks awaiting the decision of the Nobel Committee, as if all the pride and independence had gone out of him, I am embarrassed. I don't want to see a man of genius in his underwear. I think it's improper. And I understand only too well the mechanism of self-assertion exemplified by a certain little-known writer (completely without talent, in my opinion) who accompanies each of his publications with a self-advertising note to the effect that he was once nominated for the Nobel Prize. Who could have nominated him and when? It brings to mind an episode in Graham Greene's **The Comedians** where an old American tries to intimidate some Haitian policemen by telling them he had run for the US Presidency, and only his wife knows that he had represented the Vegetarian Party and did not have a dog's chance.

Having said that I must admit that "Booker Passions" (the title of an article about the Prize) are running higher and higher, and not only in Russia where it is new and exotic, but in its home country as well. From

A Subjective Substantiation of a Subjective Choice

Sergei Reingold's article "That Strange Booker Prize", published in **Znamya**, I learnt that after 1980 the Booker Prize achieved the same heady status as horse racing (which is quite something in horse-loving Britain). 1980 was no random date: it was then that a battle of giants took place between Anthony Burgess and William Golding, which the latter won and, it is said, could not conceal his exultation.

I am sure it was not the money won by the author of **The Lord of the Flies**, who went on to win the Nobel Prize three years later, that made him so happy. Sir Michael Caine, the Chairman of the Administrative Committee of the Booker Prize, told me in private that when Golding was asked how he was going to spend the money — ten thousand pounds at the time — he said he was not sure yet, but perhaps he and his wife would build a third bathroom in their second house in Portugal.

I mention money, because to my genuine surprise I have observed that even in the conditions of Russia's very real poverty, Booker passions are not primarily inspired by money, a fact in which I take a patriotic pride. So when I am reproached for the present short list of only three names instead of six, with the implication that the cruel jury has deprived three worthy candidates of $1,000 to which, according to this year's rules, the shortlisted six are entitled, I sympathise with the disappointment. But a literary prize is not unemployment benefit. If we are serious about raising the literary level of Russian writing, let us keep our dignity. Let the prize be a boost to our ambitions and not a consolation piece of humanitarian aid.

The 1994 literary harvest is really rich, and precisely that is what motivated our unusual choice.

Seven further novels (seven!) were seriously considered for the short list. Each had at least two votes and if we had had a penchant for lobbying, or if we had been aiming to fill the quota of six places in the short list, there would have been no difficulty in securing a third vote for three more authors. Here is a list of possible candidates in alphabetical order: Ion Drutse, **The Sacrifice**; Yuri Maletsky, **Refuge**; Alexander Melikhov, **Eviction from Eden**; Vladimir Retsepter, **Turning to Casanova**; Felix Rosiner, **Achilles on the Run**; Mikhail Veller, **Sergei Dovlatov's Knife**; and last but not least, Vladimir Sorokin's **Norm**, which was the only work to cause a really long and moderately heated debate. Nothing really out of the ordinary happened (they say a chairman of the British Booker jury, a famous English poet, once threatened to throw himself out the window if his favourite failed to win and thus prevailed over his opponents). Our dispute hinged not on tactics and tastes but on strategy. The prevailing viewpoint was that the poetics of Norm is a blind alley, whatever definition you give to the novel (and whatever your attitude towards its subject of the public devouring of excrement), not so much in relation to present-day prose as to Sorokin's own career as a writer. Suffice it to compare **Norm** to **The Queue**

209

to see how a method once discovered has been put on the production line and has proliferated cliches.

The three shortlisted novels are the result of a consensus of opinion rather than disagreement. All five jury members, differing in tastes and certainly not in any way biased, wholeheartedly agreed to these three. What grounds had any of them to be prejudiced: the famous writer Fazil Iskander, the famous poet Natalia Gorbanevskaya, the brilliant Slavist Andrzej Dravic, the much-respected critic Alexander Chudakov?

Georgy Vladimov, Oleg Pavlov and Evgeny Fyodorov were agreed on unanimously. Some regretted that Drutse was not included, others wished Sorokin could have been there, but we all agreed that to extend the list would not be fair, not only in relation to the shortlisted authors, but (I anticipate an outburst of disagreement) in relation to those who were not shortlisted. After a great deal of discussion we agreed that there is a considerable distance between the three shortlisted novels on the one hand, and any of those that might have been numbers four, five or six. I am not saying that there is a gulf between them, but there is a clear difference. If we decided to choose three more names from the seven candidates we would create an even greater injustice: no matter who was included others, equally good, would be left out.

The jury decided that there was no solution to this problem if we were to keep our standards high — the only policy that is not insulting to a literature aspiring to a greater future.

There has been extensive press comment on Georgy Vladimov's **A General and His Army**, ranging from ecstatic praise proclaiming it a great novel to vilification from both aesthetic and ideological points of view. In other words, this novel has already stimulated an enviable degree of controversy which has yet to peak. According to critic Sergei Chuprinin, **A General and His Army** is distinctive for its "austere style verging on defiance". Austerity as defiance! The novel stands out not only against a general sloppiness posing as freedom of style and thought, but because it is genuinely new irrespective of who first broached this subject.

Here is how Andrei Platonov formulated the literary ideal many years ago: "Literature that makes minimal use of conventional forms, traditional styles, that reduces to a minimum the oppression of the grey mass of words, and the need to grope wildly among a plethora of details... Literature that acts directly, that is, expounds concisely and economically but with utmost seriousness, the crux of the matter the author wants to communicate to the reader." This is an ideal that cannot be attained completely (precisely because ideals are too ideal), a moving towards something which has no end, but it helps the mover to avoid becoming outdated. This is quite distinct from the desire to shock with novelty for its own sake, something which is always short-lived, which wins a tactical victory only in a tiny space and

A Subjective Substantiation of a Subjective Choice

whose criterion of novelty — nothing but the very latest — does not belong in the realm of the aesthetic.

This is why novelty for its own sake so soon becomes outdated. "A new poet. Try to remember his name, you may not hear it again," said Jules Renard.

Are the works of Vladimov, Pavlov and Fyodorov "realist"? I put the term in quotes not because for many people today "Realism" is synonymous with "old" and "outdated", but because this term has been very loosely defined of late and because it is, indeed, just as conventional as terms usually are, while the huge and powerful army of critics grouped (willingly or unwillingly as the case may be) under this banner are only capable of eroding its terminological boundaries to a complete muddle. So our heated debates with the proponents of novelty for its own sake and our attempts to reassure ourselves that realism has not yet exhausted its potential are pitiful and absurd. Realism cannot exhaust itself unless, of course, it is understood in a primitive way as a copying of the "surface reality of life", or dependance on it, rather than as responsibility towards life, history, and the future. It is precisely realism, interpreted in this way, that carries within it the possibility of endless renewal and variation, and a constant pushing back of its boundaries. But however its boundaries may be varied, they are still there, and they still preserve the outline of the real world as it is graspable by the artist. To put it in simpler terms, literature abhors lawlessness.

In this respect, the works by Evgeny Fyodorov and Oleg Pavlov are good examples. The latter is a newcomer in Russian literature (although **An Official Tale** has already secured him a niche of his own), and he is a good example of how the boundaries of realism can be extended. His work clearly shows the influence of Platonov and, in part, of Saltykov-Schedrin. But the young writer is by no means simply a brilliant student of Platonov, neither is he an irresponsible and profligate imitator (like many of the forty longlisted authors, who seem to be victims of the current epidemics of Nabokovism and Platonovism, except that they dilute the dense highly concentrated style of these two masterful writers to make it easily digestible by the public). In **An Official Tale** the vividly depicted army routine is not overburdened with naturalistic description, and preoccupation with detail has been elevated to the grotesque. I say "elevated" because this is indeed symbolism of a higher order, and creates genuine art rather than just a literary game.

As for Evgeny Fyodorov, the "strangeness" of his prose has repeatedly been given strange labels. His prison camp **Odyssey** has even been branded "post-modern baroque". I would wholeheartedly agree with classifying it as a post-modern work, but with the proviso that it is genuinely post-modern, without over-intellectual purposefulness or forced diligence in realising a previously devised pattern. Yes, it is strange, isn´t it, when first-hand experience in a prison camp is presented as life as such, thus raising existential questions about the roots of evil and man's resistance to it. Fyodorov is ideologically nearer to the merciless manner of Shalamov ("Prison camp experiences can only be negative") than to Solzhenitsyn ("Bless you, prison, for happening in my life"). Besides, Fyodorov has the courage, the strength and the inner freedom to come out of hell retaining his joie de vivre (which has nothing to do with fleeting jollity).

The three finalists are highly representative of the current state of Russian literature. They are not the only ones, naturally. The jury had reason to seriously consider ten works. But these three short-listed novels, precisely because of their small number, reflect very strikingly the variety of present-day writing. They happen to belong to three different generations. Vladimov belongs to the sixties generation (although a writer of such magnitude cannot be pinned down generationally), Fyodorov was shaped early in his life by the Stalinist gulag, and Pavlov is 25. But it is not the age factor so much as artistic orientation that underlies their unlikeness.

This year's Booker jury has been lucky to have works of high literary quality to judge. The authors of these works are less fortunate, because we are allowed to choose only one winner. In a poorer literary harvest, which there have been before and will be again, each of the other short-listed authors could have been an acclaimed winner.

3 December 1995

P.S. Today Georgy Vladimov was chosen as the 1995 winner.

4 December 1995

"LITTLE BOOKER"

In 1995, the "Little Booker" Prize, which is different each year, was awarded to the best literary journal published outside Russia, for their contribution to the promotion of Russian literature abroad. The prize was divided between the well-known journal RODNIK, based in Riga (Latvia), and the less well known journal IDIOT published in Vitebsk (Belorus). In the previous year, the "Little Booker" was awarded to the best provincial Russian literary journal, and was won by VOLGA (Saratov). In 1993, the Prize was awarded for the best collection of short stories and went to Victor Pelevin. And in the first year "Little Booker" was split between SOLO of Moscow and Vestnik Novoy Literatury of St Petersburg – two new journals of avant-garde literature.

Rumyantsev & Co. Publishers

There are not many publishing houses in Russia today that are catering to the intellectual reader and aim at educating the public rather than satisfying their lower instincts. Rumyantsev & Co. is one of these few, which is slowly but steadily growing in size and reputation.

The publishing plans of this post-perestroika private venture include translations from all the European languages of classical fiction and scholarly works as well as a series of contemporary Russian authors.

The latter includes **Nikolai Klimontovich's** *The Road to Rome* (see a chapter in English in **Glas 10**), **Nina Sadur's** *South* and *Orchard* (also see Sadur in **Glas 3 & 6**), and **Oleg Davydov's** *Cuckoo's Children* and *The Flight*.

Slavists will appreciate the new series of folk tales of the nationalities inhabiting the CIS, 11 books in all, including Russian, Mordovian, Ossetian, Avar, and Urals tales. Careful textological preparation of the tales, scholarly commentary, a vocabulary of dialectisms in each volume, and detailed introductions make this series a unique publication of equal interest to the specialist and the general reader.

Dmitry Donskoy
The Genealogy of the Rurik Dynasty. 9-15th cc.
700 pages, 2 hist. maps, 125 genealogical trees

Beginning with the 10th century all the ruling Russian princes invariably belonged to the Rurik family. Apart from being related among themselves some of the princes and princely clans were also related to the royal families in Europe, Byzantium, and elsewhere. This is why the study of the Rurik dynasty sheds new light on many events in Russian history, and reveals the hidden motivations behind the internal and foreign policies of the emerging Russian state, and later the Moscovian Russia of the late 14th and early 16th centuries.

The book traces the history of sixteen generations of the Rurik dynasty embaracing the time span from 862 to the middle of the 15th century.

Donskoy drew on numerous Russian and foreign sources (chronicles, annals, archaeological, iconographic, epigraphic and other materials). Commentaries include foreign texts with translations, excerpts from later chronicles and historical studies of 16-19th centuries, a complete bibliography on the subject.

The author was able to establish kinship ties and biographical landmarks relating to 1,043 princes and princesses of the Rurik dynasty, such as their birth dates, the year of mounting the throne, marriage dates and names of the marriage partners, the circumstances of death and a list of offspring. For the first time a complete list of canonised Ruriks is provided.

Address: 17 Goncharov St (korp 1), 127254 Moscow, Russia
Tel/fax: (095) 434 1141

Nina Iskrenko
The Right to Err

Selected Work
(with ten poems in original Russian text)
Translated by John High, Patrick Henry and Katya Olmstad
With an introduction by Andrew Wachtel
and afterword by Forrest Gander
Three Continents Press, Colorado Springs, Colorado, USA

"Nina Iskrenko died February 14, 1995, after a long battle with breast cancer. Perhaps some of her spirit lives on in these poems." — *John High*

Nina Iskrenko (1951-1995) is a major Russian poet, very unlike the world famous Akhmatova and Tsvetayeva, but just as powerful and innovative. She was the leader of the Poetry Club in Moscow and an active organiser of poetic readings and literary festivals. Her contribution as a poet and activist to the "new" Russian literature is enormous, and she is gratefully remembered by her friends and fans alike

Nina Iskrenko was widely published in Russia and translated abroad, and she was a contributing editor of the FIVE FINGERS REVIEW. See also translations of her poetry in GLAS 3.

---

* * *

The one & the same old age
hangs from a lamp shade
the one & the same old idiocy
grows on a bush

When the other man
sits there in the other armchair
& the other head folds inward
in this contemplation
of you

Five Fingers Review #14
"Metamorphosis"

Spiritual ennui & poverty
Manic confusion, misplaced aggression
Salamanders in power
Disturbing psychic visions or just plain obstinacy

Cold War writing.
　　Portrait of a psychopath's mother.
　　　　Native American poetry. New work from the UK.
　　　　　　Modern myths & glyphs.

Whatever your reasons for not yet ordering
Five Fingers Review, we understand.
But don't deprive yourself
any longer.

FIVE FINGERS REVIEW #14: METAMORPHOSIS.
With 224 pages of innovative fiction, poetry and essays.
Translations from the Russian,
experimental work from the American edge.

Perfect binding, glossy coated color cover, 6" x 9".
Digital recastings of 18th-century alchemical drawings.
ISSN 0898-0233 / ISBN 1-880627-03-5. Nine bucks.

Distributed by Bernhard DeBoer Inc., Bookpeople.
Fine Print. LS Distributors, and Small Press Distribution.
Individuals may order copies through:
Small Press Distribution 1814 San Pablo Avenue
Berkeley, CA 94702, USA

phone : (510) 549-3336
fax:　(510) 549-2201

Books from SABASHNIKOV PUBLISHERS
(all titles are hardback):

The *New Russian Writing* series

Alan Cherchesov. REQUIEM FOR THE LIVING
This novel by a gifted writer from Russia's North Ossetia region can be read in many ways - as philosophical parable, elaborate allegory, or compelling, lyrical narrative. 1995, 365 pp.

Petr Aleshkovsky. STARGOROD. VOICES FROM THE CHOIR
A series of short stories set in a small provincial town in post-perestroika Russia. 1995, 256 pp.

Forthcoming titles:

Nina Gorlanova. HIS STRONG AND BITTER MEAD
The novel deals with common people who can be happy with small joys, who love people and the world in spite of everything.

Petr Gladilin. THE HUNT AT THE ZOO
A parody of the crime novel genre which combines all the elements of a true thriller with a light, life-affirming style.

Valentin Berestov. SELECTED WORKS. In three volumes
A wide range of genres is offered - from hilarious prose to satirical epigrams, from serious philosophical essays to joking songs and verses.

Nina Artyukhova. SELECTED WORKS. In two volumes.
Fascinating stories, verses and riddles for children and adults. 1995-1996, 536+736 pp. Illustrated.

The *Records of the Past* series

MIKHAIL SABASHNIKOV'S NOTES
For the first time we publish the full text of the memoirs of the founder of Sabashnikov Publishers, a distinguished public figure of the late 19th and early 20th centuries. 1995, 588 pp. Illustrated.

Other titles available in 1996:

Yekaterina Andreyeva-Balmont. MEMOIRES
The wife of the famous Russian Silver Age poet Konstantin Balmont presents the poet's biography illustrated with photographs from the family archive, Balmont's letters and poems.

Boris Golubovski. THE GREAT SMALL THEATRES
A full documentary survey of the development of Russian theatre in the 1930s and 1940s. Illustrated.

Sabashnikov Publishers
38/1, Frunzenskaya Naberezhnaya
Moscow 119270 Russia Tel.: (7 - 095) 242 42 17. Fax: (7 - 095) 242 08 47

SERGEI POTAPOV
A Painter with a Cosmic Consciousness

"...IF THERE IS A CONTEMPORARY RUSSIAN ARTIST WHO DESERVES TO BE DISCOVERED AND APPRECIATED IT IS SERGEI POTAPOV. AT A TIME WHEN TOO MANY ARTWORKS ARE DISTINGUISHED ONLY BY GLIBLY CLEVER TWISTS ON BANAL CONCEPTS, HE OFFERS GENUINE ORIGINALITY, COMBINING THE TRADITIONAL QUALITIES OF ESTHETIC EXCELLENCE WITH A PROFOUNDLY MODERN – YET ALSO ETERNAL – SPIRITUAL VISION." – CATHY YOUNG, "METAPHYSICAL LANDSCAPES" IN THE WORLD & I, APRIL 1991 (USA).

Sergei Potapov (born 1947 in Riga) graduated from Moscow's best art school, the Stroganov, in 1970. But by that time he had already developed a highly individual style of his own which he called "Post-Symbolism", to distinguish it from Russian Symbolism of the early 20th century. "To me Post-Symbolism means a synthesis of everything that was developed by the Symbolists of the past as seen through the prism of our own century." He is interested in semantic aspects of symbols rather than their subjects or ritual significance. His images represent the various states of human consciousness and astral doubles of living persons.

In the 1970s Potapov began to paint on the reverse side of oilcloth because it did not need stretching and was always available. At that time he was interested in Eastern, particularly Buddhist art. His oilcloth paintings of that time resemble mandalas — symbolic images in the shape of a circle enclosing a symmetric pattern, representing a macrocosm, where universal forces come together. Later he experienced his very personal discovery of Christianity, with the result that Eastern and Christian traditions became blended in his work. There is also a visible influence of pre-Christian Russian art which the artist sees as "dark, subterranean energy, having a terrible power in Russia."

Potapov readily acknowledges the influence of the Western symbolic tradition, particularly of Hieronymus Bosch. "In their view of the Apocalypse, of eschatology, East and West are very close. And Bosch is probably closer to the Russian life today than anyone else."

Potapov's paintings of the 1980s, although retaining their bright, decorative colour palette, are more focussed on human figures in grotesque positions calling to mind a carnival or a circus: "For a symbolic artist the circus theme reflects certain deep karmic currents leading to either a bloodshed or this unceasing exaggerated circus."

In recent years he has returned to his favourite theme of karma, of "negative energies" accumulated by generations and coming back to haunt Russia. "That is why perestroika cannot work: people have good intentions but can't fulfill them because of these demonic clots. Man dashes this way and that, in fits and starts, but he finds himself in a river of karma, of dark energy that blocks him on every side." His grotesque figures of modern-day money-grubbers and post-Soviet officials are not funny but frightening just as his nudes are not erotic but repulsive. "To me these figures are manifestations of monsters in human form. I know all too well that these things are not funny. These are Dostoevskian themes."

To date Potapov has to his credit more than 400 paintings, hundreds of etchings, and more than a thousand drawings. Because of his non-conformism and religious mysticism he had to work clandestinely in the past, and it was only in the years of perestroika that he was allowed to exhibit his work in Russia. Since then he has been invited to take part in numerous collective art exhibitions and has had seven one-man shows in Russia, Europe and Canada. His paintings and etchings have been acquired by museums and private collectors on all continents. In December 1992 he had a one-man show of 100 paintings at the Central Art Exhibition in Moscow. A detailed catalogue of the exibition is available. In 1995, Potapov displayed his work at the exhibition of European painting "The Signs of the Zodiac" in Switzerland. His painting "Virgo", (reproduced on the back cover of this issue of GLAS) was acquired by the Swiss museum of contemporary art in Chateau Gruyere.

The front and back covers of this issue of Glas feature two of Potapov's most famous paintings, "Wanderers" and "Virgo" which belong to his series "Wanderers, Nymphs and Muses".

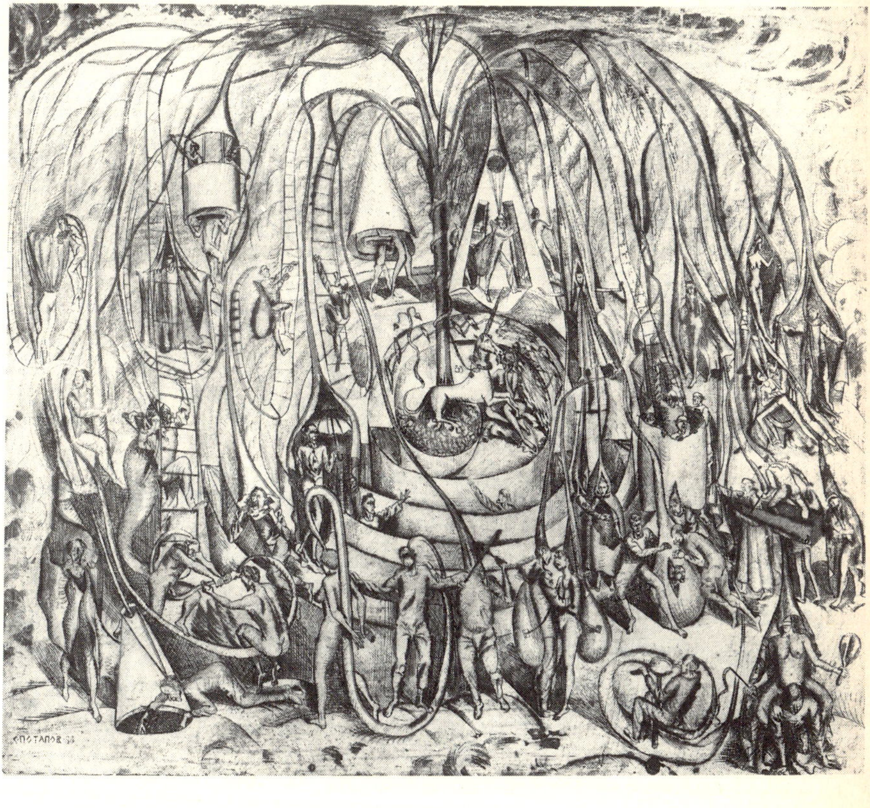

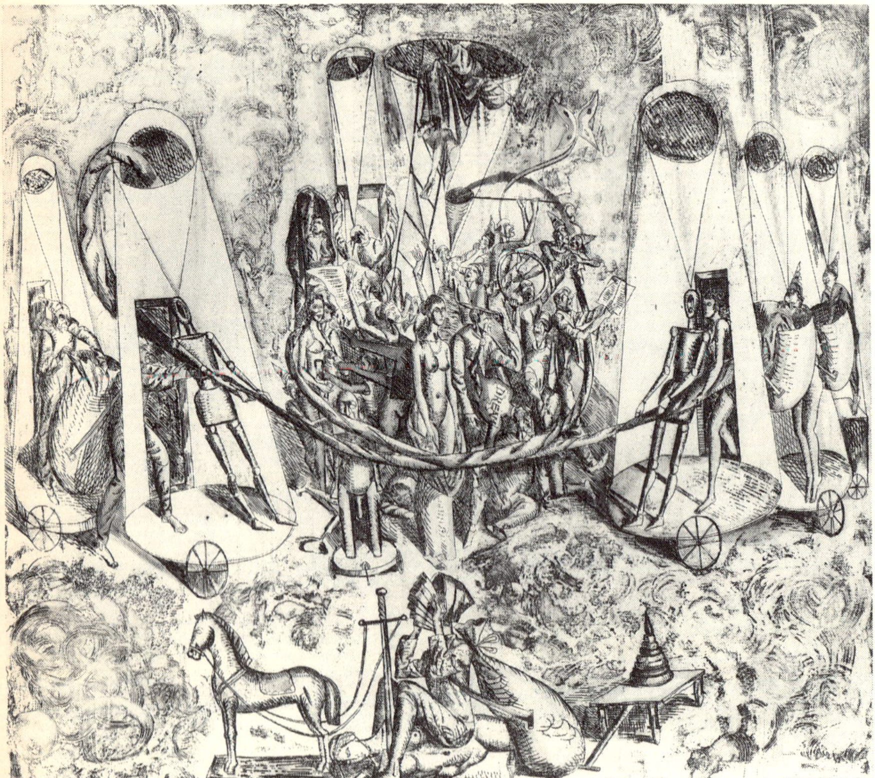
87 С.ПОТАПОВ

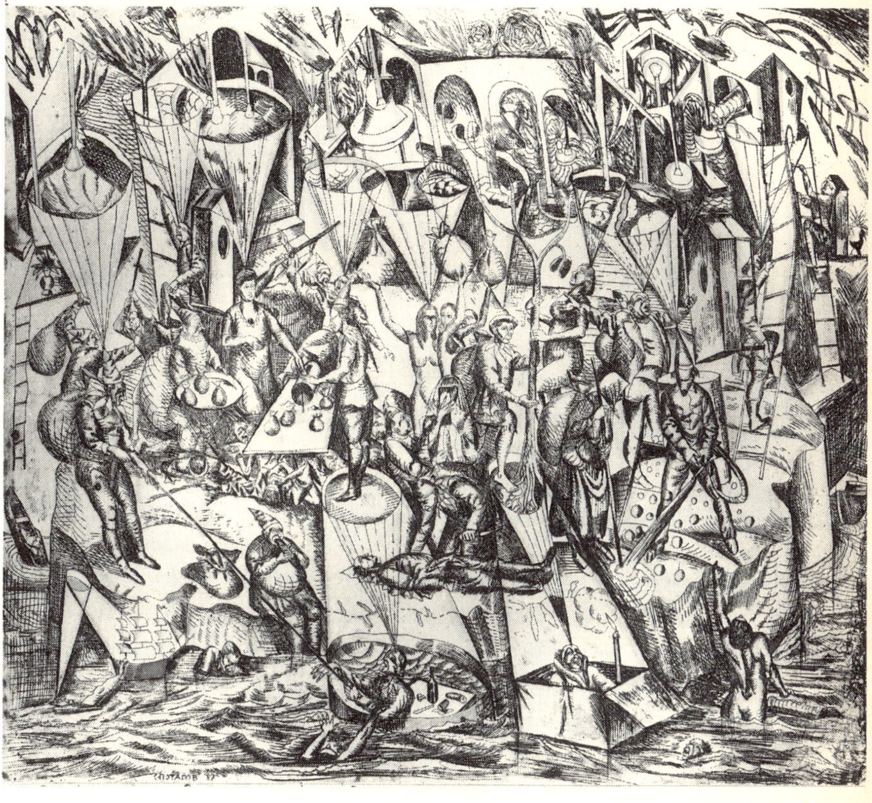

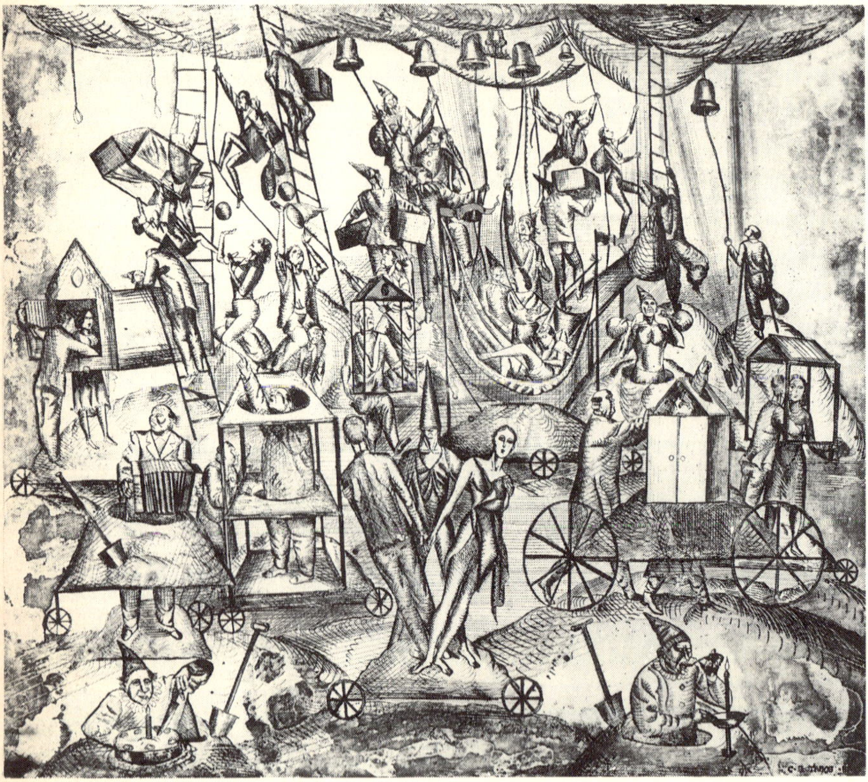

Transit
EUROPÄISCHE REVUE

Heft 10
Wien. Jahrhundertwende

Tony **Judt**
 Europa am Ende
Claus **Leggewie**
 Milleniumsdämmerung über Österreich
Robert **Menasse**
 Ein verrücktes Land
Antonio **Fian**
 Augsburg. Farce
Rudolf **Burger**
 Österreichische Nationsbildung
Christoph **Winder**
 Splitter vom Sparverein
 Texte von
Hermes **Phettberg** und Harry **Rowohlt**
Steven **Beller**
 Hitlers Wien, Herzls Wien
Rainer **Münz**
 Nachrichten aus dem neuen Deutschland
Chris **Niedenthal**
 Wiener Klischees. Photographien
Ute **Gerhard**
 Frauenbewegung in der Flaute?

Prag. Moral und Politik

Timothy **Garton Ash**
 Intellektuelle und Politiker
Václav **Havel**
 Intellektuelle in die Politik!
Eva **Hahn**
 Die "tschechische Frage" von Masaryk bis Havel
Brad **Abrams**
 Die Vertreibung und die Dissidenten
Peter **Demetz**
 Vertriebene und Emigranten

Transit 1
Übergänge zur Demokratie?
Transit 2
Rückkehr der Geschichte
Transit 3
Die Mühen der Ebene
Transit 4
Politische Kultur
Transit 5
Gute Gesellschaft
Transit 6
Dilemmas der Sozialpolitik
Transit 7
Macht Raum Europa
Magisches Prag
Transit 8
Das Europa der Religionen
Transit 9
Ex occidente lux?

Herausgeber:
Krzysztof Michalski
Institut für die
Wissenschaften vom
Menschen
Spittelauer Lände 3
1090 Wien

Bestelladressen / Order addresses:
Europa:
Verlag **Neue Kritik**
Kettenhofweg 53
D - 60325 Frankfurt/Main
Abonnement DM 38,00 pro Jahr;
Einzelheft DM 20,00 plus Porto

USA:
IBIS - international Book Import Service
2995 Wall Triana Highway, Suite B4
Huntsville AL 35824-1532
Subscription rate $ 30.00 per annum
(two issues); single issues $18.00
plus postage; MC and Visa accepted

Grant & Cutler Ltd

The UK's largest foreign language bookshop

Russian books

from the classics of the 19th century
to the very latest novels
from vocabularies
to specialist technical dictionaries
from phrase-books
to complete audio courses
from histories of the revolution
to the latest political developments

**we stock all the Russian books you need
to communicate, do business or relax**

55-57 Great Marlborough Street, London W1V 2AY
tel: 0171-734 2012   fax 0171-734 9272
e-mail: martin@grant-c.demon.co.uk